The Glory

LAUREN ST JOHN

The Glory

LAUREN ST JOHN

Orion
Children's Books

First published in Great Britain in 2015
by Orion Children's Books
This paperback edition first published in 2015
by Orion Children's Books
An imprint of Hachette Children's Group
Part of Hodder & Stoughton
Carmelite House
50 Victoria Embankment
London EC4Y 0DZ
An Hachette UK Company

Text © Lauren St John 2015
Illustrations © Jule P. Owen 2015

A CIP catalogue record for this book is available from the British Library.

ISBN 978 1 4440 1276 7

2 4 6 8 10 9 7 5 3 1

Printed in Great Britain by Clays Ltd, St Ives plc

www.laurenstjohn.com
www.orionchildrensbooks.com

Dedicated to the memory of Chiara Sanfilppo,
who loved horses and *The One Dollar Horse*.

'I was born upon the prairie where the wind blew free and there was nothing to break the light of the sun. I was born where there were no enclosures and where everything drew a free breath. I want to die there and not within walls.'

Ten Bears, Comanche Chief

PROLOGUE

Jonas B. Ellington had the worst characteristic with which any businessman could be cursed: he was a romantic. He'd lasted just one semester at Harvard Business School, where the only lecturer not tempted to throttle him had suggested he pursue an alternative career in painting, writing or, failing that, landscape gardening.

Jonas had done none of those things. Instead he'd invested the $1,000 left to him by his father, another romantic, in creating a cheap, environmentally friendly floor cleaner he'd first mixed up in his kitchen. He'd reasoned that even in the toughest times people still need to clean their floors and that the cheaper the product, the more likely they were to buy it. The environmental bit was equally obvious to him. Jonas spent every minute he could in nature and was mystified by anyone who didn't have as their life mission a desire to save the planet for future generations.

It turned out that millions of people thought the same way, if not about trees and animals then certainly about low-cost floor wash. Not having a wife to object, Jonas transformed his kitchen into a makeshift factory. From there, his Green Power cleaning product company moved to a defunct Mexican restaurant, and now it filled an entire grain warehouse in Dinosaur, Colorado.

Jonas's business acumen had never improved, but at forty-seven he had an unerring instinct for making money. He'd given a small fortune to charity but still he was dissatisfied. As he sat in his office one Friday afternoon, he thought nostalgically of his grandfather, who'd enriched Jonas's boyhood with thrilling fireside tales of the Old West. They'd shared a passion for wild mustangs.

His granddad was fond of quoting Frank T. Hopkins, a nineteenth-century horseman believed by many to be the greatest distance rider of all time. 'You can't beat mustang intelligence in the entire equine race. These animals have had to shift themselves for generations. They had to work out their own destiny or be destroyed. Those that survived were animals of superior intelligence.'

On Jonas's office wall was an oil painting of Hopkins competing in the so-called Longest Race. Hopkins claimed that, in 1886, he rode his mustang stallion Joe, from Galveston, Texas to Rutland, Vermont – a distance of eighteen hundred miles – in just thirty-one days, thirteen ahead of the second-placed rider.

Jonas tipped back his chair and studied the picture. Opinion was divided as to whether Hopkins was a conman and a fraud. There were those who were convinced that he'd no more won four hundred distance races than he'd walked on the moon. To Jonas, it didn't matter either way. Mythical or not, he loved the idea of Hopkins pitting his wits and the strength and fiery will of his mustang against the elements.

There was a knock at the door. In came Wayne Turnbull, the new clerk, a thin man with a dramatically receding hairline.

'Scantily-clad celebrities,' mused Jonas.

The clerk was startled. 'Sir?'

Jonas righted his chair with a crash. 'Sorry – Wayne, is it? – I was just thinking aloud. Not about unclothed pop stars and actresses, I hasten to add, but about society's obsession with talentless Z-list wannabes, famous for being famous. Sometimes I long for the return of the bad old days – you know, the Wild West. I don't mean gunfighters and ambushes, but the spirit of it.'

The clerk perked up. For reasons of his own, Turnbull regularly yearned for a time when the law was a crooked sheriff with a tin badge. He regarded his boss with more interest.

Jonas wore a dreamy expression. He gestured at the painting. 'Take Frank Hopkins. In the nineteenth century, he claimed to have raced a horse eighteen hundred miles across the United States, averaging fifty-seven miles a day. No historical proof, so it's probably nonsense, but that's not the point. Endurance riding is immensely popular today, but with the exception of the two hundred and fifty mile Shahzada in Australia, the maximum distance of most races is around one hundred miles. It's still a tough test, mind you. It still pushes competitors to the limit, but it can't be compared to the challenges faced by the distance horsemen of the Old West.'

Turnbull hated horses. In his experience, one end bit, the other end kicked and dispensed manure, and the middle was both dangerous and uncomfortable. Still, he saw no harm at all in indulging the boss's whims. One never knew when it might lead to a pay rise.

'Seems to me, sir, that someone should revive Hopkins's race. Retrace the route or something.'

He stopped. Jonas's eyes were lit with a diamond gleam. When he spoke his voice actually shook.

'Wayne, you're a genius. A total genius. We'll revive the race. Not the original one. Not enough romance. Galveston and Alabama have their attractions, but they're very built up. For our race, we'll devise a route that cuts through the heart of the West – from Colorado to Oregon via Wyoming and Idaho.'

Jonas did a quick search on his laptop. 'Twelve hundred miles. Now that sounds like a proper race. What do you think, Wayne? Green Power could sponsor it. We'll offer an incentive worthy of the challenge. A gold buckle with an emblem of Hopkins riding a mustang on it, plus $100,000. No, better make it $250,000. Winner takes all.'

Turnbull's mouth began to water. A cool quarter of a million dollars for a horse race. The boss was clearly mad.

'I'd need a chief organiser, Wayne. A right-hand man. Any experience with setting up events?'

Turnbull took a moment to reflect. It was true he'd organised the botched jewellery store robbery that had earned him and his accomplices a lengthy spell in Colorado State Penitentiary, but that wasn't down to any failure of leadership. It had to do with the unforeseen imbecility of the getaway driver, who'd dropped the car keys down a storm drain as they were attempting to escape. Were it not for that, his carefully masterminded plan would have seen him sipping cocktails on a beach.

'As a matter of fact . . . '

'Consider yourself hired, Wayne. Before the year is out, we'll make this race a reality. It's May now. We could aim for October, on the cusp between fall and winter. Then the weather will come into play.'

'Good thinking, sir. There's nothing like floods, snow and a gale or two to sort the men from the boys.'

'And the women from the girls, Wayne. This is the twenty-first century and this is about finding the best rider. There are as many gifted horsewomen as there are men. More, probably. I want it to appeal to teenagers too – the kind of youngsters who helped build this country. Too many teenagers today lack purpose. They're fixated with texting and the Internet. The closest they get to nature is a photograph on their screensaver. They need a real challenge. Our race will give any kid over sixteen a chance to shine.'

His pale face glowed. 'What should we call it? A great race needs a great name.'

'The Green Power Distance Derby?' suggested Turnbull, who'd never been good with words.

Jonas's eye fell on the miniature US flag poking out of a mug on his desk. Old Glory. 'What do people race for, Wayne?'

'Money,' Turnbull said at once.

Jonas frowned. 'No, Wayne. Horses, people and even huskies race for the glory of it. They want to cross the finish line knowing that they've fought with every breath and are the best of the best.'

'The Glory, sir – it has a certain ring.'

The dreamy expression returned to Jonas's face. 'The Glory it is.'

1

Dovecote Equestrian Centre, Surrey, England

On a blustery September afternoon as bright as a new-minted coin, a teenage rider cantered towards a jump. Alexandra Blakewood was exercising her eighth horse of the day, but there was nothing in her body language to suggest that she was in any way fatigued. She balanced lightly in the saddle as the dark bay thoroughbred cleared the double with room to spare and hurtled towards the next jump.

This was the part where everyone apart from Clare, Dovecote's owner and chief instructor, lost control of him, but Alex used a series of half halts to slow the horse enough to take the oxer, repeated the process with next two jumps as he attempted to rocket between each, and completed the circuit with only one rolled pole. As she eased him to a walk, patting and praising him, her grin was so wide anyone would have thought she'd just won at Olympia.

She rides like an angel, Clare thought ruefully, well aware that in every other area of Alex's life she was anything but. At Dovecote Alex was a model pupil, hungry (almost desperate, Clare sometimes thought) to learn, hard-working and the only fifteen-year-old she knew even remotely talented enough or committed enough to volunteer to school seven or eight horses every Sunday, which she did come rain or shine. Nor did she shy away from dealing with difficult horses. If anything, those were the ones she bonded with most.

But Alex had a tendency to ride recklessly and take too many chances. If she was told off, she became mutinous, although she was careful never to be rude. She knew that Clare operated a zero-tolerance policy when it came to insolence or swearing. From the terse exchanges Clare had overheard between Alex and her mum, she did not exercise the same restraint at home. Far from it. Clare had a feeling that trouble was brewing in the Pritchard/Blakewood household and that, when it came, it would be with hurricane force.

'I can't think why Mrs Priestly complains about him,' Alex said as she rode up to the gate. 'He jumps like a dream. Maybe she'd be better off with an old cob. Personally, I like horses with a bit of fire.'

Clare hid her amusement with a scowl. 'There's a difference between a hot horse who loves to jump and one who's a hazard to himself and his rider. Besides, he'll never improve his shape over fences unless you spend more time doing lateral work with him. He's weak in all the crucial muscles. As for your position on that last jump . . . '

'Yeah, but . . . '

Alex got no further. Her stepfather's 'winter gold' Jaguar came racing into the car park and skidded to a halt on the gravel. He exited the vehicle at high speed, followed by Alex's mother.

'I think they're looking for you,' began Clare, but she was talking to herself. Alex was galloping away in the other direction, approaching the first jump dangerously fast.

The hurricane Clare feared had just blown in.

'What is it that we're not giving you, Alex?' demanded her stepfather. 'Tell me that. I'd really like to know. So far this year we've bought you a second iPhone after you dropped the first in the bath, not to mention a new laptop and a wardrobe full of clothes and riding gear. We've also been on holiday to Devon and Tuscany and paid eye-wateringly expensive school fees.'

Despite repeated appeals not to do so, Alex sat with her feet up on the armchair. She buried her face in her knees to stifle a yawn. Her caramel-coloured hair, long and unruly, was still damp from her riding hat. Arguments with her parents always followed the same pattern. Her mum and stepdad would start out clearly furious but doing their best to be reasonable. Why, they'd want to know, had she done whatever it was she'd done.

At her last school, the teachers had been remarkably tolerant. Alex had regularly played truant and drawn horses on her exam papers – with few consequences. At school, that is. Her parents were another story. Alex was prepared to accept that drawing eventers on test papers was not a proven route to academic success, but she thought her mum should have been able to see past the truancy and appreciate that Alex had not been smoking, sneaking off with boys, or worse; she'd simply been holed up in a storeroom with a book. Instead, her mum started leaving pamphlets around the house about the catastrophic effects of taking drugs.

At her current school they had no sense of humour. The head teacher had blown a gasket over Alex's latest escapade. Personally, Alex thought it was quite ingenious. When a new PE teacher started at the school Alex had reasoned that if she never showed up to a single class, he'd never know she was missing. Since she already bunked off music and drama, it meant she got to spend an hour or more most days with two horses in a nearby field. She'd overheard Clare telling someone that they belonged to a couple of bankers who worked long hours and rarely exercised them.

To begin with, she'd simply sat under a tree or, if it was raining, in a stable, reading a novel, but over the course of the term she'd progressed to experimenting with different horse whisperer-type techniques and riding the horses bareback. The whole thing had worked like a charm until the previous Friday, when the owner of the horses had come home unexpectedly. Alex had managed to evade her grasp, but the uniform had been a giveaway. It hadn't taken the school long to discover the culprit. Hence the current row.

'I know you love me,' said Alex tiredly. 'And I know that I have everything I could ever wish for – apart from the thing I want most, a horse – and, of course, you're the world's most perfect parents, blah, blah, blah.'

'Don't be insolent,' said her stepfather. 'Why do you want to upset me and hurt your mum?'

As always, Alex had the feeling of watching herself from a distance, as if she were staring in at the contents of a goldfish bowl. She saw a slender girl in black breeches and a baggy V-necked grey sweater hugging herself defensively in a room straight out of *Country Living*, all overstuffed white furniture, great vases of flowers and artfully arranged rugs and paintings. It was so clean that once a week the cleaner had to spend her whole four hours dreaming up things to do.

On the sofa, her mum, Natalie, and Alex's stepdad of two years were rigid with agitation. Jeremy, who was something big in insurance, was in his version of weekend casual – ironed jeans, pin-striped shirt and shiny black shoes.

'I'm sorry,' said Alex. 'What more can I say? I've already apologised a million times. How was I supposed

11

to know that the owner of the horses would sprain an ankle running after me? I'm sorry she's injured, but I had no way of predicting that.'

'No, but you shouldn't have trespassed on her property and ridden her horses in the first place,' said Jeremy. 'You should have focused on your schoolwork like everyone else. If I hadn't known her husband from the golf club, we might have had a lawsuit on our hands.'

Her mum regarded her despairingly. 'Why do you do it, darling?'

Alex stared out of the window at the landscaped garden, every inch of it tamed into submission. Why *did* she do it? The truth was, she didn't know. Partly it was to hide how shy she was and uncomfortable in her own skin. She'd never really felt as if she fitted in and that feeling had grown worse after the divorce.

When she played truant to be with horses, she got into trouble, but what mattered was that just for a while she felt less lonely. Just for a moment she felt the way only horses could make her feel. Warm inside. Needed. Worth something.

For a while she felt less angry too, which was good because the slow-burning fury that had started as an ember after her father had walked out of the door four years earlier now raged in her like a forest fire. Having her mum weeping and fuming one day, and then planning her wedding to Jeremy the next, hadn't helped either.

Slowly, Alex had retreated inside herself. Her school

reports painted a picture of a bright but withdrawn teenager who needed to try harder. Her parents fretted that she was distant. Cold. Unemotional about things that she should care about, such as exams. Too emotional about things that were unimportant, such as horses.

As if anything could matter more than horses.

'Answer your mother,' ordered Jeremy. 'Why do you do it? I mean, you're nearly sixteen. It's high time you grew up. Why are you always in trouble?'

Alex shrugged. 'It's a laugh.'

Jeremy jumped to his feet, black hair bristling. 'Well, let's see how funny you find it when your riding lessons stop. As of this minute, you're grounded for three months. No, there's no point in appealing to your mum. She and I have already discussed this. You will not be allowed near any riding school until you learn to behave.'

Alex began to shake. 'No, please, anything but that. I'll do extra chores and study for hours every weekend. I'll work myself to the bone to get As in all my exams. I *need* to ride. I'll die if I don't.'

'Don't be ridiculous, Alex,' snapped her mum. 'Anyway, we don't have a choice. Clare had a word with me while you were collecting your bag from the tack room. I'm afraid you're no longer welcome at Dovecote after the stunt you pulled, racing off on Mrs Priestly's thoroughbred and forcing Clare to cancel a lesson to go after you. She's not having the health of

13

her horses and the reputation of her riding school ruined by a single pupil, even if you are one of the most talented.'

'And that's another thing,' said Jeremy, drowning out Alex's protests. 'Since you've demonstrated yet again that you can't be trusted, we are not going to take you to Paris next weekend. Nor are we going to leave you alone. You'll be staying with Rich and Barbara. You could do a lot worse than watch how their daughters Chloe and Tiffany behave, and try to emulate them.'

It was all Alex could do to stop herself from screaming. Rich was another big tuna in insurance and he and his identikit wife and daughters, the three of whom glowed as if they'd been scrubbed with a Brillo pad and fed on nothing but organic milk and honey from birth, were the most boring people in the universe.

After failing to persuade her parents to relent either about Paris or her riding lessons, Alex stormed up to her room, where she cried for over an hour. France she could live without, but horses were her whole world. They were the first thing she thought about every morning and the last thing she thought about at night. To keep her from them was cruel beyond words.

There was no doubt in Alex's mind that, between them, her mum and Jeremy had ruined her life. By taking away the thing she loved most, they'd destroyed the best thing that had ever happened to her.

Sitting up, she dried her eyes on her sleeve. She pulled

her laptop out from under her pillow. The screen purred to life, casting a blue halo across the bed. Alex smiled as she opened up Facebook. She'd make her parents sorry. Boy, would they be sorry.

2

'The Beeches', Virginia Water, Surrey

When the doorbell went for the seventeenth time, Alex experienced a feeling of panic so great that she wondered if she was hyperventilating.

Her plan had been to get back at her parents by throwing a party while they were in Paris. They had a cabinet full of alcohol that she'd intended to mix with fruit juice, cherries and a tin of peaches to create a giant bowl of punch. She'd bought some plastic cups and a few bags of crisps and put together a playlist. As soon as Rich and Barbara and their nauseating daughters were asleep, she'd imagined sneaking round the corner to her house, switching on the lights and welcoming her guests. If indeed there were any.

All week she'd worried that the party would be a disaster. She had few friends. Who did she think was going to show up? By Thursday she'd only had three people accept her Facebook invitation. One was from a boy who suffered from chronic dandruff and two were from girls from her last school who she could barely remember. A couple of her more popular classmates had surprised her by saying that they'd come if they could, but on the whole her invitation had been ignored.

Alex was not as upset as she'd thought she might be. Already she had cold feet. What if the party got out of hand? That evening she put another notice up on Facebook, this one advising everyone that the party had been postponed due to unforeseen circumstances. 'Postponed' sounded better than 'cancelled'. It at least allowed her to save face.

Her fury with Jeremy and her mum for banning her from riding and destroying her relationship with Clare and Dovecote Equestrian Centre had not diminished one iota. If anything, it had gone nuclear. But the realist in her was aware that she had infinitely more chance of changing their minds with a period of angelic behaviour than she did by being a monster.

On Saturday morning, her mum and stepfather had left for Paris with barely a backward glance. Alex was forced to endure an excruciating day with Rich and Barbara and their daughters. Beneath their wholesome-as-apple-pie exteriors Chloe and Tiffany were a pair of witches. They'd spent the entire time making sly digs at her while pretending to be effusively nice. She could have wept with gratitude when the whole family trooped off to bed at ten o'clock on the dot.

Unable to sleep, Alex logged on to Facebook. What she saw stunned her. The party invitation that she thought she'd deleted now had eighty-two acceptances. That was disturbing enough, especially since her second notice, postponing the party, seemed to have vanished. But the really frightening part was the number of people promising to meet each other at her house at 11 p.m. 'It'll be a BLAST!!!' said a boy she'd never heard of.

A sick feeling came over her. She sprang out of bed, dragged on jeans and a jumper, grabbed her house keys and tiptoed downstairs. Luckily, Rich and Barbara's fat golden retriever was so stuffed with treats that it barely stirred as she let herself out into the night.

Petrified that she'd arrive home to find hordes of marauding revellers, she was relieved to see the place in darkness. Shadows stretched uninterrupted across the lawn. She was digging her keys out of her pocket when a car pulled up. A woman who'd clearly been drinking wobbled up the path.

'This doesn't seem like much of a party. Are we early or something?' Without waiting for a reply, she yelled to a man in the car, 'Dominic, check the address, will ya? The place is dead.'

'There *is* no party.' Fear lent Alex her attitude. 'It was cancelled. Now get off our property before I call the police. You're trespassing.'

'Relax,' said the woman, holding up her hands as if to

ward off a blow. 'Keep your wig on. I'm going, but you need to chill.'

The engine revved and the car sped away.

Alex was so unnerved that it took her a full minute to unlock the front door. Once inside, she stood for a moment with her hands covering her face. She'd made a massive mistake putting the party up on Facebook but she seemed to have got away with it. Never again would she be so stupid. Anything could have happened. People could have trashed the place.

Shaken, she went into the kitchen and put the kettle on. It was ten past eleven. She'd have a coffee, chase away anyone else who might have missed her postponement notice and return to Rich and Barbara's. Anything was better than being alone with her thoughts.

She was lifting the milk from the fridge when the doorbell rang. Alex tried ignoring it but whoever it was leaned on it until she was forced to run for it before it woke the neighbours. To her surprise, it was the two classmates who thought they wouldn't be able to come.

'Where's the party?' demanded Gemma, looking round the living room as if she expected people to leap from behind the sofa and shout, 'Surprise!'

'I, um, I cancelled it.'

Gemma's face fell. 'Cancelled it? Have you any idea how many *lies* I had to tell to get here? Have you any idea how *complicated* it was? Have you any idea how much *trouble* I'll be in if my parents find out?'

Sensing Alex's discomfiture, Isabella spoke up. 'Hey, Gems, don't stress. The night is young. Why don't we make our own party?'

Before Alex could object, Isabella was steering her into the kitchen. 'Got any Jäger and Red Bull? I fancy a Jägerbomb. Or Sex on the Beach. Don't tell me you've never heard of it. If you have the ingredients, I'll show you how to make it. It's soooo yummy.'

Alex had never drunk alcohol in her life and had no intention of starting now but, eager to impress, she opened the cupboard where her parents kept an assortment of wine and spirits. Egged on by Isabella, she proceeded to empty a bottle of vodka, half a litre of peach schnapps and a couple of cartons of orange and cranberry juice into a bowl. Meanwhile, Gemma found the sound system and Alex's party playlist and turned the volume up so loudly that Alex had to shout to be heard.

The doorbell rang as Alex chopped cherries into the mix. Before Alex could stop her, Isabella was answering it. Four beautiful teenagers entered the kitchen, boys and girls. They were strangers but Alex was unable to pluck up the courage to ask them to leave, especially since Gemma seemed thrilled to meet them.

Hiding her shyness with a casual, 'Hey, how's it going? Can I offer you a Sex on the Beach?' Alex handed out plastic cups of drinks and plates of crisps. Thankfully, the newcomers were polite and friendly. After a while she began to relax. It seemed terribly sophisticated to be entertaining six guests, all of whom were laughing and enjoying themselves.

Then the bell rang again.

That had been over two hours ago. Now, as Alex opened the door for the umpteenth time, rivulets of sweat pooled at the base of her spine. She no longer recognised her own home. It heaved with people she didn't know. Somebody had spilled red wine on her mum's precious white sofa and the carpet was a kaleidoscope of chocolate, crushed crisps and broken glass. A cushion had burst and there were feathers everywhere. She could hear squeals and thuds from upstairs. It sounded as if someone was moving furniture.

On the front step stood four hooded youths with glittering eyes. Alex tried to slam the door, but the tallest one blocked it with his boot. They shoved past her as if she didn't exist.

'You can't come in!' cried Alex. 'The party's over. Please, you have to go.'

'Says who?' growled one. 'If you don't wanna have a good time, little girl, run home to Mummy.'

She was about to rush after them when something caught her eye. Something so nightmarish that her brain struggled to comprehend that it was real. Illuminated by the streetlights, scores of teenagers were converging like zombies on her house. There were cars everywhere, some parked on the lawn. A couple of girls were having a row with a neighbour who was in his dressing gown. As Alex stood open-mouthed on the doorstep, a gang of six or eight kids bumped past her, clutching clinking bags of booze.

She wanted to scream at them to get out of her home, but the words stuck in her throat. Paralysed with horror, she couldn't begin to think how to halt the invasion. Her mum and Jeremy were not due back until Sunday evening. She could run to Rich and Barbara's house for help, but that would mean leaving her home in the hands of the vandals for a short period when the situation could deteriorate even further. Her only option was to call the police and face the consequences.

Even as the thought went through her head, the high-pitched wail of sirens cut through the night, followed almost immediately by the sweeping searchlight and throbbing overhead whir of a police helicopter.

Alex's knees gave way beneath her and she sank on to the step with her head in her hands. Life, as she knew it, was over.

3

Alex expected screaming rows and to be grounded forever. What she didn't anticipate was the opposite. Her parents hardly spoke as they toured the wreckage of their home. They listened gravely to her tearful explanations. At one point her stepfather said in an eerily calm voice, 'Do you understand what's happened here, Alex? What you've done? What it's cost? How much has been stolen or destroyed? And it's not just about the money. The sentimental things that have been taken, such as your grandmother's wedding ring, are irreplaceable.'

A sob burst from Alex. 'I'm sorry, Jeremy. Mum, I'm so, so sorry. If you forgive me, I'll never do anything like this ever again. You have to believe me, I didn't mean any of this to happen. I tried to stop it. I took the invitation off Facebook, but loads of kids had already got hold of it and shared it with everyone they knew.'

Her mum wore a faraway expression. She was only

partly listening. That scared Alex more than any amount of recrimination would have done. 'Yes, dear. I know. Of course you didn't mean it. You never do. It's always somebody else's fault. But that's okay. In a way it makes the tough decisions easier.'

'What tough decisions?'

'Nothing for you to worry about,' said Jeremy.

'What do you mean, Mum? What tough decisions?'

Her mother massaged her temples. 'Can we not do this now, Alexandra? I have a headache.'

That night Alex found it impossible to sleep, and not just because every breath filled her lungs with the aroma of stale vomit – a legacy of the party. It seemed to have impregnated the carpet fibres and no amount of cleaning or Spring Breeze spray could shift it. She kept thinking about her mum's comment about the tough decisions. What did that mean? Were they planning to send her to a psychiatrist or would they simply ban her from being around horses for a lifetime?

Alex put the pillow over her head. Whatever they were up to, it couldn't be good. She had to try to stop it. Tomorrow she'd start anew. Clean slate. No more playing truant. She'd go down on her hands and knees and scrub the house from top to bottom if she had to. She'd devote herself to studying and coming top of the class. She'd do anything if only it meant that she could ride again.

Sleep came at her like an ocean wave. She went down so deep that everything in her resisted being dragged

24

back to the surface. It wasn't until she was physically shaken and light flooded the room that her eyes flickered open. Vision blurred, she tried to make sense of what she was seeing. Jeremy and two strangers were staring down at her. She shot up in bed with a scream.

Her mother came into the room. Like Jeremy, she was fully dressed even though the clock indicated that it was 3.32 a.m. 'Don't worry, Alex,' she said soothingly. 'These people are here to help you.'

'Help me?' Alex tried to wrench herself free of what she was sure was a nightmare. The man and woman were in matching white T-shirts, denim shirts and chinos. They were smiling. The man had his hands in his pockets as if nothing could be more natural or normal than to appear in a teenager's bedroom in the dead of night looking like a paunchy model from a Gap advert.

'These lovely people are from Camp Renew in the United States,' said Jeremy. His voice was bright, as if he was talking her through a new insurance policy. 'This is Sue-Ellen and the big fellow over there is Ken. Camp Renew is a marvellous place, Alex.'

'Y-e-s, it i-i-s,' agreed Sue-Ellen, her American drawl making three syllables of each word. 'Wait till you see our location close to the Rocky Mountain National Park in Colorado. It's tru-u-ly beautiful. A fifty-thousand-acre wilderness. We have mountain lions and bears. Ever think you'd see a grizzly in the wild Alexandra?'

'I feel as if I've fallen headfirst down a rabbit hole,'

said Alex. 'Would somebody please wake me up? What are these mental people doing in my bedroom?'

Ken stiffened but his smile remained in place. 'That's the first thing you'll learn at Camp Renew – no name-calling. Strike Cartwright – he's our warden – won't stand for it.'

Alex was beginning to feel terribly afraid. She kept trying to convince herself that she was asleep. When she awoke, everything would have gone back to normal. She jumped out of bed. The four adults reared back as if she had the Ebola virus.

Alex halted in confusion. 'Say something, Mum! What's going on? You're frightening me.'

Her mother looked white and strained in the lamplight. 'Darling, I know this must be a bit of a shock, but Camp Renew is a very special place. It's in one of the most stunningly pretty areas of the US. You're going to love it, I know you are. They have an extraordinary success rate with troubled teens. There are wonderful stories of redemption.'

Alex went cold. 'Oh my God, is that what this is about? You want to send me to a boot camp like that awful place we saw in that TV documentary?'

'Camp Renew is not a boot camp,' Jeremy told her. 'It's a therapeutic boarding school. There's a big difference.'

'Yes, there i-is,' agreed Sue-Ellen. 'We offer teens an opportunity to find their higher selves through counselling, physical effort and close contact with the great outdoors.'

'You can't be serious? Mum, is she serious?' Her mother avoided her eyes, but Alex glared at her until she looked up. 'How long are you and Jeremy planning to send me away for, exactly?'

Jeremy checked his watch. 'Alex, you'll be home before you know it. Just think of it as an opportunity to see another country. Now I'm afraid we're going to have to get moving because you need to get to Heathrow in time for an early flight. You have fifteen minutes to pack and then you'll be on your way. Ken and Sue-Ellen will be driving you. Alex, I'm sorry it's had to come to this, but Camp Renew is renowned for performing miracles and one day you'll thank us.'

'You think I'm going to thank you for having Beavis and Butthead here swoop in at three a.m. and drag me across the Atlantic to some teenage prison?'

'Darling, it's really not like that,' protested her mum. 'You're letting your imagination run away with you. There's climbing and kayaking. They do trail rides in the mountains too. I'd have no objection to that because it'll be in a structured environment where discipline and good manners are a priority.'

For a moment Alex had a vision of herself on a mustang, galloping across the wilderness, and then she remembered that if her parents were sending her to a holiday camp she would not need to be escorted there in the dead of night by two goons.

Ken tapped his watch. 'Folks, we need to hustle. The plane ain't gonna wait for us.'

Sue-Ellen glanced around the room. 'Where'd you say you put the suitcase, Mrs Pritchard?'

Alex bolted for the door, but Ken blocked her way, holding it shut with one enormous paw.

'I'M NOT GOING AND YOU CAN'T MAKE ME!' she screamed at her parents.

'This is normal,' said Sue-Ellen. 'We see this reaction all the time. When Alexandra returns she'll be a different girl. Healed from the inside out.'

Alex ran to her mother and threw her arms around her. 'Mum, please don't do this to me. I know I've messed up and I'm sorry. I'm going to spend the rest of my life making it up to you, you'll see. I'll help out around the house and spend every waking hour studying. I'm going to make you proud.'

Tears filled her mother's eyes. She looked helplessly at Jeremy. 'Are we doing the right thing, darling? Maybe we should give her a second chance.'

'A second chance? More like her fiftieth. No, Nat, what Alexandra needs is tough love. Camp Renew will give us back our daughter.'

Alex looked from one to the other. They were talking about her as if she was a piece of furniture they were planning to shift to a different room. Ducking away from her mum, she leapt once more for the exit, but it was no use. Ken was as immovable as a tree.

Alex's heart felt numb but her mind was suddenly sharp and clear. If she was going to survive this experience, it needed to be. She turned to her mum. 'I'll go if I can take Pluto.'

'Ma'am, Camp Renew has a "no pets" policy. Warden Cartwright wouldn't stand for it.'

Natalie Pritchard retrieved a small bear from beneath the duvet. 'This is Pluto. Alex has had him since she was a baby. She never goes anywhere without him, including on holiday.'

'Camp Renew is about letting go of babyish things,' asserted Sue-Ellen.

To Alex's surprise, a stubborn expression came over her mother's face. 'Maybe it is, but the bear doesn't fall into that category. He is a family heirloom, if you will, given to Alex by my late mum.'

'For goodness' sake, surely there are more important things to worry about than a bloody bear,' said Jeremy, losing patience. 'I appreciate that you and Ken are the experts here, Sue-Ellen, but frankly if a stuffed toy is going to make Alex more cooperative and help the three of you catch your flight, I for one am in favour of it.'

Sue-Ellen's face was a genial mask. 'As you wish, sir. It's just that past experience has taught us that troubled teens often use toys as hiding places for drugs and other illicit substances.'

'Alex doesn't have those sorts of problems,' snapped Natalie. 'But feel free to search the bear if you need added reassurance. Now, shall I fetch the suitcase?'

4

The Bigger Burger Cafe, Chattanooga, Tennessee

'What'll it be today – an Elephant or a Gorilla?' asked Will Greyton, dredging up his best customer service smile for the sweaty, obese man leaning over the counter.

'Which is bigger?'

'Do you mean in real life or at the Bigger Burger?'

'You got a smart mouth on you, boy. Natchrilly, I mean at this here burger joint. Which is the super-size one?'

'All of our burgers are super-size, sir, but the Elephant burger is a quadruple stack with extra bacon whereas the Gorilla is only a triple.'

'Perfect. I'll go for that.'

'The Gorilla?'

'No, the Elephant, dumbass. You trying to make a fool out of me, boy? Want me to call your manager?'

'No, sir, I don't. I need this job. Would you like the

jumbo fries with that? They come with a half-price shake.'

'Yeah, I'll have the fries and the Flamingo milkshake. That's strawberry-flavoured, I'm taking it? Flamingos being pink and all. Is it super-size?'

'It is if you have the Flamingo Supremo, but that costs fifty cents extra.'

'What a rip-off! What's in it – crushed rubies? The way things are going pretty soon I'll have to remortgage the house to buy dinner. Okay, hit me with two of them Supremos. Now my wife wants the fish and fries. Which is bigger – the Killer Whale or the Blue Whale?'

After a day of conversations about animal-sized burgers, seventeen-year-old Will often felt that the brain that had made him a straight A student at his Chattanooga high school was turning slowly to soup. Hour by hour his spirit was dying.

Only a year ago his dream of going to the University of Tennessee in Knoxville to study veterinary medicine had seemed not only possible but inevitable. At sixteen, life had been a breeze. He'd sometimes felt guilty about how easily things came to him. Apart from losing his mum to a malignant tumour when he was just three years old, he'd led a charmed existence. Academically gifted and effortlessly athletic, he'd sailed through school, achieving accolade after accolade.

There'd been pressure on him to choose between his studies and the track, where he had the potential to excel, but to Will there was never any competition. If he wanted to go to veterinary school, he needed to get the best possible grades and that, to the frustration of his athletics coach, was where his focus lay.

Besides, he'd never cared less about school sports. The only physical pursuit he put any effort into was horse riding and that was less about riding for its own sake than because he was passionate about horses – especially the grey mare given to him on his fifteenth birthday by his grandparents. She was part Arabian but Gramps had got her for the knock-down price of $100 because she was an 'accident'. A horse of lowly origin had broken into a paddock full of mares at a prize-winning Arabian stud and Shiraz had been the result. The owners had been so appalled at the scrawny, misshapen foal produced by their champion mare that they'd got rid of her at the first opportunity.

She'd initially been bought for $150 by a local rancher, who'd broken her and put her to work rounding up cattle. Her looks hadn't improved with age but in the early days his wranglers had fought over her because she could work for ten hours without breaking a sweat.

Then a pattern began to emerge. One by one, she'd sent every wrangler to the hospital. It never appeared to be intentional; on the surface, she was willing and responsive. But the outcome was always the same. She'd stumble while descending a steep slope and a minute later there'd be a broken collarbone. She'd gallop too close to a tree and crush a man's leg. Once, she'd turned too sharply while passing a gulley and almost launched her rider over the edge. His fall had been broken by a thorn bush that hid a dozing rattlesnake. He'd been lucky to escape with his life.

The rancher was sorry to have to part with his best horse but the wranglers had decided that she was cursed. It was them or her. He sold Shiraz for $300 to a company that organised trail rides for tourists. Not knowing her history, they were glad to have her. Within the first month, however, she'd dispatched three guests to hospital. Nothing appeared to be her fault, but she was the common denominator in every incident.

Not wishing to be sued for everything he had and hoping for a quick sale, the owner of Paradise Rides had sold her to a friend of a friend, Will's grandfather, for $100, claiming that the reason she was so cheap was that his guests described her as 'ugly' and 'too clever for her own good'.

Will's earliest memory was of wanting a horse of his own. When his grandfather had led Shiraz out of the barn and told him she was his fifteenth birthday present, he'd almost cried with happiness. To him, she was the most beautiful horse who'd ever walked.

Other people looked at Shiraz and saw a wiry excuse for a mare with a scraggly mane and few qualities to recommend her. Will only saw her bold, intelligent eyes and the thin, dark skin and long sloping muscles signalling that she had her Arabian dam's capacity to endure. Thanks to strong, straight legs and perfect pasterns and cannon bones, each of her gaits was smooth and efficient. Whatever other faults she may have had, laziness was not one of them. She was a good eater, too. Nothing put her off her food.

Shiraz had never met anyone like Will. Since birth, she'd been treated like a machine. Not one scrap of love or appreciation had ever come her way. Initially, she'd been nonplussed by the boy who came to visit her, always with treats and radiating calmness and kindness. Though tall, he was light in the saddle and had velvety hands. She'd tested him a few times but when she found that no punishment was forthcoming and that, if anything, he was more patient than before, she'd responded with a devotion and loyalty that deepened every day.

The two quickly became inseparable. Every Friday evening, Will and his dad drove out to his grandparents' farm in the Appalachian Mountains. After breakfast on Saturday Will would load Shiraz with a pack containing food, a sleeping bag and an ancient tent and they'd spend two blissful days exploring the mountains. In school holidays, Will moved out to his grandparents' house for the duration. He'd fill his backpack with supplies and then he and Shiraz would disappear for days at a stretch. Once they were gone for an entire week.

Then his grandparents had died within a month of one another, Gramps first, going peacefully in his sleep, and Nan barely three weeks later, supposedly of complications resulting from a fall, but really, as Will's dad put it, because she didn't want any life that didn't contain her Henry. Will had tried to imagine loving

34

someone so much that you couldn't bear the thought of breathing a single breath without them, but he couldn't make the mental leap.

At school, he'd had his share of female attention, although the few girls he'd got as far as taking on a date had lost interest the moment they'd found out how much time he spent studying. Along the way, he'd met pretty girls, smart girls and girls who were smart, pretty *and* liked horses, but he'd never met anyone who made his world stand still. These days, as he scraped grease from the deep fat fryer at the Bigger Burger, he doubted he ever would.

The death of his grandparents had been the first in a chain of events that had led him to where he was now. Next, the hardware store where his dad had worked for over thirty years had gone bankrupt. Len Greyton was a fit fifty-five with decades of managerial experience, but he could not find so much as a window-cleaning job.

Within months the mortgage company had been sending red-letter demands and Len had no choice but to raid the college fund he'd spent years building up so that his son could one day become a vet. Will had tried his hardest to convince his dad that it didn't matter, that there were plenty of other ways he could find to work with animals, but Len was devastated. He felt a failure. His sense of worth, already at an all-time low, continued to plummet, especially when Will was forced to quit school and take a job at the Bigger Burger to help pay bills. Depressed and anxious, Len's health began to suffer.

Will, who'd always felt that the very best thing about his life was having a father who was also his best friend, found it agonising to see the proud man he loved shrinking before his eyes. He kept praying for a miracle. He or his dad would get a better job and somehow, some way, everything would be all right.

In the grubby changing room at the back of the Bigger Burger, Will clocked out and changed from his orange and blue uniform into jeans, a flannel shirt, cowboy boots and brown leather chaps. It took him ten minutes to drive from the town centre to the house of an old friend of his father.

Shiraz was already at the field gate, waiting for him. As always, Will felt a mixture of love and guilt when he saw her. Guilt because she'd moved from a life of plenty at his grandparents' beautiful hundred-acre farm – land that had been in his family for generations now snapped up by a corporation, with the meagre profit being swallowed by the bank and tax man – to a quarter acre of poor-quality grazing in a run-down neighbourhood on the outskirts of town. Will supplemented Shiraz's diet with the best hay and feed he could afford, but he couldn't do anything about her environment or the fact that she was alone.

'I guess you're pining for the mountains as much as I am, aren't you, girl?' murmured Will as Shiraz buried her head in his chest and let out a shuddering sigh.

'Don't worry. We'll have to grin and bear it for a while but some day soon I'll build a new life for us and we'll go adventuring again, you and I.'

Will had no great hope that a new life would materialise in the foreseeable future, but that's what he told himself, Shiraz and his father almost every day, in the belief that if he said it often enough he would manifest something good into their path.

In the meantime, he had more pressing concerns, such as exercising Shiraz. Currently, he had two choices. He could either ride her through the neighbourhood until he reached a park with five miles of trails and hills or, if he rose early enough, he could do interval training with her on a local sports field. The park was the better option in terms of scenery and hills, but to get to it meant passing numerous yards packed with barking, snarling dogs, not all of which were chained or behind gates. Their owners were no better. Once Will had almost been speared by a youth trying out a new crossbow on an unfortunate crow.

It took a lot to rattle Shiraz, but her nerves had been severely tested recently. As he saddled her that evening, Will tried to decide whether to risk running the gauntlet of the two Rhodesian Ridgebacks on Carter Street, or to ride poor, bored Shiraz around the sports field for the eighth day running. He tried to be creative and to keep the work interesting for her by experimenting with alternating interval training with natural horsemanship techniques that he spent hours reading up on or studying in online videos, but it was never going to be enough for a fit, intelligent horse like her, a horse with imagination.

Swinging onto her back, he rode up the driveway. He was leaning down to open the garden gate when he heard a shout. Tyler, his father's ex-colleague, was crossing the lawn.

'Hey, Will, how's it going?'

'Great, Tyler. You?' Will nudged the mare through the gate as if he was in a hurry. He lived in terror that Tyler would raise the field rent, making it impossible for him to afford. What he'd do then, he dreaded to imagine.

'Same as everyone else around here, Will. Times are tough and the gravy train only ever seems to stop at the stations of the wealthy. How's your dad coping?'

Will tried to contain Shiraz as she lunged forward, desperate to be free of her suburban prison. 'Dad's doing great,' he lied. 'Everything's good.'

'And the Bigger Burger?'

Will forced a smile. 'It's bigger.'

Tyler laughed. 'They're huge, those burgers. That Elephant should be illegal.'

Having run out of small talk, he kicked at a tuft of grass. 'Truth is, Will, I've been wanting a word with you. As you know, I'm out of a job just like your pop and looking to find dough anywhere I can. A friend of mine is starting a business growing tomatoes and my field just happens to be an exact fit for his polytunnels. If I let him have it for free, he'll cut me in on the profits.'

Will felt as if he'd been punched in the gut. Knowing what was coming next, he reined in Shiraz and circled back. The mare danced in protest, hooves clattering on the tarmac.

'I'm sorry, Will. I know this puts you in a tight spot.'

'How long have I got?'

Tyler was shame-faced. 'A week.'

When his grandparents' farm was put up for sale, Will had spent an entire month trying to find affordable livery for Shiraz. At one point his dad had suggested that he sell her back to the trail riding centre she had come from. Will could never recall being anything worse than mildly annoyed with the father he adored, but at this suggestion he'd blown up.

'Dad, you and Shiraz are my best friends,' he'd said when he'd calmed down. 'I'd no more get rid of her than I would you.'

To his relief, his father had not attempted to talk him out of it. Quite the reverse. Shortly afterwards Len had dug out his address book and called everyone he knew. By the end of the day Shiraz had a home in Tyler's field.

Now Will had less than seven days to find someone else who would loan him a field and/or stable for the minuscule sum of money that remained after he'd paid the bills each month. The portions might have been elephantine at the Bigger Burger, but the wages certainly weren't. Still, as he turned Shiraz towards the sports field, he made a last-ditch attempt to think positively.

'The best bit about hitting rock bottom, girl, is that the only way left is up. It's impossible for things to get any worse.'

5

As Will turned into Hudson Street, an ambulance came screaming past him. The hairs stood up on the back of his neck. It wasn't until he rounded the corner and saw the spiky silhouettes of his neighbours gathered together outside his home that it hit him that this time the unfolding catastrophe was not someone else's problem. It was not a heart-breaking story on the evening news or something overheard at the barbershop. He was in the midst of it, living it.

The drive to the hospital should have taken fifteen minutes, but Will did it in six, running three red lights and doing two or three times the speed limit. The worn tyres of his truck skidded on an oil spill on the way and he almost ended up on a stretcher himself. All the while, his heart was thrashing in his chest.

The ER was a war zone, packed with walking wounded. Stressed and distressed friends and relatives fought tooth and claw for priority. Nurses, doctors and administrators moved briskly among them, herding the worst cases into curtained booths or whisking them into labyrinthine corridors signposted with sinister-sounding medical conditions.

Will arrived only minutes after the ambulance, but he found it near impossible to discover what had become of his dad, who had yet to be entered in the system. A stern receptionist dispatched him back to his truck to fetch his ID and only became kinder once her screen told her what had happened.

'You'll need to get the B lift to Cardiology . . . '

Will didn't wait to hear the rest. He took the stairs three at a time to the fifth floor. Though deathly white and heavily medicated, Len was able to muster a weak smile when he saw Will.

'Hey, son, don't look so worried,' he rasped. 'I keep trying to tell these good people that I'm in the wrong department. It wasn't a heart attack at all. It's indigestion. The pain came on right after I ate some of that bean chilli you made last night. I told you your cooking would kill me one day.'

That was as much as he got out before he was whisked away to the cardiac cath lab for multiple tests. Will was instructed to sit in the waiting area until he was called. 'You'll need to have your father's health insurance card ready for when he comes out,' a nurse told him.

This was the part that Will had been dreading. Two months earlier his dad had cancelled their health insurance on the grounds that Will was young and healthy and didn't need it and he himself was as 'strong as an ox'. It was easy to say in hindsight, but a frisson of alarm had rippled through Will. Unfortunately, Len's mind had been made up.

'You're the one who keeps telling me that there is a whole world of employers out there just waiting to hire me. When they do, I'll take out a new policy on Obamacare or whatever. In the meantime, we can save hundreds of dollars a month. After all, it's not as if anything's going to happen to me while I'm housebound, is it? The worst injury I'm likely to suffer is a strained wrist from changing the TV channel.'

And now here they were, in the hospital, facing a bill that would wipe out their remaining savings. Will could not have cared less about the money. His dad was alive and that was all that mattered. But he was worried about what came next. There was no way that he could look after his dad and Shiraz on his Bigger Burger salary. He'd have to find a better job. But where? *How?* Teenagers with no qualifications were not high on the priority lists of businesses offering well-paid jobs.

Outside, the night sky was shot through with the red glow of arriving ambulances. For more than an hour Will sat in desperate silence, wanting news, not wanting news. He felt utterly alone. Over the past year he'd often found himself wishing that the mother he'd never known was still alive. If she were here now, she'd know what to do. They'd go through this as a team, be strong for his dad together. As it was, Will felt much younger than his seventeen years. A mere kid. A boy ill-equipped to deal with the avalanche of grown-up problems heading his way.

In an effort to shut out the image of his dad in the hospital bed, Will picked up a newspaper. Article after article blurred before his eyes. Squabbling politicians, reality stars he'd never heard of, financial crises, natural disasters. He was about to toss the paper aside when he saw on the front of the lifestyle section a full-page picture of Shiraz outlined against a blue sky.

Will snapped to attention, the photograph sharpening into focus. It wasn't Shiraz, of course, but the horse her previous owners would have liked her to be – a pure-bred Arab with all of the ethereal beauty and perfection of her breed. The caption named her as Laughing Dove Esmeralda, twice winner of the American Endurance Riding Conference (AERC) National Championships.

LONG RIDERS HIT HOPKINS'S TRAIL IN PURSUIT OF THE GLORY

To some, Frank T. Hopkins is the greatest horseman in US history, an iconic nineteenth-century figure who many believe rode further and won more endurance races (400) than anyone before or since.

To others, he was a conman and a fraud who invented a biography so colorful it included a stint working with Buffalo Bill, a three thousand-mile 'Ocean of Fire' race across an Arabian desert, depicted in a movie

starring Viggo Mortensen, *Hidalgo*, and an eighteen hundred-mile race from Galveston, Texas to Rutland, Vermont.

It was this epic feat that has excited the imagination of Green Power CEO, Jonas B. Ellington. An endurance riding fan, he campaigned for many months before convincing international endurance riding authorities to allow him to stage the toughest horse race in the world, a monster of nearly 1,200 miles, known as The Glory.

The Glory, which starts on October 1st and offers a gold belt buckle and a purse of $250,000 to the winner, is open to any rider aged over 16, provided they can afford the entry fee of $250 and have a horse fit enough to meet the stringent checks of event veterinarians both before the race and at regular intervals throughout.

Weekend riders who fancy their chances need not apply. The race route, from Boulder, Colorado, to Hood River, Oregon, cuts through the heart of the Old West and covers some of the harshest terrain in America. Mountains, rivers, gorges, and wildlife are just a few of the challenges riders are likely to face, and that's before the weather enters the equation.

The race has been mired in controversy . . .

'Will Greyton? Dr Sanchez. How are you holding up?'

Will flung aside the newspaper and bounced to his feet, heart pounding. 'My dad – is he okay?'

The doctor folded his hairy arms tightly across his

chest. 'I'll be straight with you – your father is a sick man. He's fortunate that the heart attack he had this evening was a minor one and that our ambulance was there within minutes. Had that not happened, we'd be having a different conversation.'

'I don't understand. Dad's always seemed so healthy.'

'Outwardly, yes. He obviously keeps himself in shape. Sadly, his heart is a different story. I understand that he lost his job at the start of the year. I'm guessing you attributed some of the warning signs – tiredness, shortness of breath, dizziness – to the depression and anxiety surrounding his unemployment?

'I'm sure it isn't news if I tell you that the stress of being unemployed is probably partially responsible for his attack. But the underlying cause is coronary artery disease. Your dad needs an operation as soon as possible. Without it, his heart is a ticking time bomb. He might be fine for a couple of months or even a year, but if he does have an attack it could kill him. I'm sorry to be blunt, but it's better that you know the truth.'

He checked his watch. 'Now, I understand from Accounts that your father has no health insurance.'

Will swallowed. 'No, sir, we don't, but I promise I'll pay back every—'

'Don't worry about today's bill. We have a charity initiative for folks like yourselves and we'll swallow the costs. But here's the thing: your father needs coronary artery bypass surgery. Our budget is all tapped out and we can't fund that, nor can we help him with ongoing medication. I'll send him home with a month's supply, but after that you'll be on your own. I'm sorry. I hope you understand.'

'Yes, sir, I do,' said Will. Even though he didn't. Even though he couldn't comprehend how any doctor who'd signed up to the Hippocratic Oath, a sworn promise to heal and have compassion for the sick, could send a man with a ticking time bomb for a heart back home to gamble with his life.

'The operation my dad needs – how much will it cost?'

The doctor seemed faintly amused. 'If I were you, Will, I wouldn't think about that now. Get through the next few months and see how things go. I'm sure the adults in your family will come up with a plan.'

Will's fists clenched at his side, but his tone was even. 'Just give me a figure. It doesn't have to be exact.'

The doctor's beeper buzzed. He glanced at it and frowned. 'You'll have to excuse me . . . '

'Please.'

Dr Sanchez stopped with a sigh. 'You're asking the wrong question. This is not about how much his recovery may or may not cost. What's critical is that your dad is not stressed when he leaves the hospital. Fretting about bills, worrying that *you're* worrying, these are things that could bring on another heart attack. My strong advice is that he is kept as relaxed and happy as possible. Starting today. Now, I must run. The nurse will be out shortly.'

Will watched him scurry away down the corridor, already focused on his next case.

'Hey, kid!'

A steel-haired man in a leather jacket beckoned him over. Will went reluctantly, ready with an excuse. 'Apologies if I'm out of line, but I couldn't help overhearing your conversation. Might be that I can help you out. I had a triple bypass myself a couple of months back. For a cardiac op you're looking at twenty grand plus – more if there are complications.'

Will almost fainted. 'Twenty *thousand* dollars?'

'Crazy, isn't it? You'd think you'd get a gold-plated heart for that price, but no, it's only the old one with a few repairs. But you do get a new lease of life, that's the main thing. These days I'm fitter than my son and he's a ball player.'

'But what happens if you don't have that kind of money?'

'Then you're toast. Forget the government promises about affordable health care. If you don't have insurance or can't pay for Obamacare, you're on your own. You have to make a plan. Speaking from experience, the heart is not something to mess about with. It's life-and-death stuff. But don't worry, you'll come up with it – the cash, I mean. One thing I've learned, when your back's against the wall, that's when you find out what you're made of.'

Will thanked him but didn't return to his seat. He paced up and down, fighting back tears. Gradually, a simmering anger took hold of him. Rage at the insurance companies who'd taken his father's money for decades but would not fork out a dime now that he needed them. Rage at the owner of the hardware company whose bankruptcy meant that Len was laid off with only a month's pay after more than thirty years of blood, sweat and toil. Rage at the calculating coldness of the doctors and hospital accountants. Rage at his own youth and helplessness.

The nurse emerged from a side door. 'Mr Greyton? You can see your father now.'

The blood was roaring so loudly in Will's ears that she had to repeat herself twice. Snatching the newspaper from the table, he shoved it into his jacket pocket and followed her.

Len's colour had improved but his face was creased with worry. 'Will, I'm sorry. This is all my fault. The cost . . . What are we going to do?'

Will gave him a hug and the brightest smile he could manage. 'Dad, don't you fret about a thing. I have an idea. It's all going to be fine, I promise.'

6

Camp Renew Academy, Elk, Colorado

'Try again, Alexandra. Sooner or later you'll get the hang of it.'

Alex took the reins and a clump of black mane. 'He's not going to bite me, is he?'

Chase Miller, head wrangler at Camp Renew, gazed pityingly at her from beneath the brim of his hat. 'Clyde's not gonna bite you.'

'Or kick me?'

'He's not gonna nip, buck, kick or do anything else to you. Clyde is what we call bombproof. He's also about the sweetest-natured horse I've ever broken. Come on, have another go. Put your left foot in the stirrup . . . No, no, stand a bit closer to his shoulder. That's right. Grab the back of the saddle and spring. I said spring, not pull him over. Whoa! Okay, that was too much spring. You nearly went flying over the other side. Don't worry. We'll get there. But you need more practice. We can't have you going off into the wilderness on your own and not being able to get back in the saddle. That would not be good. The last thing we want is to lose you.'

Alex had been at Camp Renew for ten days, but it felt like ten months. Not counting sleep, and there'd been precious little of that, every minute of every twenty-four hours had been dedicated to some torturous physical or mental activity. In the rare moments when her brain and body were her own, she'd found it ironic that having unexpectedly found herself living a horseshoe's throw from sixty-five mustangs and quarter horses in breath-taking mountain scenery, she had to try her hardest to stay away from them. Her escape plan depended on it.

Perhaps as an incentive for her to embrace the American boot camp experience, Alex's parents appeared to have said nothing to the Camp Renew staff about the riding ban they'd imposed on her in the UK. She had a daily lesson, during which she pretended to be scared of horses and ignorant of anything to do with them. In the saddle she masqueraded as the kind of limp, ineffectual rider she'd always looked down on at Dovecote Equestrian Centre.

It wasn't hard to act the part. Riding Western-style

wasn't half as easy as it looked and Alex was still getting to grips with using split reins. Two separate reins were attached to a curb bit via 'slobber' straps, which stopped saliva or water coming into contact with the leather. They crossed at the base of the horse's neck, allowing them to be used with two hands or for neck reining, and were usually seven or eight feet long. The idea was that if the rider fell or dropped them, they'd remain on the horse's neck and not be trampled or broken.

The saddles were even more of a challenge. There was a multitude of straps, rings and strings, plus a breastplate to stop the saddle slipping back and a latigo, a leather strap securing the front cinch – a Western-style girth – to the saddle's rigging. You virtually needed a degree course to tack up. And that was if there was only one cinch. Sometimes there was a back cinch too.

In addition, Camp Renew's military fitness regime meant that she felt as if she'd been beaten from head to foot with a baseball bat – adding to her awkwardness in the saddle. Her muscles were no longer muscles. They were pure liquid pain. Nonetheless, there was a fair amount of theatre involved in riding poorly. Away from listening ears, she apologised to every horse forced to be an unwilling accomplice in her charade.

It was a fine line. She didn't want to be so incompetent that Chase Miller refused to let her have a horse during her wilderness experience, a key test in Camp Renew's 'behaviour modification' programme. If she found herself on foot, she'd be going nowhere fast. On the other hand, it was crucial to her plans that nobody suspected she was a good rider.

For the first few days at Camp Renew, there'd not been one second when Alex hadn't wanted to die. She didn't want to die in the drama queen way she'd sometimes threatened when frustrated with her mother. She wanted to cease to exist. In her worst moments she'd had the sense that if she fell and cut herself the blood that would leak from her veins would not be crimson. It would be black with rage and despair.

'The first thing we ask here at Camp Renew is compliance,' Warden Strike Cartwright had told her the morning after she'd arrived in the US. His voice was soft. It went through her like a knife through butter. 'Compliance is the art of doing what is required of you willingly and to the best of your ability. You get extra points for smiling.'

'And what if I don't want to comply?' Alex said bitterly. 'News flash. When you drag someone out of their bed at three in the morning before transporting them across the Atlantic as if they're an escaped murderer and then frisk them on arrival at your boot camp, they don't exactly feel like smiling.'

The warden's expression didn't change. 'Like I said, we *ask* for your cooperation, we don't demand it. This is most definitely not a boot camp and we never force anyone to do anything. But you should bear in mind that we only *ask* once.'

The silence that followed was as chilly as an Arctic winter.

Tears pricked the back of Alex's eyes. She blinked them away. 'I'd like to phone my mum. She'll be worrying about me.'

'But of course. My staff will have explained to you that you're allowed two phone calls home a month. You've only just arrived and Sue-Ellen will have already been in touch with your mother to reassure her that you're safe and well. Why don't you wait until you've been here for a little while and have some news? That way, you'll have something to tell her.'

Alex opened her mouth to protest, but shut it again quickly. There had been an ugly scene at Heathrow airport, where she'd managed to escape from her minders long enough to use the payphone outside the toilets and call her parents, reversing the charges. She'd expected her mum to have had second thoughts and be in floods of tears, ready to bring her baby home at a moment's notice. Instead Natalie had hardened her heart. In the three hours that Alex had been gone, Jeremy had discovered further damage from the Facebook party. Somebody had painted graffiti on the summerhouse and broken the stained-glass window.

Before Alex could apologise yet again, Sue-Ellen had rushed up, wrestled the phone from her grasp and reassured Natalie that this was a lapse that would not be repeated. Alex had been allowed to speak to her mother one last time, just long enough to hear her say: 'Alex,

Jeremy and I would appreciate it if you could use this period to reflect on your behaviour and make the most of the opportunity you've been given to transform and do something positive with your life. Travel safely. Don't forget I love you.'

'IF YOU LOVED ME YOU WOULDN'T BE DOING THIS TO ME,' Alex had screamed into the phone, but there was no response. The dial tone purred in her ear. As if that wasn't bad enough, Sue-Ellen had spent the rest of the journey stationed outside the cubicle whenever Alex had to use the bathroom.

So the warden was right. Alex had nothing to say to her mum apart from: 'How could you betray me like this?'

Or, 'I'll never forgive you for as long as I live.'

Strike Cartwright's stare lasered into her. 'So are we clear, Alexandra? You'll speak to your mother in a week or so, by which point you'll be more familiar with the high standards of behaviour we expect of our students at Camp Renew.'

'Yeah, we're clear,' mumbled Alex.

Too late she remembered that she was supposed to address all staff as sir or ma'am.

Strike Cartwright gave no indication he'd noticed. He turned to gaze out of the window at the range of mauve mountains that lay beyond the verdant pastures. The sky was an unfathomable blue.

'Have you ever seen a more magnificent view, Alexandra? At Camp Renew we pride ourselves on our location. We're fortunate enough to have the run of fifty thousand of the most beautiful acres bordering the Rocky Mountain National Park. You've seen the brochure?'

Alex had. On the plane, Sue-Ellen had shown her glossy photos of cute, ranch-style cabins and smiling girls white-water rafting, abseiling down cliffs and riding horses through wildflower-scattered meadows. They wore a uniform of jeans, grey T-shirts and fleece-lined hooded sweatshirts with the academy logo printed in black. Outwardly sceptical, Alex had held fast to the hope that Camp Renew would be the summer camp her mum had painted it as, albeit a little stricter.

That hope faded as soon as they'd pulled up at the gates, where two armed guards, one with a sniffer dog, signed them in as if they were entering a maximum security prison. As they'd continued towards the ranch house, where a dozen girls were doing star jumps in formation on the lawn, a sick feeling had come over Alex. She'd wanted to leap from the car and run away, but where would she go? For much of the last half hour of the journey from Denver airport, they'd driven through wilderness. Occasionally, she caught a glimpse of a house or ski lodge through the trees and once they'd passed a petrol station and a general store, but for the most part there was nothing.

The warden's gaze was still locked on the scenery, as if he was studying it for imperfections. He stabbed a finger in the direction of the forest that bearded the lower slopes of the mountains.

'Would you believe that this paradise was once the safe haven of every gunfighter, villain and desperado who'd ever escaped a lynching elsewhere? There was no law. Murder was as commonplace as grocery shopping. People shot each other simply because they were annoying.

'Here at Camp Renew, we prefer to use nature to teach our students valuable life lessons. Disrespect the wild and it can disrespect you to death. Mother Nature is a cruel mistress at times. Believe me when I tell that you won't recognise yourself when you leave here. Cussing, dabbling with drugs, anti-social behaviour or sitting slumped in front of the television eating garbage, these will be things of the past. But change doesn't come for free, Alexandra. Apply yourself or pay the price. Your choice.'

Alex glared at his profile. He was well over six foot, with a military haircut shaved almost to the skull. His face was like a granite cliff pecked by crows. The head of an elk was suspended on the wall above his desk. She felt sorry for it. If there was one thing worse than being shot and stuffed, it must be spending eternity in the office of a man who enjoyed threatening 'troubled teens'.

Strike Cartwright turned so suddenly that she had difficulty rearranging her expression. His tone was almost fatherly. 'Good day, Alex. Thank you for coming in. I wish you a happy, rewarding stay at our Colorado academy.'

He sent her on her way with a smile, but the moment

she was out of sight he picked up the phone. 'Bud? New girl, name of Alexandra Blakewood. British. Thinks the world owes her lunch on a silver platter. Here because she trashed the family home with a Facebook party. Scruffy, discourteous and needs a serious attitude adjustment. Are you getting the picture?'

He chuckled at the response. 'Exactly. Nothing that a few of your workouts won't cure. Can you factor in twenty extra push-ups and a couple of extended planks from me? Oh, and Bud, make sure she calls you "sir".'

7

Strike Cartwright was right about one thing. No girl at Camp Renew was forced to take part in a single activity. Not physically, at any rate. What he hadn't said was that the consequences of refusing escalated until life became so unbearable that you practically begged to do whatever it was you hadn't wanted to do in the first place.

Alex learned that the hard way on her second day. Roused at 4.45 a.m. to shower and do an hour and a half of homework, she chose to put her head under the covers, cling tightly to Pluto and hope that the world would go away.

'Suit yourself,' said Katie, the cheerful dorm supervisor. 'I'll let the kitchen know that you don't want breakfast.'

Alex was too tired to protest and so she slumbered on until 7.10 a.m. When she awoke she was alone in the dormitory. It was a creepy feeling. A shaft of sunlight illuminated the rustic cabin and the seven other beds, neatly made up. Remembering the warden's words, 'We only ask once,' she hurried to check the dorm worksheet, pinned on the bathroom wall first thing each morning, and saw that she was supposed to be doing chores – in this case, cleaning tack down at the barn.

Polishing saddles and bridles was not something Alex considered a chore and she'd been dying for an excuse to be near the horses, but by the time she'd thrown on her clothes and run down to the stables, hair standing on end, it was 7.21 a.m. There, Chase Miller took exception to both her tardiness and her appearance and told her so in front of five other girls, all smothering giggles.

'Where you come from, it might be okay to show up looking like you've spent a night in the barn, but it's not acceptable here at Camp Renew. I appreciate that it's only your second day and that you're probably still a little jet-lagged, but a glance in the mirror would have told you that your sweatshirt is on back to front. Here at the academy, we have a saying: "When you disrespect yourself, you disrespect others."

'Same applies to lateness. We don't tolerate it. For that reason, I'm putting you on manure duty. For the next seven days, you'll be at the stables at 4 a.m. and not a minute later to bag up horse manure. You'll do it willingly and you'll do it well or you'll lose your weekend privileges. Now my advice to you would be to return to the dorm and make yourself presentable. Strike Cartwright sees you in that state, you'll be on gruel for the rest of the month.'

Not wanting to risk running into the warden or anyone else, Alex took the path that led around the back of the barn. Only those horses scheduled to be ridden that day were in a corral. The rest were out in the pasture. Accustomed to the chestnuts, bays and greys of Dovecote, Alex was struck by the fact that almost every horse had its own unique hue. There were strawberry roans with chocolate hindquarters, Appaloosas with silvery-rose coats and cocoa spots, and dun horses with zebra stripes on their legs – a genetic legacy of the earliest horses on earth. There were also paint horses, sorrels and platinum-coloured mustangs with black manes. Just seeing them lifted her spirits.

Separated from the others was a palomino. He'd been put into a round pen, but he wasn't really there. That is to say, his whole being was somewhere else. He was facing away from the barn and the horses in the paddock, his gaze locked on the distant mountains as if he could wish himself there by sheer willpower.

Glancing over her shoulder to check she wasn't being observed, Alex crept closer. Like most of the horses at Camp Renew, the palomino was barely fifteen hands high, but beneath his striking rose-gold coat and flaxen mane he was all sinew. Alex drew in a breath. The wildness in him was a tangible force, like the scream of an eagle in flight. It emanated from the corral and sparked something inside her. She could practically hear it sizzle.

'Hey, boy,' she called through the railings. 'If it's any consolation, I know how you feel.'

The horse did not register her presence. His only interest was the mountains.

'Don't take it personal,' said a disembodied voice, almost giving Alex a heart attack. 'He like that with everybody.'

She turned to see a swarthy man of indeterminate age sitting on a barrel in the shadows. From his accent, she thought he might be Mexican. He had a mug in one hand and the remnants of a breakfast pastry in a wrapper on his lap.

'What's his name?' she asked shyly.

'Scout, they call him. A mustang. Fast and strong. See his deep chest. Heart like a mountain lion. But he much trouble. Always difficult for the wranglers. One year after they take him from the wild, he make big mistake. He throw Warden Cartwright. Tried to crush him.'

As Alex watched, the horse shook out his flaxen mane and broke into a bucking gallop, kicking up dust as he flew around the pen. Sliding to a stop, he snorted with frustration.

'Why?' Alex asked. 'Why is he so difficult?'

The man crumpled his wrapper. 'Same reason you and me is difficult. Scout don't belong here. When your body is caged and your spirit wants to wander, that's when big trouble always starts.'

Out of the corner of her eye, Alex saw the five girls

who'd been cleaning tack returning to the dormitory via the road.

She said urgently: 'What happens if Scout carries on being difficult? Will they be patient with him?'

'Hard to say. He has to pay his way like everyone else. If he don't or if the warden takes against him . . . ' He drew his finger across his throat. 'Doggy chow.'

A rooster crowed loudly. Alex almost jumped out of her skin. With an anguished glance at the stranger, she bolted up the path. The palomino watched her go.

The unexpected encounter cost Alex ten minutes and by the time she'd attempted to improve her appearance, she was late for breakfast. She reached the dining hall at 7.44 a.m., only to be informed that the kitchen had prepared no food for her and she could expect nothing until lunch. Furious at this injustice and hating Camp Renew more with each passing second, Alex threw a tantrum. Katie folded her arms and smiled throughout.

When Alex ran out of steam, she said simply: 'You'll be getting fruit for lunch but nothing else. And if you keep this up, I'll let the kitchen know that you won't be having dinner either.'

For Alex, every moment of the rest of the day was misery. Homesick and starving, she had to sit through hours of lessons before being allowed a spongy apple and an over-ripe banana at noon. Over and over her thoughts returned to the palomino and the slaughterhouse fate that might await him if he didn't learn to cooperate.

In the afternoon, she and six other girls were put to work in the vegetable garden and grounds, weeding and digging.

'Anywhere else they'd call it blackmail,' said Jodi, an African American girl whose sweet, elfin face belied her violent past. 'Here they call it positive reinforcement. It's sort of carrot and stick. Any time you put up a fight or mess up a chore, they just quietly pile on more work. On top of that Bud Baxter, the fitness instructor, will go out of his way to kill you during PE. Meanwhile, they take away your privileges. Those are things like eating chocolate brownies once a week or watching films on Sunday. Lose those and life isn't worth living. On the other hand, if you cooperate, they show you, hey, we can be nice if you let us. You'll see – one of the kitchen staff will slip you an extra piece of pie at dinner.'

Alex's stomach growled at the thought. She glanced at Jodi. 'How long have you been here?'

'Only three months.'

'*Only?* I'd go mad if I was here that long.'

Jodi laughed. 'Girl, you might as well check into the loony bin now 'cos that's the least you're gonna be here for. They don't even let you enrol in Camp Renew unless your parents pay three months' fees in advance, but Warden Cartwright reckons he gets the best results after a year. He told me I'm looking at fifteen months.'

'Fifteen *months!*'

Alex's heart went off a cliff. She tried to recall Jeremy's exact words when she'd asked how long he and her mother were planning to send her away for. For the first time it struck her that he'd evaded her question. *You'll be home before you know it, Alex. Think of it as a chance to see another country.*

In her shocked-awake state, she'd interpreted that as a week or two. Until now, nobody had contradicted her.

'I can't be here one day longer than two weeks,' she told Jodi, her voice rising. 'That's for certain. I mean, I have school. I have a *life*. I don't belong here. I made a mistake, but I'm not a juvenile delinquent. There's no way my mum would have sent me away for months on end. She just wouldn't. I know her and she wouldn't.'

Lyle, the activity supervisor, came striding over. 'Is there a problem?'

'No problem,' said Jodi, looking warningly at Alex. 'Alex here thought she'd been bitten by something, but it was just her imagination.'

Alex manufactured a smile. 'I'm fine. It was my imagination.'

Lyle's face registered disbelief. 'Great. Because, you know, Warden Cartwright likes to keep a harmonious house. Those who create discord find it tough to proceed through the levels.'

When he moved away, Jodi grabbed two rakes and Alex's arm and dragged her towards the main lawn.

'Ow! Let go of me.'

'Am I hurting you? Well, let me save you a whole lot

more pain and aggravation. You ain't gonna beat the system. That won't stop you trying but I promise it'll make things a thousand times worse. Trust me, I know. I've spent more time on Retreat than anyone else in the history of Camp Renew.'

The word 'retreat' conjured up images of a pretty forest dotted with attractively furnished cabins, where students got to spend time in idle contemplation. 'Is that some kind of reward?'

Jodi laughed harshly. 'It is if you enjoy getting eaten alive by bugs, freezing your butt off and surviving on rice cakes. You know how in prisons they talk about solitary confinement? Well, Retreat is Camp Renew's version. Only in order to sell it to the fee-paying parents, they don't stick you in a dark hole. They send you out into the wilderness. Adults love the thought of their out-of-control child getting in touch with nature. To them it's romantic. They don't realise that it's actually hell with a sky.'

Alex's eyes widened with alarm.

'Oh, don't worry. Your first wilderness experience will be a breeze by comparison. That's purely an initiation rite. Once you've been here a couple of weeks and learned a few survival skills, they send you out for forty-eight hours with warm clothes, a tent and food, plus a fishing hook in case you fancy yourself as some pioneer from the last century. It's a character test. You go on horseback and it's kind of cool once you stop being terrified out of your mind.

'After that, though, they use the wilderness as a punishment. You fail to toe the line and they send you out with nothing but a sleeping bag, a box of matches, a fishing line and a bottle of water. You're on foot. No horse. They drop you in the middle of nowhere and you stay there until you've had time to reflect on your actions. You have a radio to contact them in an emergency, but that's it. Take it from me, you learn pretty fast.'

Alex stared at her. The knot in her stomach swelled until it felt like a football. 'Where I come from, you'd never get away with that. Health and Safety would have a fit. What about our human rights?'

'You got a lawyer?'

'Has anyone ever run away? If you're out there on your own in the wilderness, what's stopping you from simply walking out?'

Jodie hooted. 'You're messing with me, right? This place is ringed by mountains and security fences and crawling with rattlesnakes and bears and mountain lions. They deliberately bring you here on back roads so you never really know where you are. Even if you did somehow avoid the guards and biting creatures and get through the electric fence and onto a main road, you're far from civilisation in a place where few cars pass. You'd be picked up by a cop patrol car before you'd gone two miles. You might as well stick a sign on your back with a target on it. But that's not all . . . '

She rolled up the right leg of her jeans. Above her trainer was a black band with a winking red light at the back of it. 'You get one free pass in the wilderness – your first. Blow it and they fit you with a tracker. You go to the bathroom and they know about it. So you can forget thinking you can run for the hills as soon as they let you off the leash. No, the best way to survive Camp Renew is to work the system. You know, suck up to the right staff members and make them think you're complying so they cut you some slack on your homework and in the activities you don't like.'

With leaden limbs, Alex picked up a sack and began to gather leaves. 'What did Lyle mean about those who create discord finding it tough to move through the levels?'

'Camp Renew's entire programme is structured around the idea that there are five progress markers on the road to personal improvement and fulfilment.'

Jodie propped her rake against her hip and counted them off on her fingers. 'Phase one is denial. You come here angry at everyone – your family, friends and the staff and students at Camp Renew. You can't believe you're here. You're convinced there's been a terrible mistake. At the same time, you're scared and lonely. So you start pretending to be a model student while inwardly hating your mum and dad and everyone else. It's fake progress. Phase two is when you start to own up to the wicked stuff you've done and get real.'

'But I've only ever done one wicked thing and that wasn't my fault . . . ' protested Alex.

Jodi pushed up her sleeves, revealing a scorpion tattoo

bizarrely at odds with her angelic features. 'See what I mean? You're in phase one: denial. Stop lying. Phase three is when you start to understand that actions have consequences. At the same time, you're getting on better with people and empathising with their problems.'

'Is that the stage you're in?'

'Could be. Or maybe I'm still in phase one and only pretending that I'm all right. Phase four is when you work on your relationships with friends and family and prove that you can honour your commitments. Phase five is when you learn and prove that you're truly a changed person and will stay out of trouble when you get home.'

Standing on the snake-green lawn, dwarfed by the scope and scale of the mountain landscape, Alex felt as inconsequential as a speck of fluff on a cinema screen. Her throat was bone dry. It was ages until dinner and she still had a riding lesson (good) and two hours of PE with the sadistic Bud Baxter (horrible) to get through before she got to shower at 9 p.m. Lights went out at 9.45 p.m. after a further prep session. As far as she could tell, the aim of the academy staff was to tire out their rebellious charges to such an extent that they no longer had the energy to disobey.

There was a note of desperation in her voice. 'How long does it take? To get through the levels?'

Jodi shrugged. 'Impossible to say. It's different for everyone. Plus the staff never tell you which level you're on. Warden Cartwright has X-ray vision and if there's even a hint of wrong-doing, there's time added to your sheet. You're looking at six months minimum, but probably closer to a year. The life you mentioned back in the UK – I wouldn't count on seeing it any time soon.'

The head groundkeeper came striding over. 'Good job, girls. Jodi, I've been instructed to tell you that you're excused from swimming today, but Miss Egress would appreciate it if you could take a turn on lifeguard duty. Alexandra, you have a riding lesson now. Hope that goes well.'

Alex nodded dumbly and set off along the path to the barn. From the moment she'd seen photos of Camp Renew's horses in the brochure, she'd clung to the thought that no matter how awful life got at least she'd be close to horses. And once she'd arrived at the academy and seen the wranglers striding back and forth to the barn in their jeans and fringed leather chaps, she'd also liked the prospect of showing them that they didn't have a monopoly on equine knowledge. That just because they could stay on a bucking bronco or rope a steer didn't mean that they could ride elegantly over a show jump and perform dressage moves that would leave people gasping.

That had all changed after her conversation with Jodi. Warden Cartwright might be able to lock Alex up, threaten her, dictate where she went or what she said or even banish her to the wilderness, but he couldn't control her mind any more than he could control that of the palomino mustang. Her affinity with horses was the one thing she had to hold on to. It was precious. If the staff at Camp Renew found out about it there was a real danger that they, like her parents, would ban her from being around the creatures she loved whenever they wanted to punish her.

No, her gift for riding and the contents of Pluto's pouch, which had thus far escaped detection, were all that remained of the ruins of her old life. They were her secrets and that was how it was going to stay.

8

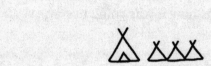

On the morning of her sixteenth birthday, Alex awoke stiff, cold and sleep-deprived in the wilderness with only Clyde for company. Not that she was complaining. As companions go, the placid bay was infinitely preferable to any of the humans at Camp Renew and the ground beneath her sleeping bag was only marginally less uncomfortable than her bunk.

It was the first time she'd ever been camping and what came to her as she unzipped the tent and inhaled an invigorating blast of pine-scented air was that it was also the first time she'd ever been truly independent and responsible for her own decisions.

It was an illusion, of course. Camp Renew was a fifty-thousand-acre fortress and she had strict instructions about where to go and how to conduct herself over the next day and a half. But it was a welcome illusion. Never in her life had she been less free and yet never had she felt more alive and at liberty to go anywhere and do anything. It almost made up for the hours she'd spent convinced she was about to be mauled by a bear.

Climbing out of her tent, Alex could just about make out Clyde's silhouette, ears pricked as he swung to watch her. It was 5.30 a.m. and still pitch dark, but within minutes she intended to be packed up and on the move. During the night a plan had formulated in her mind. She was reluctant to think about it in too much detail because every time she did so she became paralysed with the same terror that had gripped her as Chase Miller bumped out of sight in the academy trailer.

'Now don't go doing anything stupid,' he'd warned her. 'Without exception, the students who've tried to get smart have come unstuck. One was almost killed by a bear and others have lost blood, brains or limbs. Pay attention to the wilderness training you've been given. With your riding as poor as it is, my recommendation would be that you make your camp here and don't move more than a few hundred feet in any direction. Clyde will take care of you.'

This sage advice came back to Alex as she saddled the bay by torchlight. Her fingers were clumsy with cold, but sweat crawled down her spine. *Don't think, don't think, don't think. Just act.*

After securing her tent and sleeping bag behind the saddle and slinging her bags over the saddle horn, she mounted and nudged Clyde along the dark track.

Perhaps because the Camp Renew staff were concerned about her survival skills, they'd deposited her no more than a couple of miles from the academy. If Alex's hand-drawn map was to be believed, that meant she was around five or six minutes' ride from the pastures where the horses were turned out each evening – less if she loped. That was the wranglers' word for cantering – loping.

It was easier said than done. The initial part of the plan worked beautifully. She hoped that if she gave Clyde his head he'd go directly to the slopes where he spent his nights, and so it proved. As she neared it, she dismounted, unsaddled him and removed his bridle, leaving his rope halter underneath. After tying him to a fence post, she took a handful of carrots from her saddlebag and let herself into the paddock.

Within seconds she was at the centre of a kicking and biting melee. It was a miracle she wasn't seriously injured, especially since it was still quite dark. Cursing herself for her idiocy, she sprinted away from the hungry mob. But excitement had spread through the herd. Every horse she approached with the bridle either shoved its hindquarters in her direction or sped away with a toss of its mane.

Alex began to panic. A faint seam of rose had appeared in the sky and a glance at her watch showed that she had forty-five minutes at best before one of the wranglers came to drive the horses to the academy. On the fringe of the excited herd, but slightly separate from it, was the palomino. Alex felt a pang of conscience. Scout was another reason she'd lain awake the previous night. Her heart clamoured at her to take him with her, to save him before the wranglers lost patience and he was turned into pet food. Her head insisted he was a one-way ticket to A&E. If the wranglers couldn't manage him, what hope did she have? She needed a dependable horse that would not go nuts in traffic or anywhere else and leave her stranded.

She set her sights on a pinto cow pony. One of her dorm-mates rode him regularly and he was quiet and well behaved. Better still, he stood his ground as she approached. She had one arm around his neck and was lifting the bridle over his ears when another horse jostled him and he took fright.

Alex was close to tears. It was no use. She was a nervous wreck and understandably the horses had picked up on it. What choice did she have but to return to her campsite and stay there until Chase Miller came to fetch her the following day? He'd take her back to the prison that was Camp Renew and there she'd stay until Warden Cartwright deigned to release her. If Jodi was to be believed, that could be a year or more.

The previous day she'd spoken to her mum for the first time since getting off the plane in Denver two and a half weeks earlier. Alex had hoped to persuade her mum to relent, but it transpired that there was no such thing as an unmonitored call at Camp Renew. Dorm superintendent Helga Ward, a former drill instructor in the Navy, had sat glowering across from her throughout. Handed a script of therapist-approved conversational topics, Alex had been instructed in no uncertain terms to steer clear of emotive subjects that might lead to conflict. There'd been no chance of her begging to go home, as she'd planned.

'The house is so awful and empty without you,' said her mother, already a stranger. 'It feels as if you've been gone forever.'

One part of Alex melted when she heard the emotion in her mum's voice. The other part became even more enraged than it already was. If her mother missed her one per cent as much as she claimed she did, she'd have been in Colorado a fortnight ago, apologising for putting her daughter through such a horrific ordeal and taking her home on the next plane.

But Alex could say none of that. Nor did she get a chance to, because in the next breath Natalie said: 'How are the horses? Have you done any riding?'

In Alex's mind, keeping her riding talent a secret had become an obsession. Afraid that her mother would give her away, she burst out: 'I've been getting up at four every morning and shovelling manure. That's not exactly my idea of fun. They didn't put that in the brochure, did they, Mum? Or the fact that they have mustangs so wild even the wranglers struggle to stay on?'

With Helga giving her a thunderous glare, she added quickly: 'But that's okay because I'm finding other things I like. There's an indoor rock-climbing wall and we've been learning how to build fires and make emergency shelters in the wilderness . . . '

Helga tapped her watch meaningfully. Alex was glad to hang up. Home seemed like something that had happened to someone else in another lifetime.

Now even the horses had rejected her. Turning her back on them, she sank onto the frosty grass, a black dot beneath the fading night sky. That was it. She'd officially hit rock bottom. She might as well wait for the wranglers to show up and take whatever punishment was meted out. She was past the point of caring. In the place where her heart used to be was something as cold and heavy as flint. All she'd needed to do was catch one horse among the sixty-four in the pasture. *One.* A toddler could have managed it, but she'd failed.

Alex took out her crumpled map. Over the past few weeks she'd done her best to build up a picture of the ranch that lay beyond the electric fence of the academy campus by asking different people questions. From the teachers she'd learned the geography of the nearby mountains and rivers. Chase Miller had pointed out where the horses' night pasture was, and by asking Jodi and several other girls about their wilderness experiences she'd been able to sketch in a lake, a gulley and a cave where a family of bears reputedly resided.

But the most helpful information had come from

Ernesto, the Mexican cattleman she'd met when she first saw the palomino. When she asked him how he got his cows to market, he'd explained that the wranglers drove them to a corral near the main road, where they were picked up by a lorry.

'Is the main road far?' she'd asked, remembering Jodi's comments about escape being impossible because of the ranch's remoteness.

He laughed. 'Is nothing, is close. Maybe three miles,' pointing towards a dip in the blue hills. Nervous that he'd said too much, he'd then rushed to do his chores.

At that stage, running away had still been a pipe dream. The inescapable fact was that she was in a heavily guarded academy situated on a remote ranch teeming with dangerous creatures. Any attempt to strike out alone would be lunacy.

Even so, an hour before she was due to depart for her wilderness adventure, Alex had unpicked Pluto's side seam and taken out the roll of cash hidden in his belly. Just in case. For four years she'd saved every penny of lunch and pocket money she'd been given in the hope of eventually buying a horse. The biggest windfalls had been the birthday and Christmas cash sent by her father, now living with his former secretary and new family in Perth, Australia. Guilt money, Alex's mum called it. The occasional phone call aside, it was the only contact Alex had with him.

To stop herself blowing the money on clothes or electronics in a weak moment, she'd got into the habit of sewing up Pluto's pouch every time she added a sizeable amount to the stash. Now, of course, her priorities had changed. If a chance of escape presented itself, her £580 savings might be her passport to freedom.

Ironically, it was one of her jailers who'd planted the seeds of a getaway plan in her head. Driving out to the wilderness camp Chase Miller's truck crested a rise and Alex saw, between the blue hills, a ribbon of road. But it was not that which caused her blood to quicken. It was the four horseboxes flashing by.

'Is there an event on somewhere?' asked Alex and could have kicked herself. She was supposed to be ignorant about all aspects of equestrianism. 'I mean, is there a rodeo on or something?'

Chase braked hard to avoid a leaping deer and turned right, up a steep track. 'Most likely they're headed for Boulder. That's a university town a little ways from here. Some businessman with more money than sense is putting on a long-distance horse race with a winner-takes-all pot of $250,000. Every loon in the country thinks they have a shot at it. People who've maybe sat once on a horse. How they think they're gonna ride all the way to Oregon beats me. It'll be a bloodbath.'

Alex was riveted. 'Is Oregon far?'

'Twelve hundred miles.'

'Twelve *hundred* miles?'

'Uh-huh. Longest endurance race since Frank Hopkins supposedly rode from Texas to Vermont in the nineteenth century. On horseback, that's about a month's hard riding. So they say. Personally, I think ninety-nine per cent of the field will drop out in the first thirty miles. Those fruitcakes don't have a clue what they're getting into. The only saving grace is that J.B. Ellington – he's the Green Power CEO who's puttin' the race on – is a horse fanatic. No rider will be allowed to cross the start line unless their animal is passed fit to race by a veterinarian.'

'Are any of the wranglers entering?'

Chase pulled into a clearing and parked. 'Over my dead body. A couple of 'em had their hearts set on it but two things stopped 'em: the entry fee, which is about $250, and you don't get it back if you quit after the first mile, and me tellin' 'em they'd have nobody but themselves to blame if they took part in such foolishness. The story I'm getting from Boulder is that it's chaos. Not enough volunteers and all of these darn fools that don't know one end of a horse from the other.'

Impatience clouded his face as he watched Alex incompetently pick up a bridle by the bit. 'I don't know why I'm worrying about those idiots when I got enough problems of my own right here. Girl, I hope you're gonna survive out here. *You* barely know one end of a horse from another.'

It was this conversation that had kept Alex up half the night. That and the screeches of the forest creatures. Half of them sounded as if they were being murdered in cold blood and the other half sounded as if they were doing the murdering. She'd fully expected to be a menu item.

To distract herself, she'd found herself returning again and again to the race Chase had spoken of. He'd mentioned that there were not enough people who understood horses staffing the race. If she could get to Boulder, perhaps she could find work there until she figured out what to do next.

But to do that she needed a horse and that horse couldn't be the palomino or Clyde. The mustang was too wild and she needed Clyde as a decoy. If she 'borrowed' one of the other horses and hid Clyde, it might buy her enough time to get away.

That had been her plan, at least. It hadn't occurred to her that she wouldn't be able to catch a single horse. The cold dampness seeping through her jeans was a painful reminder that she would not be going anywhere except back to the campsite with Clyde. Her pie-in-the-sky scheme had failed.

At that very moment something tickled the back of her neck. She went still. Horse breath, sweet as a new-cut meadow, warmed her right ear. Slowly – by the tiniest degrees – she turned. Half a dozen horses were arranged in an arc behind her, eyeing her curiously. Only one had had the courage to step forward.

Alex stood up carefully. During the week she'd been on manure duty, she'd found an opportunity every single day to sneak a few sugar cubes to Scout, the palomino. He'd never acknowledged her in any way, so she'd had no choice but to leave them on the ground. Yet here he was, stretching out his golden neck, nostrils fluttering.

She ran a hand over his muzzle. He quivered, breathing in the scent of her, ready to run. When she put the bridle over his head he snorted in alarm, but he followed her willingly enough to the gate. With every step she debated whether to release him. She'd seen the wranglers attempting to ride him. Most days he was a nightmare. But the clock was ticking. An image of Strike Cartwright swam into her head. *Apply yourself or pay the price, Alexandra.*

She would never get a better chance to get away from Camp Renew. Either she took the risk that she'd be able to manage the palomino or she resigned herself to a year or more at the mercy of the warden.

Outside the gate, Scout stood impatiently while she tacked him up. Clyde's saddle was so heavy she could barely lift it. There were an infernal number of straps. Eventually she was done. She put a foot in the stirrup. Scout's ears flattened against his head and he sidled away. She hopped after him. Conscious that at any minute one of the wranglers might come galloping down the track, she was frantic to leave the scene of the crime. At the same time she knew that the only way to persuade him to do as she asked was to be patient. She took a deep breath and kept her movements slow and confident.

On her next attempt, Scout leapt forward. It was only because Clyde's lead rope pulled taut, momentarily checking the palomino, that Alex managed to scramble aboard. Scout's quarters sank beneath her and he reared. Alex threw herself forward and clung on. When his forefeet slammed down, every instinct told her to abandon the whole mission. Her hands were shaking so much that she could barely hold the reins. But there was too much to lose.

'On with you and let's have no more of your nonsense!' she boomed, doing her best impression of Clare at Dovecote Equestrian Centre.

To her astonishment, the palomino moved forward without further protest. Clyde lurched into a trot in their wake. Before she knew it the pasture was receding into the distance.

In order to avoid leaving tracks or running into vehicles, Alex travelled parallel to the gravel road. She rode at a medium trot, wary of going any faster in case Scout took it into his head to buck or bolt. He did neither. Gradually, Alex relaxed. It was so enjoyable to be back in the saddle and riding her best again, to not have to pretend to be horse-phobic and incompetent that, despite her predicament, she found herself smiling. Clyde trailed obediently behind.

After a couple of miles she crossed a stream flanked by trees. Dismounting, she positioned Clyde so that he was invisible from the road but also sheltered and with access to water. Then she wound leather hobbles around his forelegs. His movement was restricted to bunny hops – quite startling to the uninitiated but an everyday event

83

to a ranch horse. If he panicked or made even a small attempt to escape them, they'd break immediately. By that time, hopefully, she'd be far away.

From her saddlebag she took one of her two small sacks of feed and put it on the ground for him, saving only a handful to keep Scout sweet as she remounted. Clyde tried to follow but was brought up short by his hobbles. He whinnied after them. In the silence of the dawn, the sound seemed to ricochet off every hill.

With every step she expected a wrangler or security guard to jump from the bushes and arrest her. She thought too that Scout would be reluctant to leave his friends. She was wrong on both counts. Nothing and no one interrupted their progress. The palomino's ears were pricked and he moved with the keenness of a husky at the start of the Iditarod. Perhaps, like her, he had no friends.

A voice in Alex's head clamoured at her to stop. To turn back before it was too late. She had no real plan beyond the gate, beyond getting away. This was not an adventure – not in the least. It was suicide.

She decided to let Scout make the decision. If at any point he hesitated she'd retreat to the safety of her camp.

He never faltered. Barely eight minutes after they'd said goodbye to Clyde, the cattle pens came into view. Beyond them was the ranch gate – wide open. And beyond that was the grey thread of road and the promise of freedom.

Alex could not believe her good fortune. It wasn't

supposed to be this easy. There had to be a catch. An alarm that would send out a siren screech. A guard with a gun, concealed and waiting. She approached the corral with caution, keeping to the cover of the trees with their vivid autumn leaves. There were several outbuildings, but it was impossible to tell whether or not they were occupied. Alex's mouth was parched with fear. Beneath her, the palomino was equally tense, eyes out on stalks. In another two minutes they'd be through the gate and onto the relative safety of the road.

Once again, she glanced over her shoulder. Against the backdrop of violet mountains, a red tendril of dust was curling into the sky. As she watched, a new column rose to join it.

Someone was coming! A vehicle was heading in their direction and it was travelling at speed. There was no time to hide. At any moment it would fly over the rise and there they'd be, sitting ducks.

'Run, Scout, run!' yelled Alex, shoving the reins up his neck and using her legs to drive him forward. Her terror infected the palomino and he accelerated with a power and speed she'd never experienced on any horse, not even one bred to race. They hurtled towards the exit, Scout's shoes clattering on the gravel. Behind them, the plume of dust barrelled through the clear morning air like steam from a runaway train.

At the last conceivable second Alex saw why the gate was open. An iron cattle grid more than twelve feet deep from front to back barred their way. To attempt it would be madness. If Scout fell even fractionally short he'd risk smashing a leg and/or maiming her. Desperately she tugged at the reins. The curb bit was harsh and he ducked his head to get away from it, but she realised with a shock that he had no intention of stopping. Afraid of hurting him, she gave him his head. He'd surely refuse or run out when he saw the gaping metal mouth of the grid.

Then, suddenly, it was too late. They'd passed the point of no return. On the next stride Scout gathered himself. Alex barely had time to grab a handful of mane before he took off. The roar of an approaching engine carried through the trees. Any second now it would be upon them. There was nothing she could do but close her eyes and hope.

9

Potts Field, East Campus, University of Colorado, Boulder

Will used a rag to give Shiraz a final polish and stood back to admire the result. To him, she'd never looked better. A crash course of good nutrition and intensive training had lent a layer of sleek muscle to her angular frame in just a couple of weeks, and her freckled grey coat was almost shiny. Best of all was her change in mood. The apathy that had begun to creep through her like a virus in the confines of Tyler's field had gone. Her rose-petal nostrils savoured each new scent. Her intelligent eyes took in every new sight and scene with a delight that would have been infectious had Will not been so plagued with guilt about his father.

'Would you mind moving? You're blocking the way.'

Will barely had time to jump aside before a groom

leading a high-stepping Arabian with a gleaming liver chestnut coat shoved past him and into the next stall. The near-perfect conformation and condition of the gelding, a testament to good breeding and a large bank balance, was like a slap in the face to Will and Shiraz.

The groom secured the stall door and carefully poured a bottle of mineral water into a bucket for his charge. When he looked up and caught Will and Shiraz watching him, his gaze flickered over the mare with distaste.

'I think you might be in the wrong place. As I understand it, the professional riders are down this end. Amateurs and their mules are over on the other side.'

Will nearly fell for it. So awkward and out of place did he feel that a jibe from a stranger came across as an order that should be obeyed. But he wasn't going to stand for anyone insulting Shiraz.

He said coolly: 'That's funny because, as I understand it, Jonas Ellington, the man who created The Glory, made it clear from the outset that he wants this to be an open race – open to everyone and not just the elite few. Shiraz and I are quite comfortable here, thanks. This is the stall we've been allocated and this is where we'll stay.'

To his surprise, the man gave a quick, tense smile. 'Fair enough. Sorry. I'm Mike Berry, Dietrich Anders's groom. My nerves are shredded. We've had quite a time of it trying to get our horses in and out of quarantine, rested and in shape for the race after a long journey from the Netherlands. Then, of course, we get here and it's like a three-ring circus. Anyone who owns a mammal with more than three legs is trying to pass the veterinary inspection. I could have sworn I saw a cow.'

Will left Mr Berry complaining to a fellow groom and went out exploring. It was true that the riot of activity on Potts Field, more usually home to the University of Colorado's track and field teams, resembled a staging post in a Wild West movie, but in his opinion the organisers were coping admirably with the hordes. They'd been besieged with entries.

The size of the purse had attracted top endurance riders from countries as far afield as the United Arab Emirates, Australia, South Africa and Europe. While some big names had stayed away, unwilling to risk their own health or that of their champion horses over 1,200 miles of brutal terrain, even for a quarter of a million dollars, plenty of others were up for the challenge. Naturally, they were among the favourites to take the prize. But not everyone was convinced they'd last the distance. Across the US people were putting bets on local horsemen who knew the terrain and had horses who were not soft from a cushy life in stables but were forged in steel.

Also in the mix were the unknown quantities – people like Will. The *non*-professionals. They were the burger flippers, paper pushers, teachers, lawyers, dentists, IT geeks and extreme sports fanatics who just happened to have got their hands on a horse which by hook or by crook had made it through Green Power's stringent vet checks. Judging by the number of out-of-control horses

Will had seen since he'd arrived the previous afternoon, for some it was a gamble too far.

There were four blocks of fifty temporary stalls, available on a first come, first served basis, and rope enclosures in a large paddock for any remaining horses. The starting field would be three hundred and two. Critics of the race argued that it was too many, but their voices had been drowned out by the vociferous support of the participants and tourist and business communities of the states through which the race would pass: Colorado, Wyoming, Idaho and Oregon.

Beyond the stable blocks were two exercise arenas. As Will approached there was a loud thwack as one horse kicked another in the shoulder, eliminating it in an instant from the race. Over in the second section a white-faced woman was clinging to the bridle of a plunging Appaloosa. The horse had a barrel-shaped body that would be crippling to ride for any distance and the kind of short, bulky musculature that would play havoc with its cooling system during any period of extended exertion. The race began at dawn the next day. Will felt for them. He doubted the pair would make it to lunchtime.

Then again he had an irrational fear that something would happen to finish his own chances before The Glory had even started, so he didn't feel inclined to judge.

The wafting aromas of the food court made his stomach rumble. He quickened his pace, hurrying past a snaking line of market stalls booming country music. The drifting barbecue smoke mingled with the smells of new leather, molasses and a variety of oils and liniments. Riders buzzed like bees around the stands selling everything from ultra-light endurance saddles to Ariat endurance boots and vitamin-boosting smoothies for horses and riders.

A woman selling warm weather gear caught Will's eye. 'Sure you got everything, hon? It's a long race and if winter moves in early, it's going to be hellish cold.'

Will shook his head and hurried on. He was perfectly well aware that he didn't have everything he needed, but there was not a lot he could do about it. For the journey from Tennessee to Colorado, he'd found a ridiculously cheap last-minute horsebox hire deal on the Internet, but the fuel had cost him much more than he'd bargained for. Once he'd paid his entry fee, he had just $96 to last him for the duration of the race – no problem at all if he was forced to quit after a couple of days but a huge one if he survived the entire month and anything major went wrong.

But, Will told himself, it wouldn't. Failure was not an option. He'd staked everything on this. He had to win. *Had to.* If he didn't, there'd be no possible way for him to keep Shiraz and no money to pay for his father's operation. Worse, it would mean that he'd lied to his dad for nothing.

The surgeon had made it clear that stress could cause Len to suffer another heart attack. Far more than the race itself, it was that which kept Will awake at night.

His dad was under the illusion that the only reason Will had quit the Bigger Burger and left Chattanooga barely a month after Len's release from hospital was because he'd been offered a trial period as a highly paid wrangler in Colorado. If he ever found out that Will had instead spent the last of his college savings on the entry fee for one of the longest and most treacherous horse races ever attempted, the shock could kill him.

That was the reason Will hadn't eaten since arriving in Boulder the previous afternoon. Guilt. He was nauseous with it.

Exiting the tented village Will saw a crowd gathering around the demonstration arena, with more people joining all the time. A roar of appreciation went up. There was so much jostling that several minutes elapsed before he spied a gap near the entrance and was able to see what held them in thrall.

A devilishly handsome man in a red shirt and breeches was reclining on the bare back of a galloping stallion. As if that wasn't remarkable enough, he was also shuffling a pack of cards. He sat up, wrapped his legs around his horse's sides and flashed a grin at his audience. Among his admirers was an especially pretty redhead. Spotting her, he did a theatrical double take. Without touching the reins, he stopped his mount within a couple of strides and made him back up – all the while comically fanning himself with the cards. The girl went the same shade as her hair.

There were more oohs and aahs as the showman

somersaulted off his horse and presented her with the splayed deck, indicating that she should take a card. They cheered when she held up an ace. The man and his horse performed matching deep bows.

Will was entranced. The trick rider was impressive but he was nothing compared to the shimmering majesty of his horse. Will identified the stallion's breeding at once. No other horse in existence had a coat with the striking metallic colouring of the Akhal-Teke from Turkmenistan. This particular one had a mother-of-pearl-shell glow known as perlino. His high head carriage was reminiscent of an Arabian's and there was a greyhound leanness to his flanks. This was a horse genetically evolved to endure.

'Who's the rider?' Will asked his neighbour.

'You don't recognise him? You're not from around these parts, are you? Allow me to educate you. You have the privilege of watching Jack Carling, one half of the legendary Carling Brothers. That's Wyatt, the older one, over on the other side. They're Wyoming boys, born and bred, and they're about to teach some of these fancy foreigners and supposed endurance experts a thing or two about great horsemanship.'

The brim of Wyatt's Stetson was pulled down, hiding his eyes, but he had the same taut muscled frame and arrogant grace as his brother.

Having autographed the ace with a flourish and given it to the pretty redhead, Jack commanded his horse to lie down. Everyone laughed.

'As you can see, Desert King here likes to take a nap now and then. But don't be fooled, y'all. King is what's called an Akhal-Teke. He comes from darkest, furthest Turkmenistan. Do not expect me to find that on a map. I barely know the way to Cody and I grew up there. As some of you already know, Desert King ain't just a pretty face. In 1935, some of his ancestors carried a group of Turkmen two thousand five hundred miles from Ashba . . . Ashba-something to Moscow in eighty-four days. For three of those days they crossed two hundred and thirty five miles of desert without water.'

'Should I bet the house on you and the King to win?' someone shouted.

'I wouldn't go that far. Lotta things can happen out on the road. Lotta miles and a whole lotta trouble between here and Hood River. Plus I got my big brother to contend with.'

He saluted Wyatt, who grinned lazily in response.

'All I'm saying is that Desert King is bred to tackle big distances and twelve hundred miles woulda been a walk in the park for his forebears. I wouldn't bet against a Carling being in the mix when the action gets hot and heavy around the thousand-mile mark. No, sir, I would not.'

With that, he urged the stallion to his feet. There was much cheering and well-wishing as he walked from the arena and a groom rushed to take his horse. The crowd dispersed. Only Will stayed where he was. He'd noticed

94

something as Desert King stood up and was debating what to do about it.

Finally, he came to a decision. He ran to catch up with Jack Carling. The horseman was signing autographs as he walked. Will waited until the last fan had gone and followed Carling to the car and lorry park.

'Excuse me, Mr Carling.'

Carling turned with a smile, pen at the ready.

'Thanks, but I'm not here to get your signature.'

'You a reporter?'

Carling jingled his car keys, his gaze shifting over Will's shoulder.

'No, I'm not. Sir, I hope you don't think I'm out of line but I thought you might want to know that when your horse got to his feet in the arena he favoured his left side, as if something was tender. I mean, I'm sure the vet would have picked it up if there was a ligament issue, and I'm probably a thousand per cent wrong, but . . . '

He tailed off.

Carling was contemplating him with a sort of shocked admiration. 'And you are who, exactly?'

Will was taller than Carling and not easily scared but there was something about the way the man's nostrils whitened with tension that set alarm bells ringing. He fought the urge to take a step backwards.

'Will Greyton. I—'

'Since you've got the audacity to call into question my ability to care for my horse, Will Greyton, I'm assuming that you're older than you look and are actually a qualified veterinarian or an equine specialist? A farrier maybe?'

'No, sir, I'm just—'

'Or a race official? Are you a race official?'

'No, I—'

'Gosh, I'm all out of ideas. What *is* your job?'

'I'm unemployed at the moment. I left my job to compete in this race.'

'What job did you leave?'

Will wanted to crawl into the ground. 'I worked in the fast food industry.'

Carling stroked the stubble on his jaw. 'Ahhh, I get it. Somehow you've got yourself a pony with a bit of life in it and you've been gutsy enough or dumb enough to quit your minimum wage job frying chicken or whatever to chase the dream. Now you're on a mission to become a hero. I feel sorry for you, and because I'm a nice guy I'm going to offer you a friendly piece of advice. Quit. Seriously. Withdraw from the race and go home before you get hurt real bad. You're so way out of your league you're practically on Mars. The chances of you lasting more than an hour in this race are laughably remote. But they do say that every dog has his day so, in case you make it further, let me give you another tip.'

He leaned in so close that Will could smell the chewing gum on his breath, mingled with the spicy amber of his cologne. 'Keep your opinions on other people's horses to yourself. There are a whole lot of rattlesnakes in Wyoming. You wouldn't want to find one in your sleeping bag.'

He walked away with a spring in his step, whistling jauntily.

Will stared after him. Turning at last to go, he found his path blocked by an official.

'What was that all about?'

'Nothing,' Will said shortly.

The official had black eyes and a ring of curly brown hair that clung gamely to the desert of his skull. His red badge proclaimed him as Wayne Turnbull, Chief Clerk. He tipped his head in the manner of a crow examining a choice morsel. 'Didn't look like nothing. Looked like a whole lotta something to me.'

'Appearances can be deceptive. Actually, we were discussing Wyoming wildlife. Would you excuse me? I have a race to prepare for.'

'What's your name, boy?'

Will's blood started to simmer. He'd had better days at the Bigger Burger. It was on the tip of his tongue to ask, 'What's it to you?' But it made no sense to get on the wrong side of the chief clerk before the race had even started.

'Will Greyton.'

'You got a rider card on you?'

Reluctantly, Will tugged it from his pocket.

The clerk turned it over in his bony fingers. 'William Greyton of Chattanooga, Tennessee. Rider number 115.' He made a note on his pad.

'Mr Greyton, at race headquarters our number one priority is to run a clean, fair race. Troublemakers will be weeded out and disqualified, with no right of appeal. Now I don't know what your beef is with Jack Carling, but if I were you I'd get over it in a hurry. I could report you for this incident. I could end your race right here and now. It's tempting, but I'm going to put your behaviour down to youth and inexperience and let you off with a friendly warning. Along with some other famous riders here, the Carling Brothers are poster boys for The Glory. Their pictures are on most of our advertisements. They're also mighty popular in Wyoming. Stay out of their way or things could get real unpleasant for you real fast.'

He handed Will his pass with a crooked grin. 'Have a great day.'

It was a sunny day, mild for the season, but Will was chilled to the marrow. He decided to give the food court near the race headquarters a wide berth. Quite apart from the fact that he'd had all the 'friendly' warnings he could cope with in one morning, he'd lost interest in the cheap and healthy tofu stir-fry he'd planned to eat for brunch. The race started in less than twenty hours. If he was to have any chance of restoring his equilibrium before then he needed several cups of good coffee, a couple of eggs and a giant plate of pancakes drenched in maple syrup. It would make a big dent in his $96 but he didn't care.

Cutting through the crowds Will couldn't help noticing that everywhere he turned people were laughing and chatting and enjoying the pre-race bustle. Many of the professional riders knew one another and even the most humble entrant seemed to have a big circle of supporters. Nobody looked as if they were concerned about finding rattlesnakes in their sleeping bag.

As he left the park and set off in the direction of the Pearl Street Mall, he suddenly felt as if, Shiraz aside, he didn't have a friend in the world.

10

Betty's Diner, Pearl Street, Boulder, Colorado

The banana and caramelised pecan waffle that Alex was working her way through was so large, so laden with maple syrup and cream, and so delicious that it was not until she swallowed the last bite that she felt the first stirrings of dread.

From her corner seat by the window she had an unobstructed view of the Bank of America across the street. For much of the meal every time a customer emerged from its high wooden doorway she'd smiled in the expectation that it would be Crystal and Trey. As the minutes had ticked away, her enthusiasm had changed to mild concern. There was either a queue in the bank or they'd had to spend ages waiting for the appropriate person to deal with a foreign currency transaction. Either way, they'd probably be annoyed that it had been such a hassle. They'd also be upset that the cheeseburgers and fries they'd asked Alex to order for them were stone cold, and their root beer floats had lost their froth.

'I'll leave the check here for whenever you're ready, hon,' said the waitress, tucking the bill under the sugar bowl with one hand and topping up Alex's coffee with the other. She frowned at the uneaten food. 'You want me to put those in a to-go box for you?'

Alex cast another anxious glance out of the window. 'It's fine. My friends will be here any minute.'

She spoke with cheerful confidence, as if saying the words out loud would make them true. The alternative was too ghastly to contemplate.

The thought that kept gnawing at her was that it had all been going far too well for comfort. From the moment Scout had come up to her in the paddock, one marvellous fluke of fate had followed another. First, they'd crossed the ranch without being spotted. Then Scout had saved them from immediate capture by performing a world-record leap over the cattle grid. He'd swerved right immediately afterwards, sending Alex flying, but she'd managed to grab the saddle horn as she went and had more or less landed on her feet.

By some miracle, the vehicle she'd heard approaching had stopped at the cattle pens. If it had continued for even a short distance and left the ranch via the gate, the driver couldn't have failed to see Alex struggling to remount an excited Scout.

Once she was back in the saddle and could take

in the empty road tapering into the distance, the momentousness of what she'd done overwhelmed her. She knew nothing about the route ahead. How far did the ranch stretch? Were there CCTV cameras hidden on fence posts or in the bushes? How often did the police do their patrols?

She almost turned back. Almost. It was Scout who kept her going. He set off down the road with a certainty that was oddly reassuring. For the first time that morning Alex allowed herself to focus on the palomino and not her non-existent escape plan. Immediately, she was struck by how comfortable he was to ride. He moved at a mile-eating pace, faster than a walk and slower than a trot. She'd heard it described as the 'mustang shuffle'. His canter was like a gentle rock in a luxurious armchair. 'Lope' was an accurate term for it.

Several cars passed them. A child stared curiously from the back window of one. Alex was tense with anticipation, expecting at any second to hear sirens. She felt totally exposed. Tall fences and a thick line of trees hemmed her in, making it impossible to hide. Five more minutes and another car passed – an old banger, clanking as it went. Alex rode with a sense that a guillotine blade was about to fall.

Eleven minutes after escaping from Camp Renew she rounded a bend to be greeted by an extraordinary sight. An SUV and trailer were parked on the side of the road. The trailer gate was open and ten goats were scattered on the bank, one or two standing on their hind legs nibbling at leaves. As Alex approached, she saw a young couple perched on a boulder, smoking and laughing.

The boy got down unhurriedly and ground his roll-up into the grass. Judging by his downy stubble and grey woollen hoody, he was barely out of his teens. 'You look like a girl who knows a bit about farm animals. Any experience rounding up goats?'

In that instant Alex realised that a) she hadn't thought up a cover story for herself, and b) this was a gift of an opportunity that, if missed, would be lost forever.

'Depends.'

He laughed. 'We could pay you in chocolate brownies if that's any incentive.'

'How far are you going?'

He named a town that was gone from Alex's head as soon as he said it. That was her first mistake.

'Heard of it? Don't worry, not many people have. We're delivering the goats to a friend of a friend. Cash on safe delivery. At least, we were. But a little while ago, Crystal here became convinced that she'd dropped her phone in the trailer while we were loading them. When she went back to check, she didn't bother closing the gate. Cue mass goat breakout. Turned out the phone was in her purse all along. That was twenty minutes ago. As soon we try to sneak up on 'em . . . '

'If you give me a ride to Boulder, I'll help you catch them,' said Alex, doing her best to come across like a self-assured cowgirl and not a teenage delinquent on the run.

Crystal hauled herself to her feet using her boyfriend's sleeve. Her clothes had a cloying herbal scent and she had a high, pure voice that put Alex in mind of a glass wind chime. 'What'll you do with your horse?'

Alex couldn't help giggling. 'No, I mean both of us. If we can travel with you as far as Boulder, I'll make sure you catch all your animals.'

After loading Scout, who to her amazement and great relief put up only the most token resistance, she lured the goats into the trailer with the aid of the remaining horse feed. Banishing from her mind her mum's many warnings about never, ever getting into a car with strangers, she hopped into the SUV.

In Boulder her luck continued to hold. During the journey her companions had formed the impression that she was competing in the race herself. It was an idea that hadn't crossed Alex's mind until that moment, but she'd seized on it as a more plausible reason for an English girl to be riding alone to Boulder with her bedroll and tent than a stint as a volunteer.

Along the way, they'd asked lots of probing questions. Where was she from originally? What was she doing in Colorado? What were her parents' jobs? Why hadn't she used a horsebox to take her horse to Boulder rather than risk wearing him out before the race had even started? How did they feel about her taking part in such a dangerous event?

It was unnerving. Alex tried to put them off by saying that her stepfather had a contract with a local insurance company and she was being home-schooled, but they wanted to know which insurance company and where was it based and where did she and her family live. Most disturbingly, they also wanted to know where she'd found her pretty horse. In the end, she had no option but to primly inform them that she was not in the habit of telling her private business to complete strangers.

The couple lapsed into a wounded silence, broken only once by Trey. As they drove through the outskirts of Boulder, he said casually, 'Not far from where we picked you up, there's one of them boot camps for out-of-control teenagers. They get kids coming from all over the world . . .'

His eyes met Alex's in the rear view mirror. 'Ever heard of it?'

She stared back unflinchingly. 'Sounds familiar, but I'm not exactly sure where it is.'

Which was the first true thing she'd said all morning.

The traffic was at a standstill as they pulled into Boulder, prompting much grumbling from Crystal and Trey. Alex hardly heard them. She was too busy taking in the sights. Red brick buildings and funky cafes and shops, and the Colorado Rockies rising above them, dove-grey and ribbed with forest, snow dribbling down their upper slopes like ice cream.

Cruising along streets lined with colourful posters,

clowns and banners advertising The Glory, Alex's fear of imminent capture was replaced by a dizzying excitement. Less than a month after her parents had banned her from being around the creatures she loved, she was in a town given over entirely to a celebration of all things horse. There was an electricity in the air that crackled in through the open window. Alex could feel it in her chest. It exerted a magnetic pull, as seductive as any travelling circus. Already Camp Renew seemed as alien a concept as her life back in England.

They followed signs to Competitors' Parking, Campground and Stables, situated on the University of Colorado's East Campus. As Alex hopped out of the SUV, country music, drifting barbecue smoke and the noisy energy of the milling competitors and grooms came at her in a heady wave. There were horses of every shape, size and colour. Some leaned eagerly from temporary stalls. Others were being washed, tacked up or exercised. At the far end of the stable block a farrier lifted a molten orange horseshoe and the smell of burning hoof reached Alex's nostrils.

It was horse heaven.

Wistfully, she wondered how she'd have fared if things had been different and she could have entered the race for real. What an adventure these riders were going to have. Their lives would never be the same again.

After unloading Scout, she turned to Trey and Crystal. 'Thank you so much. I don't know how my horse and

I would have managed without you. We'd have been exhausted before we'd even started.'

Trey grinned. 'Hey, no problem. Buy us brunch and that'll be all the thanks we need.'

'Sorry, guys. I would, but I have a million things to do.'

'We'll wait,' said Crystal. 'The goats will be fine if we give them some water while you're dealing with your horse. After that, we can head for the Pearl Street Mall. I know a cool cafe.'

'But I only have British money,' said Alex, her anxiety returning in a rush. 'I'll need to change it to US dollars and I don't have time to go hunting for a bank . . . '

Trey eyed her curiously. 'How long did you say you've been in the States?'

She avoided his gaze. 'Fine. I'll check in with the stables and be with you ASAP.'

Once again, she managed to brazen it out, persuading the stable manager who demanded her race registration card that she'd forgotten it at home, but that she'd be sorting out a replacement just as soon as she found a safe place for Scout. Fortunately, he didn't get officious on her. Within minutes the palomino was in a stall vacated by an injured horse. She left him munching happily on hay. The helpful manager led Alex to a secure storage area, where she was able to leave her tack, tent and saddlebags.

'I'm guessing that you have an endurance saddle tucked away in one of your bags,' he said as he locked the door. 'You do know you wouldn't last twenty miles in this race using a Western saddle, dontcha? That thing's gotta weigh over twenty kilos.'

Alex gave him a non-committal smile. 'Absolutely.'

There was a sinking feeling in her gut. The hour of reckoning was approaching. The race started at 8 a.m. the following day. Somehow she needed to have a job as a volunteer or have figured out what to do next by then. First, though, she needed to buy brunch – or lunch – for her new friends.

Those same friends had now spent thirty-nine minutes in the Bank of America.

After it had transpired that no financial institution in Boulder would exchange so much as five pounds without photo ID, which Alex didn't have, Crystal had offered to do it on her behalf. The notion of handing a near stranger her precious £580, which one teller had told her would come to over $800, was nerve-wracking, but Alex reasoned that they weren't the thieving type. They had a peace sign hanging from their rear view mirror. Besides, she'd be standing right beside Crystal when she received the money. What was the girl going to do – rob her in the middle of a bank?

But that wasn't how things had worked out. Trey's next suggestion was that she go ahead to the diner while he and Crystal stood in line in the bank. When

Alex had tried to object, the other girl scoffed at her.

'What, now you don't trust us? Please. We trusted *you* and let *you* into our vehicle when you could have been an axe murderer. We've delivered you and your horse to the stable door in Boulder, like you wanted, and we've now spent an hour walking the streets trying to find *you* a place to change *your* money. I mean, you're the first person I've ever met who doesn't have a credit card and photo ID. It's kind of weird, to be honest with you. Makes me suspicious. All Trey and me are asking is that you order us a couple of burgers and fries while we do you *yet another favour*, because we're starving. And now you're acting as if we're the Mafia about to run off with your cash or something.'

She pointed at Betty's Diner across the street. It had a candy-striped awning and blue shutters. Leaning against a lamp-post outside was a blue-painted bicycle, its basket filled with flowers.

'You'll be *right there*,' Crystal said. 'Right there! Trey can spit further than that. You can watch us from the window and call the cops if you're worried.'

Not wanting to seem petty and ungrateful, Alex retreated to the diner without further protest. Trey and Crystal had, after all, dropped from the heavens like angels and plucked her from the side of the road. If it wasn't for them, she had no doubt that she'd already be in the custody of Warden Cartwright, the police or both.

At Betty's everything looked and smelled so delicious

that Alex, seated in a booth for four, was suddenly ravenous. On impulse, she ordered a host of side items – a fruit salad of mango, pomegranate and blueberries, onion rings in batter and fried green tomatoes. The diner was heaving with people and service was understandably slow. While she waited for the meal to arrive, she studied the other customers.

Boulder was a university town popular with hikers and skiers, so many of the Fifties-style booths and tables were occupied by gangs of students and fresh air fiends in grungy leather jackets and T-shirts, walking gear or scratchy Fairtrade jumpers. In among the fruit smoothies and half-eaten plates of *huevos rancheros* (black beans, spicy tomato salsa, melted cheese, tortillas and fried eggs) were an abundance of laptops and iPads. The remaining diners were almost all in town for the race. They were officials, volunteers and competitors, a motley assortment in every type of riding wear imaginable, from jeans and cowboy boots to Lycra pants and trainers, breeches and Ariat endurance boots.

Only one other person was alone. Her view of him was partially blocked by a pillar, so that initially all she saw was the curve of his bicep beneath his flannel shirt and the novel he was reading, which had a white mustang on the cover. She knew it immediately as *Thunderhead*, one of her favourites. Intrigued, she watched as the boy turned the page, propped the novel against the sugar bowl, pushed back his sleeves and cupped both hands around his coffee mug.

Something peculiar happened to her then. Something that had never happened before, not ever. Gradually, she became aware that she was mentally tracing the outline of his hands and the lattice of veins on them. Though they did nothing more extraordinary than hold a mug, they conveyed a grace and strength that caused her fleetingly to imagine them on her body.

Equally mesmerising were his forearms, tanned the palest gold. He wore an inexpensive black sports watch on one wrist and a thin woven band on the other. The inside of his left forearm bore the trace of a scar.

Alex was still trying to make sense of why a partial view of a strange boy should make every nerve ending in her body tingle as if it had been brushed by fire when he leaned forward and caught her staring.

For most of her teenage years Alex had lived with a secret fear. While the onset of hormones had turned her classmates boy- or girl-mad, their every waking hour seemingly devoted to the hungry pursuit of real-life, famous or virtual members of the opposite sex to date, moon over or cyber-stalk, she'd felt nothing. She'd never loved anyone, never felt even the smallest tug of attraction for anyone, never pined over anyone or cried for anyone, and she'd never thought of any boy (or girl) outside of a book or film as hot. Handsome or pretty, yes, but not H.O.T.

She'd been kissed only once and that was at a charity dance at her school earlier in the year. It had been a sweltering night and the gym, packed with sweaty dancers, had quickly become a sauna. More out of desperation to know what it was like to be kissed than anything else, Alex had allowed herself to be led behind a hedge in the dark grounds by a sixth former. His mouth tasted of cigarette smoke and cheap canapés. It was all she could do not to gag.

Afterwards, his friends had nicknamed her Frosty. Privately, Alex was afraid that they were right. There was an iceberg inside her and she was going to have to go through life alone, never feeling anything.

But that was before the boy in the diner locked gazes with her.

If Alex hadn't been sitting down already she'd have fallen down, because the lower half of her body turned to liquid. She had to grip the edge of the table for support. Her first impression was that he was seventeen or eighteen and good-looking in an all-American way. Hair the colour of cut wheat, strong jaw, clear skin, regular features. A well-defined chest, disconcertingly visible beneath the white singlet that showed through the open neck of his shirt.

So far, so predictable. But the eyes that held Alex's were the intense grey-green of the ocean far from safe shores. They burned with intelligence and a mix of emotions too complex to identify. She only knew that as they made contact with hers a bolt of attraction that seemed downright indecent, given that they were in a crowded restaurant, went through her, melting her.

No question about it, he was H.O.T.

Her immediate reaction was a violent, *'No! This is not happening. I will not allow it to happen now, of all times, when there is not a thing I can do about it*. She gave him a fierce glare. The slow smile that had begun to steal across his face was stillborn. He retreated behind the pillar.

The arrival of the scrumptious waffle had helped to put him out of her mind. Now, as she sat surrounded by congealing food, she could focus on nothing but Trey, Crystal and her money. Had Camp Renew put out a missing persons report on national television? Perhaps Trey and Crystal had seen it on the news while waiting in the bank. Were the cops on their way?

The waitress was at the table again. 'Hon, we have a line. If your friends are a no-show, I'm gonna have to move you to a table for one.'

'They're coming.' Alex's eyes were glued to the door of the Bank of America. 'Maybe we could put their food in the warming drawer or something?'

'You betcha.' Expertly, the waitress scooped up the plates and stacked them against her arm. 'I don't mean to rush you, but my shift is ending and I need you to settle up. What'll it be – cash or credit?'

In that instant Alex knew with a sickening finality that something had gone wrong at the bank. Something irreparable.

'My friends have my cash. I can't pay until they come.'

'Can you give them a call, see where they've got to?'

'I don't have a phone.'

The waitress's demeanour changed. 'What are you telling me, ma'am? Are you saying you can't settle your account?'

Before Alex could muster an explanation, the manager was at her table waving the $48 bill and there was talk of calling the police. The diner fell silent. Everybody was staring at her.

She stammered: 'Th-these people who have my money, the truth is, I don't really know them. I think they may have stolen it. But maybe it's just very busy in the bank and they're still waiting to be seen.'

'I thought you said they were your friends?' the waitress accused.

'I was in the bank ten minutes ago,' a customer piped up. 'There were only two customers ahead of me – some old guy and a woman in yoga sweats.'

Alex found it difficult to breathe. The money was her lifeline, her passport to freedom. Without it she'd have no choice but to reverse-charge a call to her parents or Camp Renew and beg to be rescued. And what did that mean for Scout?

'Racine, get Officer Gregson on the line for me, please,' the manager said irritably.

Through a blur of tears, Alex saw the boy from behind the pillar rise and approach her table. He was tall and moved with a quiet confidence. Alex's face flamed as he neared. Her humiliation was now complete.

He smiled at the manager. 'Excuse me for interrupting,

but I think I can help.' Squatting, he reached under the table. When he stood up he held a $50 bill in his hand. He offered it to Alex.

'I thought I saw you drop this earlier but something distracted me and I forgot all about it. I'm sorry I didn't tell you sooner.'

The manager's mouth opened and shut. The waitress stopped in mid-dial.

The boy took $10 from his wallet and handed it to Racine. 'Thanks for looking after everyone so well.'

And with that he was gone, crossing the restaurant in five rangy strides. The door tinkled shut behind him.

The diners came to life in a swelling symphony of animated conversation, clashing plates and cutlery. Alex handed the money to Racine as if it were searing a hole in her palm.

The manager recovered her powers of speech. 'And they say chivalry's dead. I guess everyone's a winner now.'

'I'm sorry. I didn't mean to cause any trouble. I trusted the wrong people with everything I had and now it's gone.'

'Hey, I'm sorry too. We get a lot of runners – tourists and such who skip out without paying. We gotta come down hard on them or it becomes an epidemic. Would you like me to call Officer Gregson? He can take a statement from you, try to track them down.'

Alex picked up her jacket. 'Thanks, but no thanks. I have no one to blame but myself.'

'Wait till I fetch you a piece of cherry pie to go. Nothing like pie to make a bad day better.'

11

Day 1, 1st October, Centennial Park, Boulder, Colorado

Jonas B. Ellington blew on his hands in a futile attempt to warm them up, saying a silent prayer that the weather report was inaccurate while he was at it. The meteorologists were predicting . . . well, he wasn't really sure what they were predicting. Someone at the National Weather Service had been through the extreme climate lexicon. Depending on which channel you believed, in days to come Colorado and Wyoming residents faced the prospect of drowning, freezing or getting blown to Alaska.

Right now it was frosty but glorious. The early morning sunshine had rendered every grey crag and mauve contour of the mountain pristine, and lent a rose-tinted glow to the horsemen and women gathering in the park beneath it. The sky was a spirit-lifting blue. Few spirits were raised higher than those of the photographers and camera crews shooting the start of this, the longest recorded horse race in US history.

Jonas had been at the park before the first competitor arrived. He'd personally welcomed at least fifty riders before being called away by the race clerk and various other race staff members and volunteers to attend to last-minute queries and crises. Three hundred and three horsemen and women had entered the race, but already today six had withdrawn. A woman on a runaway Appaloosa had had to be stretchered out of someone's front yard, one of the foreign endurance horses had gone lame overnight, and four people had contracted stomach bugs.

Two-thirds of the two hundred and ninety-seven riders who remained were warming up or milling anxiously around the start. Among them were famous distance champions like the UK's Manny Wilder, Dutchman Deitrich Anders and Kaamil Nader from Dubai. There were also the cocky but undeniably brilliant Carling Brothers on their eye-catching Akhal-Tekes, one a perlino and the other a golden buckskin, a couple of top eventers, and wranglers and rodeo riders from all over the country.

But it was the ordinary riders that interested Jonas most, and one rider in particular. She hadn't yet shown up, which was surprising, but he was positive she would. He hoped she would, anyway. It was nice that his race had attracted some of the cream of the world's equestrian talent, but it wouldn't be the same without gritty underdogs like her. Outsiders. People with the imagination and daring to pursue dreams that ordinary mortals considered impossible.

'How are you feeling, sir?' Turnbull had come up behind him, unnoticed. He had a coffee in one hand and an apple Danish in the other. He took a bite out of the pastry. 'Nervous?' he asked, spraying crumbs.

Jonas smiled. 'Not nervous, no. Trying to take in that it's finally here, finally beginning. It's surreal but wonderful. How about you, Wayne? Looking forward to the month ahead?'

'Indeed I am, sir,' said Turnbull, which was partially true. The thought of having to deal with all of these loud, confident horsemen and their psychotic, odiferous mounts for the duration of the race was not a happy one but, if he could get through it, what riches were in store for him! Four more weeks, give or take a few days, until his patience was rewarded. He could hardly wait.

Twenty-five minutes before the race was due to start, Alex was across town at the stables checking Scout's feet, legs and tack for the umpteenth time. Unwilling to risk riding him to Centennial Park in the initial scrum of kicking, bucking and adrenaline-fuelled horses, she'd hung back, giving the palomino a pouch of electrolytes and doing her best to connect with him.

She could tell that he didn't know what to make of her. Accustomed to human-centric horses that thrived on attention and affection, she found it hard not to take his mistrust to heart. At the same time she understood it. In the library at Camp Renew, she'd read how every year wild mustangs were rounded up in terrifying helicopter stampedes, chased for hundreds of miles to the point of collapse or death and kept in long-term holding pens far from freedom.

To Alex, who'd always considered the American mustang to be the ultimate symbol of freedom, the brutal reality of their existence had come as a shock. In decades past, they'd been culled or packed off to slaughterhouses in order to keep their numbers down, but since 1971 they'd been 'protected' under the Wild Free-Roaming Horses and Burros Act. Their numbers had swelled dramatically at the same time as the grazing and water on which they depended became ever harder to access.

There were an estimated thirty-eight thousand feral horses still on the land and almost as many in the cramped hell of holding pens. Just two thousand were adopted each year. Some of those went through *Extreme Mustang Makeover*, a televised reality show where trainers had a hundred days to make them rideable. Others, like Scout, were bought by private homes, riding schools or businesses – with varying results. All the more reason why she had to find a safe haven for the palomino.

Alex glanced at her watch. Her stomach churned unpleasantly. Everything had happened so fast. The first thing she'd done after leaving Betty's Diner was rush into the bank. The staff were polite and happy to help. Nobody matching Trey and Crystal's description had passed through their doors. Alex was forced to confront the painful fact that the couple had fled with her cash as soon as her back was turned. While she'd been ordering their burgers, they'd been in Potts Field, retrieving their goats and driving off into the sunset. She had nothing on them – no address, no surnames and no number plate. Even if she had thought to take down those details, she couldn't exactly go to the police.

For the best part of forty minutes Alex sat with her head in her hands on the steps of the bank, too devastated to cry. She imagined calling home and attempting to explain to her mum and Jeremy how catastrophically she'd messed up this time – running away from Camp Renew, stealing a horse, getting into the car of two strangers, trusting them with nearly £600 in cash, ordering a feast she was unable to pay for and having to be bailed out by a teenage diner.

She could hear the disappointment in her mum's voice as clearly as if she was on the phone now. Jeremy would be standing stiffly at her side, wearing a familiar expression of concern mingled with contempt. He'd lecture Alex about how, whenever she let them down, she was really letting herself down.

121

Abruptly, Alex stood. She'd rather crawl back to Camp Renew and plead for forgiveness than give her parents ten more reasons to write her off as a loser.

But there was a problem. If she returned Scout to the ranch she could be handing him a one-way ticket to the slaughterhouse. That wasn't an option. The only way of guaranteeing his safety was to get him as far from Camp Renew as possible. Better still, she could set him free in the wild where he belonged.

A thrill went through her. Chase Miller had told her that the race passed through Wyoming, home to some of America's largest wild mustang herds. Without money or a driver's licence she had no hope of getting the palomino there on her own, but if she entered The Glory . . .

The tall, elegant African American woman behind the desk at race headquarters was sympathetic but intractable. No fee, no race. She opened a folder and fanned through the contents with impossibly long nails decorated with horses' heads.

'Babe, my heart bleeds for you. There are people in this world who'd steal a white stick from a blind man. Much as I'd like to help, there is nothing I can do for you. I got three hundred and two entries here. Each of these individuals has had their trials and tribulations getting here. Kaamil Nader has travelled all the way from the United Arab Emirates. From the boiling deserts of Arabia to the snowy mountains of Colorado and Wyoming. Imagine! But every one of these riders has managed to find the $200 entry fee, plus an additional $50 if they want us to crew their race.'

'Crew their race?'

'You're new to the sport of endurance riding, aren't you, hon? See, in a normal fifty- or hundred-mile race what usually happens is that most riders travel with their own support team. The crew drive ahead to the vet check points and are ready when the rider arrives. They help cool the horse and they carry all the supplies – feed, spare tack and clothing, towels, hay, grooming equipment, bedding, rugs. You name it, they've got it.

'Our race is a bit different – well, a lot different. For those riders who are not taking their own support staff, we're doing the heavy lifting. We don't crew for you as such, but every fifty miles there'll be a rest area with showers and supplies and plenty of feed and alfalfa hay for the horses and hot meals for the riders. Water too, and buckets. Those are two things endurance competitors need a lot of.'

'What about a scholarship?' Alex was unable to keep the desperation out of her voice. It was nearly 4 p.m. and the strain of the long day had taken its toll. If she couldn't find a solution for Scout before the race left town at eight next morning, they'd be going back to Camp Renew whether they liked it or not.

She took a breath and tried again. 'Have you considered

giving any young or disadvantaged riders a scholarship if they have the talent but not the money?'

'You mean the kind they give to football players so they can get to university for free?'

Behind the desk was a sofa on which a man in glasses and a crumpled grey jacket sat reading an equestrian magazine. Throughout the conversation he'd never once looked up. But neither had he turned the page.

'I mean, a grant. A loan. Sponsorship. Anything, really. Look, I've got to enter this race. I absolutely have to. Tell me what to do and I'll do it. If you want me to muck out or groom horses at these vet check, rest-break places, I'll do that. If you want me to get down on my knees and beg, I'll do that too.'

The man on the sofa put down his magazine. 'That won't be necessary.'

Alex stared at him in surprise. He stood up. 'What makes you think you're talented enough to deserve a scholarship?'

'I . . . I just . . . '

He approached the desk and picked up the entries folder. 'As Gloria explained, we have three hundred and two riders. Every one of them would, I'm sure, have appreciated a grant. Why should we give one to you? You seem . . . unprepared. Do you have even the faintest clue about the challenge you're considering, about the terrain you'll have to cross, the conditions you'll have to endure? In the weeks ahead there will be times when grown men will weep like babies because the cold, pain and exhaustion are too much to bear. What makes you think that you're tough enough, strong enough or brave enough not to quit at the first hurdle?'

So impassioned was this speech that reality slapped Alex in the face like a wet fish. Under any other circumstances, she'd have fled, but her feet seemed glued to the floor. For the second time that day, something deep within her stirred. It was a different type of longing but it tugged at her spirit just as powerfully. It was a yearning for wilderness, star-flung nights and the great unknown. Above all, she wanted to *feel*.

'I'm none of those things,' she admitted. 'I'm not tough enough, I'm not strong enough and I'm definitely not brave enough. To be honest, I don't have a great track record at succeeding at anything. Kind of the opposite. Having my money stolen today was only the latest in a series of disasters, almost all of them my own fault. I've screwed up a lot, hurt people, disappointed them.

'But I do have one thing going for me and that's my bond with horses. I love them. I live for them, really. The difference between me and most of the other riders is that I don't care about the money. I'm not in it for the glory. Of course it would be nice to be rich and famous but that's not why I want to do it. I *need* to do it to prove something to myself and I *have* to do it to save my horse – he's a mustang. If we can't enter your race, he faces a hideous future. Actually, he will have no future at all. You see, he's . . . on loan. The people who own him are running out of patience with him. Most likely they'll send him to his death.'

She pushed her hair from her eyes. 'But if you let me enter your race, I believe we can justify your faith in us and my horse will be saved. Am I going to wish I'd never attempted it? Of course. But I can promise you this. If you trust me with this chance, I'll give it everything I have. My whole heart. And so will my mustang; I know he will.'

The man was watching her thoughtfully. From a distance he had a boyish appearance. Up close, his gaze was shrewd and there were silver threads in his hair. Laughter lines framed his mouth.

'Your accent – it's British, isn't it? What are you doing in the US?'

'It's a long story.'

The silence that greeted this statement was almost as lengthy. 'Gloria . . . ' he said at last. 'We're going to need another pass.'

Gloria raised her eyebrows but made no comment. She picked up a pen. 'Name?'

Alex thought quickly. 'Sarah Wood.' Her middle name and part of her surname. It would do unless they asked for ID. Fortunately, they didn't. They did, however, want her date of birth and home address. Alex gave Jeremy's work contact details, reasoning that unless she was hospitalised no one would be any the wiser.

'Name of your horse?'

'Uh . . . Goldie.' It was the best she could do at short notice.

'You're not going to make me regret this, are you?' her benefactor asked.

'I hope not.'

He gave a wry smile. 'Well, that's truthful, at least. Your horse will need to be passed by our veterinarians, but assuming he's fine you're in.'

A grin spread across Alex's face. She felt euphoric. The further she and Scout got from Camp Renew, the more chance they'd have of staying out of Warden Cartwright's clutches. But it was more than that. For the next four weeks it would be just her and the palomino. Alex couldn't imagine anything more exciting or wonderful. She could do this, she was positive she could. At Dovecote Equestrian Centre she'd ridden for eight straight hours every week and barely been out of breath. This race was the equivalent of a month of Sundays.

Okay, two months of Sundays. But after that she'd return Scout to the wild.

She said fervently, 'I give you my word that I won't let you down. Not unless it's a matter of life and death.'

'Let's hope it won't come to that.'

He handed her a race guide and the laminated pass. 'There's a rider briefing at seven tonight. I suggest you pay close attention. In life, rules may be optional, but in the race they're for your own safety and that of others. Do NOT lose your pass. The green star on the top right-hand corner gives you access to the food and supplies Green Power will be providing at the fifty- and hundred-mile rest stops. I'm assuming you have most of the tack, clothing and equipment you need to get you through the miles in between or you wouldn't be here, wasting our time, but if you go to the Easy Rider stall, they'll check everything for you and make sure you have the basics. No luxuries. They can run the items past Gloria and she'll authorise those she considers necessary. Tell 'em I sent you.'

'Why are you doing this for me?'

'Because he can,' Gloria told her. 'It's his race. Meet Jonas Ellington.'

During the long cold night she'd spent on the floor of Scout's narrow stall, praying that he didn't trample on her, either accidentally or on purpose, Alex had tried to envisage what lay ahead. But nothing could have prepared her for the sight that greeted her at Centennial Park the following morning. Nearly three hundred horses assembled in the shadow of the mountain before a bright, buzzing crowd and a wall of black lenses.

Scout was bouncing with electric energy. Alex struggled to keep him out of view of the cameras, behind the group she'd ridden in with. The talk around the stable yard that morning had been how the start was often the most deadly part of any endurance race. Falls and injuries were commonplace.

She was glad she'd managed to force down a coffee and a couple of breakfast bars and also that she'd taken time to warm up Scout and get him accustomed to his new, light tack. Casting conscience to the winds, she'd traded in his saddle for a second-hand treeless one with a sheepskin seat and aluminium endurance stirrups with a springy foam footpad. His leather bridle had been replaced by a blue nylon one and his reins had leather stops along their length to prevent them slipping in the wet.

Fortuitously, the outdoor gear given to Alex at Camp Renew – riding tights, a lightweight polar windcheater, thermal vest, long johns and socks, sleeping bag and tent – was suitable for the race. The only exception was her academy-branded fleece, which she'd dumped in a bin. Even the boots Chase Miller had given her were endurance-type boots, albeit cheap ones.

For a new fleece and everything else, she was indebted to Gloria's Green Power credit card and the patient expertise of the owner of the Easy Rider stall. He'd thrown in a worn Akubra hat after she'd admired it. She and Scout were as ready as they'd ever be.

Beside the start line was a large digital clock. Less than five minutes remained. An official tried in vain to bring order to the chaos. The star riders were given no preference in position, but they were conspicuous in their proximity to the assembled media. Alex moved Scout as far from them as possible, almost colliding with an angular grey mare in her rush to escape the lens of a roaming photographer.

Turning in the saddle to apologise, she found herself

eye to eye with the boy from the diner. He was wearing a dark brown Stetson and a sandstone Carhartt jacket with a sherpa-lined hood. To say that he looked unimpressed to see her would be an understatement.

'What are *you* doing here?' he said coldly.

Alex's apology died on her lips. 'I've entered the race, just like you.'

'You're British, aren't you? Has anyone told you how tough this race is going to be, and how long? We're crossing four states – Colorado, Wyoming, Idaho and Oregon – and word is that winter weather is moving in. It'll be brutal. Are you sure you're up to it? It's not like a hack around Hyde Park in London.'

Alex didn't know whether to be impressed by his grasp of geography or outraged at his audacity. 'Who are you to tell me what I can or can't do? You don't even know me. Are *you* up to it?'

'Hope so. We're about to find out. Anyway, how can you afford it when you couldn't even . . .'

'When I couldn't pay for my meal at the restaurant, you mean? Oh, but I could. Don't you remember, I'd dropped my money under the table? You found it for me. I was planning on thanking you if I ever crossed paths with you again because it's the single kindest thing anyone's ever done for me, but now I realise that you're the type who does something nice for someone and doesn't ever let them forget it.'

He reddened. 'Look, maybe we've got off on the wrong foot.'

130

Alex smiled sweetly at him. 'Don't worry. When I beat you, which I will, I'll pay you back every cent. With interest.'

The volume of the crowd rose by several decibels, drowning out the boy's response. He and Alex were driven apart as a big roan stampeded forward, his portly owner standing in his stirrups as he fought to hold the gelding back. Over a crackling loudspeaker Jonas Ellington was wishing everyone luck and encouraging them to ride a safe race, put their horses first and 'Don't forget to have fun!'

The countdown began. 'Fifty-five, fifty-four, fifty-three . . . '

Arriving at the Centennial Park, Alex's stomach had been a sizzling ball of nerves. She'd been frightened of the race ahead and even more frightened of not competing – of being spotted by the cops or someone from Camp Renew and dragged back to face the music. Now she felt only fury and an obsessive determination to show the opinionated boy, the parents who'd betrayed her and Warden Cartwright that, if nothing else, she could ride, and if she could ride then anything was possible.

The spectators had taken up the chant. 'Twenty, nineteen, eighteen . . . '

Alex edged Scout forward so that his nose was in front of the boy's part-Arab mare, three or four riders to her left. The boy responded by urging his horse forward. So tightly packed were the competitors that he was almost kicked in the foot for his trouble. Alex found a gap and eased the palomino ahead once more.

'Nine, eight, seven, six . . .'

She glanced sideways. The boy was crouched over the grey mare's withers, his face set in chilly determination. She willed him to look at her and felt unaccountably disappointed when he didn't.

Then the mass of horses bolted forward and all was a blur.

12

Will felt the saddle slip as soon as Shiraz launched herself into the fray. Instinctively, he tried to rebalance it by pushing down hard on one stirrup while holding tight to a handful of mane, but when the mare swerved around a bucking horse it tipped past the point where he could correct it. From then on, it was only going to end one way. He went down amid a flurry of hooves and yelling. His hat was lost. He curled into a ball and did what he could to protect his head. The thunder went on and on. A grenade of pain exploded in his shoulder.

He lay on his stomach until all he could hear was the whisper of wind and a few strangled moans. When he sat up, the park resembled the set of a second-rate Civil War film. Red-coated volunteers were dashing about collecting stray horses. Paramedics patched up whimpering riders. A stretcher-bearer headed in his direction. Will waved him away. The humiliation of having made it no further than a hundred yards from the start before being carried off in an ambulance would have been too much to bear.

Already the rumps of the racing horses were little more than a sketch of motion on the horizon. He wondered whether this latest setback – an amateur error that nobody who'd had more than two riding lessons should ever make – was a sign that he should quit and return to Tennessee before something really catastrophic happened. Then he remembered that he couldn't afford to go home. Thanks to the girl in the diner, the one who was already comfortably ahead of him, as per her prediction, he couldn't afford to walk to Chattanooga, let alone get Shiraz home.

Why he'd given her the money after the way she'd glared at him, he couldn't have answered if his life depended on it. He only knew that he hadn't had a choice. His body had acted independently of his brain. The impulse to help her and, just for a few seconds, be close to her, had overridden all common sense.

Unfortunately, he'd had a sleepless night due to nerves and money worries and that and the shock of seeing her in the last place he expected had brought out the worst in him, as she'd been quick to point out. *You're the type who does something nice for someone and doesn't ever let them forget it.*

At the memory of her words, a scowl marred Will's good-natured face. He wondered if she'd seen him fall.

His thoughts were interrupted by a laconic voice.

'Judging by the purposeful way she's dragging me in your direction, I'm guessing this is your horse?'

Will heaved himself to his feet just as Shiraz came rushing up to him, whickering. She shoved him hard with her nose a couple of times before nuzzling him joyously, as if to say, 'You're a terrible person for allowing us to get separated like that, but I'm very pleased to see you.'

Despite the pain in his shoulder, Will couldn't help laughing. It was only when he turned to thank her rescuer that he realised that the man holding her reins was J.B. Ellington himself. Mortified, Will almost snatched the reins from him.

'She is my horse, yes. Thanks very much. I don't know what went wrong . . . I thought I checked . . . I mean, I was so sure—'

'Forget it. It happens to the best of us. I took the liberty of repositioning the saddle and tightening the cinch. Check it before you ride. You are going to continue, aren't you? You're not going to let a little thing like this stop you?'

'Well, I—'

'Good. Because you've got yourself a fine horse here. Built for the distance.'

Unused to anyone praising Shiraz, Will brightened. 'Yes, sir, she is.'

Jonas grinned back. 'Great. Then I'll expect to see you both in Hood River in about a month.'

As soon as he'd gone, Will located his Stetson and

dusted it off. He double-checked Shiraz's girth and vaulted easily into the saddle without using the stirrups. He'd seen it done in a Western as a boy and had practised it over and over as soon as he was tall enough to reach the back of his granddad's patient old mare. Until now it had served him well. It was quicker than conventional mounting and put no pressure on the horse's spine. But it did mean that he hadn't noticed that Shiraz's girth had been loosened in the five minutes it took him to go to the bathroom shortly before the start of the race – five minutes when she'd been alone, tied to a railing.

An image of Jack Carling's handsome face, contorted with fury, swam into Will's mind. He supposed he could count himself lucky. 'At least there were no rattlesnakes involved,' he mused to Shiraz as he eased her into a trot.

Viewed in a positive light, having things go wrong this early in the race was no bad thing. He'd been feeling low and lacking in confidence. This near-disaster had given him a jolt. It had fired him up, made him more determined. If he did nothing else in this race, he was going to finish ahead of the Carling Brothers. They might have their precious Akhal-Tekes and their reputation, but he had Shiraz and a cause worth more than money. He was racing to save his dad – the dad who even that morning he'd lied to, telling him that for the next few weeks he'd be camping out on a fictional ranch and would be in touch only periodically.

Will had to win. *Had* to. There was no other way he

could salve his conscience, help his dad or get back to Tennessee. And in the unlikely event that the English girl proved to be as good as her boast, he had to get the better of her.

Battered shoulder aside, Will could never remember enjoying a day's riding more. It didn't bother him that the competitors who'd set off as if they were auditioning for the Pony Express were already at least five miles ahead. Most were unlikely to have grasped the abiding principle of distance racing: it was not about finishing first. It was about finishing first on the best-conditioned horse. 'To complete is to win' was the endurance rider's motto.

If Will's reading on the sport had taught him anything, it was that breaking the land speed record was no use at all if your horse failed the vet check.

That didn't mean that Will had any intention of languishing at the rear of the field. Shiraz was as eager to shake the city dust from her feet as he was and they hit the Sanitas Valley Trail at something just short of a gallop. Initially, cheering spectators lined the route but their cries soon faded and Will felt his earlier panic and frustration subside and the deep peace of the mountains reaching down to him. As Shiraz settled into a steady trot, he found himself grinning like a crazy person at the prospect of a whole month of this – just him and his beloved mare and landscapes so vast they could have been inhabited by giants.

At that early stage, nearly every rider he came across seemed to be smiling. The day was so pretty it was impossible not to be happy. The clean morning air brushed his face like chilled silk. The gold and crimson of the willow and tundra grasses that lent colour to the upper slopes of the mountain stood out in sharp relief against the blue sky and rich evergreen of the ponderosa pine and Douglas fir.

Shiraz was on a high too. There was no sight that thrilled her more than an open road and she stretched out with relish, the competitive side of her wanting to pursue the horses ahead, the loner in her liking the space. She needed no one but Will. Why they were here and what lay ahead, she couldn't fathom, but she loved the unknownness of it, the constant stirring of adrenaline. It reminded her of their adventures in the Appalachians.

Will's first priority was to establish a comfortable, sustainable pace. They'd practised over the past few weeks in the familiar environs of the park in Chattanooga, but it was another thing altogether doing it out here, on undulating ground, with the mountains leaning in.

As far as he'd been able to calculate, Shiraz walked at nearly 6 mph, trotted at between 7 and 12 mph and cantered at 9–14 mph. As a general rule of thumb, riders needed to average 7 mph in order to complete a hundred miles in twenty-four hours. That allowed them to factor in a three-hour rest along the way. Some horses found cantering the most economical gait in terms of energy. Shiraz was most comfortable trotting. Will closed his eyes to try to gauge her speed. When they passed the ten-mile marker, he felt momentarily elated. It excited him, didn't terrify him, that they had a whole 1,190 miles to go.

Far more than the dangers that lay in wait, he worried that his inexperience would cost them. Everything he knew about endurance riding, he'd gleaned from the Internet and a rather dated book he'd bought for fifty cents in a second-hand bookshop. It had taken much painstaking searching on eBay and specialist equestrian sites to find affordable gear for Shiraz. Following some trading and hard bargaining, he'd scored a mismatched but decent selection of lightweight tack. In the end, he'd literally been scratching for change down the back of the sofa.

Somehow he'd scraped together what he needed, thanks to his friend Tom, a keen climber, who'd loaned Will his camping gear. Tom was the only person who knew the truth about Will's mission. To everyone else, Will had stuck to his story of how he'd be spending the autumn working as a trainee wrangler at a ranch in Colorado in the hope of earning some extra cash.

With Tom he'd had no choice but to be honest because the race organisers required an emergency contact number and that contact couldn't, for obvious reasons, be his dad. Conscious that he was already asking a lot, Will had refused everything except Tom's tent.

Tom had ignored his protests, pressing all the equipment he could spare on to Will. 'This is non-negotiable. You'll be riding into winter. Wanna die of hypothermia? Fat lot of use you'll be to your dad then. Take the sleeping bag and anything else you need. If it gets muddy and ruined, you can buy me a new lot with your winnings.'

Another reason why victory was Will's only option.

Thirty miles into the race, Shiraz's heart rate – measured by Will using his new heart rate monitor – was maintaining a steady rhythm. Even so, Will changed legs and diagonals at intervals to prevent Shiraz from over-working one set of muscles. His own shoulder was sore but not unbearable.

The trail, marked by ribbons, took them along the fringes of the Rocky Mountain National Park, where every bend in the road threw up a calendar-shot vista. Will breathed in the scent of pine and once, eye-wateringly, skunk. The place names became ever more romantic: Point of Pines. Olde Stage Road. Left-hand Canyon Drive. Indian Peaks Wilderness.

At lunchtime, he rested Shiraz near a musical stream, sponging her down and letting her drink her fill. For centuries the Arapaho Indians had inhabited the wilderness during the summer months, hunting elk, black bear, mule deer and snowshoe rabbits, and fishing for trout in the clear, rushing rivers and fifty turquoise lakes. The most daring among them had scaled the highest crags in search of prized eagle feathers for their headdresses. Many peaks bore the names of the tribes that had lived, fought and died in the Colorado Rockies and beyond: Apache, Kiowa, Navajo, Shoshoni, Arikaree, Ogallala and Pawnee.

Will leaned against a rock and let the spirit of those peaks soak into his bones. Throughout the race, they'd be riding into the past.

Sitting there, he had a momentary fantasy that this is how The Glory would unfold for him – twelve hundred miles of immersive history, jaw-dropping scenery, fine weather and amiable contestants, followed by a sprint to the finish. But he knew it was exactly that, a flight of imagination. A gladiatorial battle lay ahead. The stunt that Jack Carling or some other rival had pulled with Will's saddle was just a taster.

Early afternoon, he caught up with a group of beetroot-complexioned riders, wilting in the saddle. Two were on their phones calling for rescue, horses already spent, bay bodies foamy with sweat. A man with Albert Einstein hair was cursing a thrown shoe. Will thought about offering him one of his Easyboots, the temporary boots he carried with him to prevent lameness if the same thing happened to Shiraz, but he knew that would be suicide. The first casualties had already gone by in horseboxes, faces grim at the wheel.

The toughest thing about endurance riding, Will was fast discovering, was that there was too much time to think. Usually, that was something he enjoyed. Today his thoughts kept returning to the Annoying English Girl. Every time a lorry passed him carrying a retired competitor, he found himself hoping it wasn't her. That she hadn't fallen, hurt herself or given up so soon. And as he overtook the slower riders and began rapidly to move through the field, he kept involuntarily scanning their faces, searching for her.

It made him angry. Why was he fretting about a girl he didn't know? She wasn't his responsibility. If she'd entered the race broke and unprepared, it was her own lookout.

And yet during the course of that long first day, her face, vulnerable and flushed with high emotion as she pleaded with the manager at the diner, then proud and lit with some inner fire as she laid down the gauntlet to Will at the start, came into his mind again and again. Chances were, she wouldn't make it through the first twenty-four hours. And if that were the case, she'd be gone. She'd return to wherever she'd blown in from, as enigmatic as the wind.

Considering how much trouble she'd caused him, Will should have been glad. Oddly, he found himself plagued by the thought that, if she quit the race, he might never learn her name. For some reason that bothered him.

And if she didn't disappear, if, somehow, she survived, he had no intention of letting her beat him. She'd got a head start on her handy-looking palomino mustang, but

Will was more than confident that he could catch up with her, more than a little bit surprised that he hadn't overtaken her already.

Checking the map one final time, he turned Shiraz down a soft track and urged her into a canter.

13

The 'War Office', Camp Renew, Colorado

'IMPOSSIBLE!'

Strike Cartwright's fist hit the desk with such force that all six of the men and women in his office rose off the ground in fright. As head wrangler and director of equestrian operations at Camp Renew, it was Chase Miller who'd borne the brunt of the warden's wrath over the past twenty-four hours, but as far as Cartwright was concerned they were all culpable.

'What you're saying is not just laughable, contemptible, unfeasible and quite ludicrous, it is also impossible,' he ranted at the gathered assembly – Miller and two tired and grubby wranglers, dorm superintendent Helga Ward, the head of security Mike Tanner and beefy Bud Baxter. In addition to devising gruelling fitness programmes, it was Baxter who was responsible for all wilderness training at the academy.

'Here we have a British girl, cosseted from birth, a girl who – according to you, Chase – could barely tell one end of a horse from another, and to you, Bud, was equipped with only the most basic survival techniques, and you're claiming that this total alien to the Colorado wilderness has vanished without a trace.'

One of the wranglers, an earnest youth clutching a wide-brimmed hat, spoke up unwisely. 'Sir, Mr Warden, we've been up half the night searching for that girl, ever since we found Clyde wandering yesterday afternoon, but there's fifty thousand acres out there. She could be anywhere.'

Cartwright's knuckles went white. 'Vic, or whatever your name is, if you want to remain in my employ any longer than the next thirty seconds, you need to adjust your attitude. A sixteen-year-old delinquent in our care is missing. I don't care if you have to lift every stone between here and New Mexico, you will find her and you will bring her to me or your life will not be worth living. Besides, she's on foot. If Chase is correct, she has a day's worth of food with her at best. How far can she have got on rehydrogenated macaroni cheese?'

'The girl is not the only one who's gone missing,' Miller cut in. 'Warden, do you recall the palomino mustang we discussed?'

Cartwright remembered the palomino well. He'd earmarked it for himself until it had thrown him and tried to trample him a month earlier. From that moment on, its fate had been sealed. He gave Miller an icy glare. 'I thought I told you to send it to the glue factory. That beast is like an equine volcano, waiting to erupt. How many times do I have to tell you that some horses, like some children, are born wicked?'

'Warden, we wanted to give him one final chance before we gave up on him. Only he's disappeared. Harper here went to round him up this morning and he was gone. We've kept a lookout for him all day while we've been hunting for Alexandra, but we've yet to see hide or hair of him. Could be a coincidence. Or not.'

'Are you seriously telling me that a girl who's been riding for all of two weeks and is apparently quite terrified of ponies has rounded up a half-wild mustang, climbed on board and ridden into the sunset? With no cash and no passport? Give me a break. And where are they now? Trotting unnoticed through the 16th Street Mall in Denver?'

'I admit it's unlikely, sir.'

'Isn't it more reasonable to assume that the lunatic horse has fallen down a gully while hunting for greener pastures? Forget about him. Focus on the girl. Where could she be?'

'Perhaps a hungry vild animal came upon her . . . ' suggested Helga, leaving the gruesome image hanging in the air. Even Strike Cartwright shuddered.

'There's something else,' said Miller. 'Something weird. Clyde's saddle is missing. We can't find it anywhere.'

The warden's bald head snapped upright, like a

tortoise spying a lettuce. 'Double the size of the search party – only trusted people, people who can keep their mouths shut. I don't care whether you have to use a crystal ball or abseil off a cliff edge, just do it. Search caves, search under beds and, most importantly, search your memories. Is there anything Alexandra said or did that might give us an insight into—'

There was a timid tap at the door. Strike Cartwright's unfortunate PA teetered into the room on heels that were much too high. The warden turned on her with a snarl.

'Stacey, what have I told you about interrupting me? Why do I have to repeat everything fifty times? Have I really hired the stupidest girl alive?'

'B-but it's important, Warden Cartwright. The girl's mother is on the phone and she's asking to speak to you.'

'I don't care if it's the Pope calling, I AM NOT . . . Err, which girl's mother?'

'Alexandra Blakewood's mother, Natalie Pritchard, s-sir. What should I tell her?'

The warden used the special quiet voice he reserved for extreme emergencies. It had a more motivating effect on people than shouting.

'You're going to tell her I'm having root canal surgery, Stacey. You're to say that it's the worst case the dentist has ever seen and that I will be unable to speak for at least three days. Possibly a week. Am I clear? Oh, and Stacey, engage your peanut brain and think up ways to keep her happy. Tell her that we're delighted with her daughter's progress so far. Tell her that we have secret observers close to the wilderness camp and they've reported that her precious angel has been putting up tents and building campfires with the best of them.'

Wounded, Stacey tottered back to her desk, her glasses misting up.

The warden slammed the door behind her and karate-chopped the container of pens on his desk. They flew in all directions, one almost spearing Vic in the eye.

'If Alexandra Blakewood is not in my office by nightfall, your jobs will be on the line. FIND HER! And, remember, not a word to anyone outside the search team.'

After they'd fled, the warden brooded at his desk. From the minute he'd laid eyes on her, he'd known the Blakewood girl was trouble. There'd been something in the way she'd carried herself, the way she'd looked at him. She fell into the same category as the palomino – born bad. Of course, unruly horses were easily dealt with. They could be broken or turned into pet food. Teenagers were more problematic. One had to use more subtle methods.

His phone chirruped. Cartwright answered it without thinking.

'Do I need to remind you what day it is?'

A centipede of dread crawled down the warden's spine. 'No, Seth, you don't.'

'Good. Because on October 30th your final payment to Horizon Investments becomes due. All of it. Every cent. Mark it in your diary in red.'

'Now Seth, be reasonable. I'm doing my best, but—'

'Hate to break it you, *amigo*, but your best ain't good enough. Hasn't been for well over a year. I've shielded you until now, but our shareholders are about out of patience. They've encouraged me to draw the line with you. By the end of next week – *at the very latest* – I'll expect to see $300,000 drop into the company bank account. Our CEO joked to me the other day that for every dollar missing, we'll be taking a finger. He's funny like that. He said that if you're more than ten dollars short, we'll be moving on to your bigger body parts. Maybe you should start thinking about which you can live without.'

The connection was severed.

Strike clutched the empty penholder in a death grip. No doubt about it, the path of the righteous was a thorny one. Here he was devoting his every waking hour to making the world a better place while fate dealt him one cruel blow after another.

Ironically, the Blakewood girl was critical to his hope of repaying the money. In a bid to attract more business, Camp Renew had been offering new students a heavily discounted trial period. Few parents bothered to read the small print, which committed them to massive fees if their child stayed any longer than a month. On 28th

October, Alexandra's parents would be pressured into paying $50,000 in advance when Strike broke the news to them that their daughter's rehabilitation was likely to take at least twelve months. They were unlikely to part with the cash if she'd fallen down a ravine or been mauled by a bear.

Added to which, his other creditors might vote with their feet if Camp Renew was the subject of lurid headlines. A British girl meeting a grisly end would not be good for business. An already tricky financial situation could get very ugly indeed.

Warden Cartwright leaned back in his chair and stared thoughtfully at the stuffed elk on the wall. Desperate times called for desperate measures. He'd been a hunter once. He could do it again. If the wranglers did not produce her in double-quick time, he'd go after Alexandra himself. Gut instinct told him she was in hiding, nothing worse. She would not escape him. He'd track her to the ends of the earth if he had to.

14

Day 2, Camp Laramie, Wyoming

The blast of a far-off truck horn penetrated Alex's consciousness. A nightmare slunk into the shadows of her mind. Her chin jerked from her chest and she realised with alarm that she'd dozed off in the saddle – for how long, she didn't know.

She was furious with herself. Anything could have happened! What surprised her was that it hadn't. The palomino was still stretching forward on autopilot, the way he had been from the very beginning, his gait long and loose, ears pricked, heading for a specific destination. She had the feeling that he was leading her, not the other way around, and she wondered what would happen when their paths diverged.

Everything hurt. Bits of her were chafed, bruised, pummelled, cold and just dog-tired. Her joints ached.

Her eyes burned in their sockets. She'd have killed for a steaming bath filled with bubbles.

Switching off her helmet light, she squinted hopefully into the early morning mist. It rose like steam from the waving prairie grasses. Beneath a sky of blasted clouds was the outline of what could only be Laramie, Wyoming.

To the east of Laramie was a flickering glow. The hundred-mile race camp! By Alex's estimate it was twenty minutes' ride away at most, although it was hard to be sure. Distances could be deceptive in these gigantic landscapes.

Overjoyed to be within reach of her first major milestone, she leaned down and hugged the palomino, burying her face in his flaxen mane. Already she thought of him as her best friend. It was Scout who'd got them this far. His instincts had kicked in. They'd not manifested themselves in his behaviour, thankfully, but his senses had been on high alert. He'd trotted and loped through a night so starry that the trees were lit with a phosphorescent glow, his entire being attuned to potential threat. Provided she could stay in the saddle if he shied or bolted, she'd been confident he'd carry her to safety.

But Scout was not the only reason she'd kept going when exhaustion kicked in. She'd been unable to stop thinking about the boy from the diner, or the gauntlet she'd so rashly thrown down. *She'd beat him. She'd pay him back with interest.*

What had possessed her to make such ridiculous claims? It was obvious to anyone who watched him for longer than three seconds that he was born to ride. The ease with which he and some of the other local horsemen flowed with their ponies made her English riding technique seem mannered and stiff. She envied them. Her Dovecote instructor, Clare, had been right. Alex knew nothing.

But each time the doubts returned to plague her, she remembered Jonas Ellington. Based on five minutes' acquaintance, he'd taken a leap of faith and sponsored her. Even though she'd confessed to being a failure. Even though he knew her story was full of holes. Even though she was barely sixteen, naive and inexperienced, and his race was the sort that made grown men 'weep like babies'.

'See you in Hood River,' J.B. Ellington had said. He believed in her more than her own parents did.

It made her want to live up to that belief.

Today Laramie was a peaceful college town flanked by mountains, but the race programme, which offered a detailed history of the route, had described a period in which the soil had run with blood as the Plains Indians, settlers and ranchers had vied for gold, grazing, fur and a place in the new America.

It was on these High Plains that the Oglala Latoka

chief Red Cloud had clashed with the United States Army's Colonel Henry B. Carrington and the drums of war had sounded. And here too that the Union Pacific Railway had come trickling like mercury, linking isolated communities and bringing migrants in search of a better life.

Since her parents' divorce, Alex had been reluctant to admit that she had anything in common with her dad, but there was no denying that she'd inherited his love of black and white films – Westerns in particular. Laramie's wild past was straight out of *High Noon*. For years the town had been ruthlessly controlled by its first marshal, a violent gunman known as 'Big' Steve Long. He and his two half-brothers harassed local settlers until they signed over the deeds to their property. Those unwise enough to refuse were shot by Long, often in the brothers' own saloon, the appropriately named Bucket of Blood.

In October 1868, days after he'd killed his thirteenth man, he and his brothers were cornered and lynched by the Albany County sheriff, N.K. Boswell, and his Vigilance Committee. According to the race programme, a riveting guide to the route through which The Glory would pass, it was by these brutal means that a law and order of sorts was established. From that time on, the town began to prosper.

Scout tossed his head and began to dance and fuss. Alex blinked and her vision cleared slightly. As if pulled by invisible strings, the outlines of a dozen horses and riders emerged from the gloom up ahead. They moved jerkily, hurrying towards the camp. Soon more hoofbeats sounded behind her. Five tired horses loped by. Outraged at being overtaken, Scout fought to go after them.

For the first time in hours, Alex came alive. Dust spat from Scout's heels as he galloped across the plain, resisting her efforts to stop him. She stood in her stirrups to take her weight off his back. It was only when they neared the hundred-mile post that she managed to slow him to a fast trot. By then, she was so tired and weak she was almost past caring. If she could make it through the vetting process there'd be strong coffee and, with any luck, a big breakfast. And somewhere to wash. Please God, let there be somewhere to wash.

As she and Scout clattered into the camp, sending volunteers and a couple of slower horses scattering, she caught a glimpse of the boy and his horse, ghostly silhouettes in the mist. Alex was simultaneously annoyed that they'd got here ahead of her and quite ridiculously pleased to see a familiar face.

She swung off Scout, rider card in hand. Her aching legs almost gave way beneath her. The timekeeper approached and took her horse's number, marking the time she'd entered the vet gate. From that second on, the clock was ticking. Alex knew from the rider briefing that Scout needed to be 'pulsed down' to the heart rate parameters laid down by the head vet (64 beats per minute) within thirty minutes or her horse would be pulled from the race. Filling a bucket of water for him, she praised him as he hungrily snatched mouthfuls of hay from a nearby bale.

She was about to get a drink herself when the boy came flying out of nowhere. He grabbed her arm and Scout's bridle. 'Are you out of your mind?'

Alex pulled away from him, eyes spitting sparks. 'I could ask you the same question. You're *hurting* me.'

'Not as much as you're about to hurt yourself. You'll fail the CRI check and be disqualified unless you get your horse cooled down ASAP. That's not going to happen if he eats, for starters.'

Alex felt as if she'd been caught out not studying for an exam. She'd attended the rider briefing, as she'd promised Jonas Ellington, but she'd left before the end. The volume of information had been so overwhelming that she felt it was doing her more harm than good. Endurance racing had nothing in common with eventing, as Alex had supposed. There were a dazzling variety of rules and terms to remember. Everything seemed designed to prove that she was clueless.

Alex had decided her best hope was to focus on getting the riding part right – pacing Scout, building a bond with him. This had been borne out by her experience of navigating the vet gate at the fifty-mile stage. The steward had pretty much done everything for her and the veterinarian there had actually praised Scout's conditioning. The whole process had been so easy that it hadn't occurred to her there was a science to it.

Correctly interpreting her silence, the boy was incredulous. 'Are you always this helpless?'

Alex's temper flared.

'Are you always this obnoxious?'

A faint smile tweaked his mouth. 'Remove his tack and, whatever you do, don't let him eat any more hay. It'll slow his heart rate recovery. Drinking is okay. You might want to put his wool rump rug over his hindquarters. You don't want them seizing up in the morning air. If you've paid to have the race team crew for you, they'll give you a dry saddle pad and cinch over there. I'll be right back.'

As infuriating as it was to be rescued by him for the second time in forty-eight hours, Alex didn't doubt he knew what he was talking about. She rushed to do as he asked. Moments later, he came sprinting over with an armful of large water bottles.

'They're cold but not icy because if he gets chilled it'll keep his heart rate elevated.'

Alex poured all except one bottle over Scout's neck, shoulders and front legs, as directed, soothing him all the while. She deliberately stood so that the palomino shielded her from the boy, trying not to look at his hands holding the reins. Her legs were wobbly enough. She didn't need to breathe in the clean, sandalwood scent of him or see his blond hair, still wet from his shower, standing up in spikes.

Their next task, he advised, was to get Scout moving again in order to flush the lactic acid from his muscles and prevent them from cooling too quickly and cramping. Pain, it appeared, was another of the infinite number of things that could elevate a horse's heart rate. Alex sponged Scout's chest and forelegs as they walked.

'Ideally, you want his chest to be cool to the touch,' explained the boy, voice muffled as he bent down to check. Was it her imagination or was he keeping as far from her as possible? Not that Alex blamed him. After nearly twenty hours in the saddle, she was sweaty, grimy and had hat hair. Once again he had her at a disadvantage.

He halted Scout. 'His legs look good. No visible swelling. Would you like to check his heart rate or should I? I assume you have a heart rate monitor?'

She was sure he was thinking she was incompetent again, but if he was it didn't show. 'Ideally, you want his HR to reach race parameters within ten minutes of you dismounting. That's the reason most riders ease up on their horses as they approach the vet gate.'

Alex felt a twinge of despair as she craned to see the monitor. Would she ever do anything right? Ever?

But the boy was preoccupied with the figures on the little screen. 'Wow, 62 bpm already. That's impressive. I've never seen a horse recover so fast. Must be his mustang genes.'

He astounded her by adding: 'Well ridden. You must have paced him perfectly.'

Not as perfectly as *you* paced your horse, thought Alex, who was still trying to work out how he'd been through the vet gate, showered and had time to rest and recuperate, despite getting off to a slow start the day before. She knew that because she'd been among the early leaders (the sensible front-runners rather than the Pony Express lunatics) and for the first few hours had watched for him constantly. Nor had she seen him at the fifty-mile hold. And yet somehow during the night he'd made up for lost time.

Perhaps he read her mind because when he spoke again his tone was coolly impersonal. 'Keep him moving gently until he's down to 58 or 59 bpm and you're ready to present him to a vet. That's the TPR line – that's temperature, pulse and respiration – snaking into the distance over there. I don't envy you. It's disorganised chaos. The stewards and vets are being tough, as they should be, but it does mean there's a lot of weeping, wailing and gnashing of teeth. After that, you'll be released into hold. Good luck.'

He strode away without another word.

'Wait!'

He turned reluctantly.

'Thank you, but I don't understand. We're rivals. Why are you helping me?'

Unexpectedly, he flashed her a mischievous grin. 'It's *because* we're rivals that I'm helping you. Didn't want you being evicted from the race quite so soon. I'm kind of looking forward to our duel. But don't worry. I'm not going to be making a habit of it – assisting you.'

As he started to walk she called out, 'What's your name? I like to know who I'm up against.'

A split second's hesitation. 'Will Greyton. What's yours?'

'Uh, Sarah. Sarah . . . Wood.'

'You don't sound too sure.'

'That's because I prefer being called Alex.'

Immediately, she was livid with herself for telling him. 'It's my nickname,' she said lamely. 'I'd rather you didn't mention it to anyone. It could cause confusion.'

He lifted a hand in mock salute. 'See you down the road, Alex Wood.'

'Not if I see you first,' Alex told his departing back.

She debated whether to try a heart rate monitor on herself. Her pulse seemed to be beating unnaturally fast.

15

As soon as Will walked into the overflow camp that night, he knew he'd made a mistake. The faces of the men sitting round the flickering copper fire were hard and unwelcoming. He knew the type. From time to time they'd come looking for work or wanting to shoot deer on his grandfather's farm in the mountains. Ruffians, his granddad used to call them. 'Never turn your back on 'em, never let 'em see they've got a rise out you,' was his advice to Will.

'First time I've ever come across an albino mule,' was the opening gambit of one of the men. He nodded towards Shiraz. 'I'd have thought that any race with a fancy title like The Glory would at least pretend to have standards. Seems they let anyone enter, no matter how wet they are behind the ears.'

'See, that's where you always go wrong, Zach,' said one of his companions. 'Thinking. Smoke starts pouring out o' the top o' your head. 'Sides, you can hardly talk. That bag o' bones o' yours looks like one o' them abstract artists went berserk with a pot o' paint.'

A third man tore a strip of flesh from a T-bone steak with sharp white teeth. 'Zach's just joshing with you, kid. Don't pay him no mind. Park your pony and come get some grub.'

The other horses were in a spacious and sturdy corral, but Will made his own a little way off, wrapping ribbon-tape around a stand of five trees. He didn't bother electrifying it. Shiraz was accustomed to it. As long as he slept close to her, she was quite content. The race guide had been at pains to point out that the overflow camp was a strictly no-frills operation, but there was no shortage of hay, horse feed, carrots and apples, buckets and fresh water. Will put plenty of everything out for Shiraz. She'd eaten and drunk steadily through the day, but he wanted to be sure she had as much as she needed.

After pitching his tent beside her improvised corral and reapplying ice gel to her legs, he returned to the fire without enthusiasm.

'The cook packed up and left a while ago and we've finished all the meat, but there's plenty of beef chilli and crackers,' said the man who'd made the abstract artist comment. 'Tuck in.'

'I don't suppose there's any vegetarian food?' asked Will.

This caused much hilarity in the assembled group. Predictably, Zach laughed loudest and longest. He

162

dragged deeply on his cigarette and blew smoke rings. 'Do you know, I've heard of them anaemic, muesli-eating folk, but I've never met a live one.'

'Well, now you have,' Will responded pleasantly.

'Give it a rest, Zach,' said T-bone steak man. 'He made it here, didn't he, unlike a lot of others. Word is, out of a starting field of 303, only 174 got through.'

Out of the shadows rode a latecomer on a Morgan stallion, distracting them. Will took the opportunity to raid the cook's station for food. Returning with a handful of crackers, a bruised banana and a can of baked beans, he found the new arrival, a friendly Texan, installed by the fireside.

'Name's Jim, but most people call me Slim,' he told Will with a wink. 'Can't think why.'

Will liked him at once. Despite his self-deprecating remark, he was big-boned rather than fat and his round pink face had an endearing sweetness to it. His day job was running an IT company. Unlike everyone else in the group, he did have some endurance riding experience. 'Only a couple of fifty-milers, so it hardly counts . . .'

He was besotted with his Morgan stallion and went on at length about the horse's lineage and how nobly he'd coped with the trials of the day. 'My wife says I should have married him instead of her!'

'How much would a fine animal like that be worth?' T-bone steak man asked casually.

'More than my house, Axel, my friend,' responded Slim Jim. 'More than my house.'

Shortly afterwards, Will excused himself and went to his tent. The baked beans, eaten cold from the tin, sat unhappily in his stomach. He found it difficult to sleep. Every muscle in his body ached. At some point he must have dozed off because when he next looked at his watch it was 2.12 a.m. As his ears adjusted to the night sounds, he heard Shiraz moving restlessly.

Instantly, he was wide awake. Colic, every horseman's greatest fear, was never far from his mind. He parted the tent flaps. Shiraz was at the furthest point of her pen, nostrils flaring as she stared into the darkness. Will dressed in a hurry and went out to calm her, but for once she barely acknowledged him. In the big corral, the other horses were milling around anxiously. Something was upsetting them.

After settling Shiraz as best as he could, Will crept through the trees, nervous of encountering a bear. As he neared the corral, he heard low voices. Straining his eyes, he made out the silhouettes of Zach and Axel. They were leading the Morgan stallion. Closing the gate behind them, they began to walk him in the direction of the main trail.

Will waited until they were almost level with him before stepping into their path. 'What exactly are you doing?'

Zach let forth a volley of expletives. 'Mind your own business.'

Axel gave a forced laugh. 'Kid's going to think you have anger management issues – not without cause.' He made a show of fussing over the stallion. 'See, we were about to turn in when we saw this big boy looking all agitated. We were concerned he might have colic so we decided to take him for a stroll, sort his guts out.'

'He doesn't,' Will said shortly.

'Doesn't what?'

'He doesn't have colic.'

Zach's hand moved towards his belt and Will saw something glint, though whether it was a knife or a gun, he couldn't be sure. 'Are you calling us liars?'

'I'm not calling you anything. I'm stating a fact. The horse doesn't have colic. I spent several vacations working at an equine veterinary practice. I've seen at least thirty horses with colic. The symptoms are unmistakable. That being the case, it might be a good idea to put the nice man's horse back in the corral. I can do it for you if you like.'

Zach's fingers twitched with fury. Axel put a warning hand on his arm. 'Save it. This is not the time nor the place.'

He tossed the lead rope to Will. 'It's a thankless business being a good Samaritan, but a man's gotta try.'

Zach shook a finger at Will. 'You wanna watch yourself, Billy the Kid. Curiosity kills.'

Will wanted to respond, but he decided to take his grandfather's advice. On both counts.

With the stallion safely in the corral, he woke Slim and told him that a mountain lion had been seen in the area and he should keep a close eye on his horse. The

165

Texan thanked him profusely. As quietly as he could, Will packed up his tent and saddled Shiraz.

The Out-Timer was staying with his wife and children in a mobile home near the entrance of the camp. With such a small number of riders to oversee he hadn't expected any 2.43 a.m. departures, but though half asleep he stamped Will's rider card cheerfully enough. The hold restriction was twenty hours. Since Will had exceeded that by forty-three minutes, he was relaxed about letting him go. Will would have preferred to rest Shiraz for longer, but it was too much of a risk. Men like Zach were capable of anything. The mare seemed to feel the same way. He had to hold her back, so keen was she to be out of the camp and gone.

He'd been riding for barely five minutes when he saw an SUV and horsebox parked by the roadside. The camp was in an isolated spot. Will could think of no good reason why anyone would wait in such a lonely place, at such an unsociable hour. To be on the safe side, he guided Shiraz down a slope and into the trees. As they threaded their way carefully through the dark forest, Will glanced up. The flare of a match illuminated the driver's profile. It was Wayne Turnbull, Chief Clerk of the race.

Will leaned forward and laid a quieting hand on Shiraz's neck. 'Zach's right, girl, we'll have to watch our backs. With enemies like that, we're going to need all the friends we can get.'

166

16

Day 3, Medicine Bow National Forest Route, Wyoming

From the outset, Jonas Ellington had been determined that The Glory stay true to the spirit of the distance races of legend. That implied a high level of risk – something that sent health and safety people screaming from the room in early meetings. Jonas had been deaf to their pleas. The only point he and most endurance riding associations were agreed upon was horse welfare; there'd be compulsory twenty-hour breaks every hundred miles and forty-eight-hour breaks every seven days. In all other regards, there was friction.

The subject that caused the most explosive debates was Jonas's insistence that flexibility be built into the race. 'We have to leave room for riders to be creative.'

'You mean cheat,' a veteran official said sourly. 'If you

don't define the route down to the last inch, you'll have people ducking and diving and taking shortcuts all over the place. How would you like it if the person who wins your quarter million dollars has only ridden a thousand miles while the person in second place has ridden, say, one thousand two hundred and thirty?'

'I'd like it just fine,' replied Jonas, 'if the rider has used his or her initiative to shave ten miles off the route here or there, provided that they cross the finish line on a happy, healthy horse.'

'But it's not possible for us to police every forest, mountain or desert between Colorado and Oregon. What's to stop riders from loading their horses onto lorries and sneaking ahead, or even swapping out their tired horses for fresh ones? Your "be your own judge" approach is a licence for trickery.'

Jonas laughed. 'For starters, riders will be required to have their race cards stamped every fifty miles. In addition, we'll carry out random checks – for doping and for people "sneaking ahead", as you put it. Apart from that, there's nothing but their own conscience. And that's fine with me too. Any man, woman, boy or girl who collects the trophy knowing in their heart that they cheated will have to live with that lie.'

The media were equally puzzled by Jonas's approach. 'Why leave it to chance?' asked one journalist. 'Using GPS tracking technology, every rider could be monitored every step of the way. Then you'd know for certain that the winner was the true winner.'

But Jonas would not budge. Horse well-being aside, he believed that every rider in the race should be accountable only to themselves.

'There's a reason The Glory is being held in the West,' he told the reporter. 'Historically, this is a landscape that for the best part of a century probably witnessed more feats of equestrian daring than any other on the face of the earth. In the mid-nineteenth century you had men like Tom Ponting and Washington Malone, who took two entire years to drive a herd of cattle from Texas to New York – fifteen hundred miles on foot and six hundred by rail, without the smallest shred of proof that they'd survive, let alone succeed.

'But theirs was only one story. There were dozens. A Californian cattleman had his outfit drive his cows up the Rio Grande to the Continental Divide in Colorado, through Wyoming, Utah and Nevada to San Francisco, another two-year expedition.

'Then there were the cowhands who roamed the West gathering wild longhorn cattle. Daily, they risked death by Indian ambush, stampede, snakebite, disease, drowning, or in bar-room gunfights or midnight encounters with rustlers. Some did these things out of necessity and some were trigger-happy outlaws. But a goodly majority were driven by dreams, idealism or a fierce pride. Those are the best of the qualities on which our country was founded and the winner of my race will, I hope, embody them all.'

It was Jonas's 'flexible' approach to both rules and the route that had convinced Will to attempt the race. Now, as he clung to the branch of a prickly lodgepole pine, praying that it wouldn't break and drop him into the path of the angry moose waiting below, he wished the Green Power CEO had been the type to demand that riders follow an exact route. If Will hadn't taken a shortcut he wouldn't be in this position.

It was also the fault of Alex, or whatever her name was. Third time unlucky. If she hadn't cast a spell over him in the diner, he wouldn't have felt an irresistible urge to save her and hand over most of his remaining cash to her. If she hadn't bumped into him at the start and thrown his concentration, he might have noticed that Shiraz's cinch was loose. And if he hadn't been so desperate to avoid her at the Laramie race camp that he'd moved to the overflow camp five miles further down the road, he would not now be contemplating an inglorious end.

He could just picture the headline in *The Tennessean*:

STAR CHATTANOOGA STUDENT TRAMPLED TO DEATH BY WYOMING MOOSE

'I thought he was working as a ranch hand in Colorado,' said Will Greyton's bemused father, shortly before being hospitalised with a second cardiac arrest.

But in reality Will knew that he had no one to blame but himself. For reasons he couldn't begin to fathom, he'd been so thrilled that Alex had made it as far as Laramie he'd had to restrain himself from throwing his arms around her. Having guessed correctly that she'd be unfamiliar with vet-gate procedure, he'd suddenly worried she might not make it any further – hence his bossy intervention.

What he hadn't considered was that when she turned her fiery gaze on him, accusing him of being obnoxious, a lightning bolt of attraction had ripped through his body, taking his breath away. Even exhausted and windswept, she was the most gorgeous girl he'd ever seen. His immediate impulse had been to run in the other direction as fast as his legs could carry him, but he'd volunteered to help her so he had to continue. He'd done that by focusing on taking care of her horse and trying to come across as coolly professional.

Afterwards, he'd been so disconcerted by the effect she had on him that he'd taken Shiraz to the only hidden part of the Laramie camp, a small section behind the staff quarters. He'd spent the day napping and making Shiraz comfortable. Not wanting to run into Alex or the Carling Brothers at the riders' barbecue that evening, he'd later led the mare to the overflow camp.

It was his actions there that had indirectly caused him to be charged by the moose. After leaving, he'd ridden for nine straight hours, only breaking to give Shiraz electrolytes and water. He'd planned to have an extra-long rest at the next vet gate, one hundred and fifty mile miles into the race.

His troubles had started when he trotted round a curve in Medicine Bow National Forest and saw a vehicle that looked suspiciously like the chief clerk's. Years of working as a cattle horse had given Shiraz the reflexes of a cheetah. One sharp nudge from Will and she sprang sideways into the forest. They'd been out of sight within seconds. Unsure whether or not they'd been spotted, Will continued through the trees until he was close enough to see the SUV's number plate.

Even as he confirmed that it was the same one he'd seen earlier that morning, the car door opened and Wayne Turnbull lit a cigarette. He'd leaned against the vehicle and looked at his watch. He seemed to be waiting for someone.

Will's skin had prickled. For most of the morning he'd stuck to the conventional route, passing several groups of riders and a couple of patrolling marshals. What if one of those people had reported on his progress? What if the someone the chief clerk was waiting for was Will? There was nobody else in sight. If any kind of confrontation occurred, there'd be no witnesses.

Paranoid or not, Will had decided that it might be wise to take an alternative route. Twenty minutes further on, he'd found a pretty clearing and taped off a small corral for Shiraz. He'd been settling down to have something to eat when the moose came charging out of nowhere.

Ignoring the mare, it had pounded straight at Will. Only his athleticism had saved him.

Having escaped being pounded to a pulp by the breadth of a moose whisker, Will had at first been grateful simply to be in one piece. He'd even laughed about it. The whole situation struck him as hilarious. It wasn't like surviving a bear attack. With its jowly face and Christmas card antlers, the moose was too comical to take seriously. Will felt as if he'd stumbled wide-awake into a skit from a cartoon. He'd expected the creature to get bored of the chase within minutes and move away.

An hour later he was less amused. Two hours on, the moose's persistence was distinctly unfunny. And after three hours and a half hours, he was agonisingly uncomfortable. Any which way he turned, he was stabbed by pine needles. He'd tried chucking a few pine cones down, but had succeeded only in incensing the moose further. It had pawed the base of the tree and glowered up at him with unadulterated hatred.

Nearly four hours on, Will was in a state of mild panic. Apart from a couple of crackers, he'd eaten nothing since the can of baked beans the previous evening and he was severely dehydrated. Without a jacket, he was growing steadily colder. The temperature had plummeted. Grape clouds were rolling in and a storm threatened. His predicament was no longer a joke.

He was even more worried about Shiraz. The food and water he'd given her would have been finished hours ago. From time to time, she let out a plaintive whinny, but there was not a lot she could do for him. Much as she adored Will, even she drew the line at confronting an aggressive moose.

Will was faced with three unenviable options. To chance descending the tree would be unwise; numerous tourists and hikers had been killed underestimating the power and ferocity of the moose's charge. But it would be equally life-threatening to stay where he was and risk being incinerated by lightning and/or catching hypothermia. The headlines in his imagination were getting more extreme by the hour.

MYSTERY SKELETON FOUND IN WYOMING TREE IDENTIFIED AS MISSING CHATTANOOGA TEENAGER

'If I'd known he was planning to enter that lethal horse race, I'd never have allowed it,' said Will Greyton's devastated father Len, shortly before being rushed to hospital with a suspected heart attack brought on by stress.

A whip crack of thunder shook the tree. Will almost fell off his branch in fright. Even the moose looked unnerved.

There was nothing for it. He had to get down. Breaking off a heavy stick, he threw it at the moose in the hope of scaring it. Once again it had the opposite effect. The creature head-butted the tree and let out a bellow of rage.

Will stayed where he was, defeated. The blood, sweat

and tears he'd expended preparing for the race, the savings he'd gambled and the lies he'd told his father were all for nothing. A dumb moose was about to ruin everything.

Shiraz gave a clarion whinny, shattering the silence. Another horse responded. Someone was coming! Against all odds, someone else had taken this particular shortcut at this particular time.

'Help!' yelled Will. 'Help!'

The rhythmic clip-clop of hooves quickened. From his eyrie Will caught a glimpse of a white blaze and golden coat through the foliage. He froze. No. No, it couldn't be. There were numerous palominos in the state of Wyoming as well as in the race. Surely fate would not be so diabolical a mistress as to add to his misery by sending a girl to rescue him. *The* girl. His nemesis.

It seemed she would.

The palomino burst through the trees, flaxen mane flying. He came to a screeching halt when he caught sight of the moose. A lesser rider would have gone over his head but Alex barely moved in the saddle. She took in the situation at a glance – Will clinging to a branch and the cartoon moose standing bemused below. An explosive giggle burst from her.

'How long have you been up there?'

'Not long.'

'How long's not long?'

'Does it matter? Look, I'd really appreciate it if you'd maybe—'

'Go on, humour me. How long?'

'Why is it important? Ages. I've been up here for ages. Does that satisfy you? Okay, three hours and forty-six minutes to be precise. I'm starving, dying of thirst and I'd really like to get down before the storm comes . . . '

He stopped. Alex was doubled over in the saddle, crying with laughter.

'I'm glad you find it funny,' he said crossly when she paused for breath.

'I'm sorry. It's just . . . Are you always this helpless?'

There was no malice in her words. She was teasing him, but only gently.

'Are you always this obnoxious?' he retorted, unable to repress a grin.

She smiled and the effect was quite startling. Her face, usually so serious and defensive, came alive with an extraordinary radiance and warmth and her dark eyes sparkled like sunlight on water. All of a sudden he was glad he was halfway up a tree and unable to move any nearer.

Light rain began to fall. Alex sobered. 'Right, no more joking, I promise. Tell me how to help.'

'Be very careful. The animal might look sweet and shy but it's actually psychotic. Whatever you do, don't get off your—'

But it was too late. She'd already dismounted and was tethering the palomino to a tree.

The moose, though agitated, had stood its ground throughout. It swung its antlers in Alex's direction, contemplating the new threat.

'Alex, stop! It'll kill you. Get back on your horse. I'd rather spend the next week up here than have you . . . '

But Alex had launched into a spontaneous impression of Gene Kelly's dance routine from *Singin' in the Rain*, her favourite film. She was not a terribly good dancer, especially in riding boots and stiff from the ride, but she could definitely carry a tune. 'What a glorious feelin'. . .' she sang as she twirled through the clearing. Will almost forgot about the moose, he was so entertained.

Fat drops of rain smacked down on the trail. The forest was lit with an other-worldly light. The air crackled with the electric energy of the approaching storm. A strange feeling came over Will. He'd never known anything like it and not for all the money in the world could he have put a name to it. He was only sure that if he lived to be a hundred he'd never forget the peculiar magic of this moment.

Thunder rent the heavens, bringing Alex's dance to an abrupt halt. She was perilously close to the moose. Before Will could yell at her to get back to safety, she was clapping her hands at it. 'Shoo! Shoo! Go pick on someone your own size.'

The moose stared at her with a mixture of rage and bewilderment, tossing its antlers for effect. But it too was tired and thirsty. It was also rather bored with the game. Humans, it concluded, were more trouble than they were worth. With a last defiant grumble it sauntered on its way.

Will slithered down the tree. His hands and arms

were trembling. It had to do with dehydration, cold and low blood sugar levels rather than fear but it made him look even more of a wimp than he already did.

'Don't say anything.'

Alex zipped her mouth. 'Wouldn't dream of it.'

'Thank you. I mean that sincerely. I'm not sure what I'd have—'

'You'd have been fine. But don't worry. I'm not going to be making a habit of it – assisting you, I mean.'

Will laughed. The rain was increasing in intensity. Before he could think of anything else to say, she was untying her horse and swinging lightly into the saddle.

'Alex, the storms out West, they can be violent. You're welcome to stay and shelter. You know, if that's something you'd like.'

She smiled, but he could see that her mind was already on the task ahead. 'That's nice of you, but according to the map the next hold is only four or five miles further on. There are unlikely to be any wild animals there so it's probably a safer bet all round. See you down the road, Will Greyton.'

Will touched the brim of his hat, but she was easing the palomino into a lope and didn't look round. Within seconds he was alone. He glanced skywards and the rain pelted his upturned face. As he ran to check on Shiraz and hastily pitch his tent, he felt bereft and happy all at the same time.

17

Day 5, Medicine Bow Forest to Badwater Creek Camp, Wyoming

'Isn't it amazing how you can travel thousands of miles by air, road and horse and end up talking to someone from just up the street?'

Alex didn't think it was amazing. She thought it was pure ill fortune that, having escaped Camp Renew and ridden approximately two hundred and forty-two exhausting miles, she should end up running into a forty-something woman who'd spent most of her life in the same county as Alex.

The only thing that prevented a calamity was that Verity Morden was a chatterbox. Alex had heard all about her endurance riding successes, her computer software engineer husband and their extensive menagerie – three 'divine' children, six horses, two dogs, a cat and an abundance of guinea pigs and chickens – along with their move from Egham, Surrey, to Bodmin Moor, Cornwall ('Heaven for endurance riders . . . '), before Verity got as far as asking Alex a single question about herself.

Remembering the adage about how the key to a successful lie is keeping it close to the truth, Alex confessed to living in Surrey, but in a place some distance from her home area. 'Richmond!' she said brightly.

Verity was riding so close that Alex could smell her orange blossom shower gel. With her button nose, inquisitive gaze and crisp, well-behaved hair, she reminded Alex of a Norfolk terrier. On her other side was Verity's American friend, Gill Redmond, winner of multiple endurance championships. Alex could not stop staring at her horse, a stunningly pretty Anglo-Arab called Laughing Dove Esmeralda – stable name, Little Dove.

'Yes, but which street do you live on, Sarah?' demanded Verity. 'And don't think I won't know. Before I quit work to ride and raise our kids, I was an estate agent. There's not a corner of Surrey I don't know like the back of my hand.'

Backed into a corner, Alex sidestepped the question. 'I'll wait until I know you a bit better before I give out my home address.'

But Verity was only getting warmed up. 'Which school do you go to, Sarah?'

Alex forced a smile. 'School's not my favourite subject. I'd rather not talk about it if that's all right with you.'

Unfortunately, Verity's other questions were not so easily dodged. Like Trey and Crystal in Colorado, she wanted to know what 'Sarah's' parents did for a living, and what insurance company her stepfather worked for, and how she'd persuaded her mum to agree to let her enter The Glory and where she'd got her mustang horse, Goldie.

Alex stuck with insurance as her stepfather's profession, but invented a new company. Once again it was a bad choice. It turned out that Gill, now fifty, had spent most of her life working for an insurance broker and travelled frequently to the UK, for business and to compete, which is how she knew Verity.

Her brow crinkled. 'Rainy Day Insurance? I'm surprised I haven't heard of it. Is it a big firm? Where are their offices?'

Questioned by Verity about 'Goldie', Alex claimed that he belonged to American friends of her parents, but that led to a fresh minefield involving Goldie's stabling and her own riding background and whether or not her parents' friends would be visiting her en route.

Ideally, Alex would have made an excuse and galloped away, but the race contestants had thinned dramatically. Just one hundred and forty-seven riders remained. Whereas the first night's ride had been exciting and fun, because there'd been a constant stream of fellow horsemen or patrolling marshals, the fourth night's ride had featured several deeply spooky moments. Alex had made up her mind to find safe, reliable companions to

181

accompany her on future evening rides. The downside was that any extended period in the company of others would invite unwanted questions.

With every step, Alex felt more exposed. It didn't help that they were riding across high desert, barren plains enlivened only by sagebrush and fleeting glimpses of far-off antelope. Every now and then they'd see a ramshackle clapboard house like something out of *Little House on the Prairie*, its warped exterior silver-grey with age. One had rusting cars on blocks in the yard, grass growing up through the chassis. It had the air of a place abandoned for decades. As they neared it Alex was startled to see washing on the line, blown horizontal by the biting wind.

Amid the bleakness, there were snapshots of extraordinary beauty. Early afternoon, the sun sliced a hole in the purple clouds, illuminating crimson cliffs set against crumpled hills cloaked in green velvet.

Alex drank in the scene during a rare moment of peace. But all too soon Verity was back, posting perfectly on her perfect Arab. 'Where did you ride in England, Sarah? What's the name of the stables?'

On this occasion, it was Gill who came to Alex's rescue. Unlike her garrulous friend she was a courteous, self-effacing woman. Alex had the sense that the friendship was somewhat one-sided and that Verity, a highly ambitious woman with her eyes on an international endurance riding career, had latched on to Gill because of her success.

Finally, Gill said, 'I don't mean to butt in, Verity, but we're approaching Powder River. Nowadays, the Powder River Basin – on the other side of these mountains, close to Big Horn – is mainly known for coal mining, but once it was the sacred hunting ground of the Lakotas and the Northern Cheyenne and Arapahoe. I was wondering if Sarah would be interested in hearing about Red Cloud's War?'

As Alex nodded eagerly and guided Scout to Gill's side, Verity reminded herself that the race was a long one. There'd be plenty of time to play detective.

At the fifty-mile vet gate a short while later, she was back on the case. Alex was in Pulse and Recreation. In order for the vet to carry out a Cardiac Recovery Index (CRI) check, he first recorded Scout's pulse. Alex then had to do a trot-up with Scout, one minute after which his heart rate was checked again. The two values had to be within four beats of one another or Scout and Alex would be disqualified.

Before the vet could complete the CRI assessment, he had to examine Scout's respiratory and gut sounds, capillary refill, teeth, legs and joints, mucous membranes, saddle area and feet. A horse had to be judged metabolically stable and free of 'Synchronous Diaphragmatic Flutter' (thumps) or any gait aberrations, to be passed sound. He judged them Fit to Continue.

Watching Alex smile with relief, Verity remarked to Gill, 'It wouldn't surprise me if she's a teenage runaway.'

Her friend gave a shocked laugh. 'Verity, the only runaway here is your imagination. Sarah seems a lovely girl. Smart, funny, horse-mad. Anyway, where would she have got the entry fee from? Or the horse, for that matter?'

'Stole them? Who knows. That's not the point. The point is, she was evasive about both her school and her address and you've never heard of her stepfather's so-called insurance firm. As for that cock and bull story about her parents' American mates lending her a half-wild mustang out of the goodness of their hearts. As if. She's sixteen years old.'

'So what. You and I know loads of teenage endurance riders.'

'Yes, we do. Mostly they compete in junior or novice events, or in races under forty miles. What we don't know is a single parent who'd allow their teenage daughter to compete in a month-long race across four States. Alone. With no back-up crew. In *October*, for goodness' sake.'

'Some parents are more liberal about these things. CNN's forever reporting on the latest teenager to sail solo around the world or plant a flag on the top of Mount Kilimanjaro.'

Verity's lips tightened. 'Trust me, there's more to our Sarah Wood than meets the eye.'

Gill was saved from replying when a P/R volunteer came to take Little Dove's heart rate.

Over the next couple of hours Verity was kept busy tending to her horse, but as soon as she got a moment she asked around the camp to see if anyone knew anything further about Sarah Wood's background. No one did. Most people were too busy attending to their own aches and pains and those of their horses to have the energy to have anything other than the most token interest in a rider with so little chance of finishing on the podium.

'Personally, I'm impressed by any sixteen-year-old who has the guts to enter a race this gruelling,' said Manny Edwards, a fellow Brit. 'Haven't you got better things to do than fuss about where this girl does or doesn't come from and where she's obtained her horse?'

Gill had asked something similar. Verity found it difficult to answer. Partly, she was curious about Alex because she thrived on social intrigue. An avid reader of mysteries and detective novels, she prided herself on her ability to unearth the secrets or lies of her friends, neighbours and acquaintances.

But in Alex's case it was more than that. Verity knew horsemen and Alex, though lacking experience and quite obviously clueless when it came to endurance riding, had a real gift. Watching her move with the mustang, who would have challenged the best riders she knew, was like watching horse ballet. She was fit too. Five days into the race and she was going strong. If she survived she could be a threat and Verity wanted as few obstacles between her and a top-ten finish as possible. One of the Endurance GB selectors had told her on the quiet that it would almost certainly guarantee her a spot on the British team.

Verity resolved to take a photo of Alex as soon as the rain slowed. She reviewed the questions she'd asked so far. The easiest tactic was to pretend to be forgetful. She'd ask the same things over and over. Sooner or later, 'Sarah Wood' would slip up.

Had she known the forces of darkness she was about to unleash, Verity might have thought twice about investigating Alex. Sadly, she did not.

Those forces were at that moment gathered in the War Office, as Strike Cartwright's domain was known. Chase Miller and Alex's Atlantic escorts, Sue-Ellen and Ken, had presented the warden with a small, slightly tatty bear.

'What is it?' barked Cartwright.

'It's a teddy bear . . . ' said Ken. Seeing the warden's expression, he continued quickly: 'It was Sue-Ellen who noticed that the bear had lost weight.'

'Excuse me?'

Sue-Ellen took up the story. 'Alexandra's mom told us that her daughter never goes anywhere without Pluto – that's the bear's name. She sided with Alexandra in demanding that the toy come to Camp Renew. Claimed it was a family heirloom. 'Course, we told her that troubled teens often hide contraband, but she was in denial – as all parents are.'

'Yes, yes, cut to the chase.'

'Long story short, we examined the bear and all seemed

in order. When we got to Camp Renew, the sniffer dog was cool with it too. Now as you know, sir, Ken and I have been in Alaska the past few days, rounding up a monstrous girl who'd taken up with some Hell's Angels. Talk about drugs, sex and rock 'n' roll.'

'Sue-Ellen!'

'Yes, sir, anyway, we arrived back a couple of hours ago to hear that Alexandra was missing. I asked Helga to show me her bunk area. The bear was propped against the pillow. Right away, I sniffed a large smelly rodent, especially since Pluto was a whole lot slimmer than the last time I saw him.'

Ken showed the warden the bear's pouch. 'Weren't nothing in it except this.' A British pound coin clattered onto the desk.

Cartwright used his quiet voice. 'The conclusion being that there was cash in the bear? Probably not pocket change since it would have been heavy and jingled. More likely to be folding money. Possibly hundreds, if the bear was plump. Enough for Alexandra to evade us for quite some time if she's resourceful.'

Sue-Ellen was crushed. 'All I can say is, the kid must be a very good seamstress to have fooled us.'

The warden's fist hit the desk. Pluto flew into space. 'Don't waste my time with EXCUSES!' he screamed. 'Take some responsibility. Thanks to you, we've been stitched up. Literally. As of this second, you and Ken are suspended, unless you can think of some way to redeem the situation fast.'

'There is one thing, sir,' Sue-Ellen ventured shakily. 'Chase mentioned that Alexandra couldn't have gone anywhere by pony because she didn't like them much and was a timid rider. For me, that was rodent number two.'

The warden clutched his head. He knew it was all his own fault. Some flaw in his interviewing technique had resulted in a workforce consisting entirely of morons. 'What are you talking about?'

'Sir, the girl's bedroom was plastered from floor to ceiling in horse posters. There was even one of Clint Eastwood in *Pale Rider*. And she had a stack of pony magazines on her bedside table.'

The warden gave the head wrangler a withering look. 'So you've been played too, Mr Miller. We've all been played, every last one of us. She's ridden out of here on one of our own horses, with cash in her pocket, laughing at us . . .'

He exhaled with a venomous hiss. '*But* . . . and it's a big but, all is not lost. This region is alien to her and we have her passport. If the bear was stuffed with pocket money, most likely it was pounds. She might have had trouble changing it. Sue-Ellen, you visit every bank between here and Boulder. Find out if there was a teenager with an accent trying to change foreign currency without ID. Ken, you go north and do the same. Chase, any idea as to what she might have done with the horse. Sold it?'

The wrangler was a wreck. 'There is one other detail, sir.'

'How many other details can there be?'

'I told her about The Glory, sir. It didn't occur to me . . . see, I didn't think.'

The warden glowered at him. 'Why would you? No one else in this place ever does. What's The Glory? A hotel? A restaurant?'

'It's a long-distance horse race that started in Boulder at the beginning of the week. There's no way she could have entered it, no way a kid could survive an hour of it, for starters, but she seemed very interested in it.'

'Did she now? The chances of her having made it as far as Boulder without being picked up by the cops are less than nil, but even the most far-fetched theory needs to be examined with a microscope. Get a list of contestants. Know anyone who's entered this race?'

'A wrangler from the Double ZZ ranch, nicknamed Gap on account of his teeth.'

'Is he a good rider?'

'Not bad, but he's accident-prone and temperamental. Can't see him lasting past the first serious gulley.'

'Get hold of him. Offer him money to keep an eye out for Alexandra. She'd be easy enough to spot.'

'I'm on it.'

'Oh, and Chase, I want the best horse at Camp Renew put in the barn. One with staying power. Make sure it's well fed and watered. It might be needed if I have to track Ms Blakewood off-road. Into the mountains, say.'

Miller blanched. '*You*, sir?'

'You got a problem with that?'

'Absolutely not. Great idea. I'll round up Midnight Magic.'

'Excellent. None of this goes further than this office. Instruct Helga to spread the rumour that Alexandra is safe and well but has had to be rushed home due to a family illness. If one word of her disappearance gets out Camp Renew will be finished and you'll be finished with it. Failure is not an option. An avalanche-sized lawsuit is barrelling down the hill at us. Every second counts. Go get her.'

After they'd gone, Cartwright contemplated setting fire to Pluto as an act of vengeance. He aborted the plan, reasoning that the toy might come in handy later. An illicit substance or two could be planted in the pouch as proof of Alexandra's deviousness and mental instability.

He flipped open his laptop. An email marked 'Urgent' pinged into his inbox. The third from Horizon Investments Inc. in as many days. They were threatening to foreclose on a personal loan. Deleting it, Cartwright did an Internet search for The Glory. What he found excited rather than alarmed him. His hunter instincts were awakened, as was his greed. A staggering $250,000 went to the winner. He rather hoped that the English girl had been idiotic enough to enter. There was a chance he could kill two birds with one stone. No delinquent teenager had ever outwitted him and Alexandra Blakewood would not be the first.

Energised, he leapt from his ergonomic chair and strode out of the office, slamming the door so hard behind him that the wooden board holding the elk's head was jolted out of place. Sawdust trickled to the floor.

'What was that?' demanded Natalie Pritchard. She was standing at the window of her Surrey living room, staring out at the grey rain. The banged door in Colorado had reverberated down the Atlantic phone line like a bomb going off.

'We're renovating,' Stacey improvised, glaring after the warden. 'How may I help you, Mrs Pritchard?'

'You know how you can help me, Stacey, because this is the fifth time I've called. I want to speak to my daughter. If you won't put me through to her, I must insist on talking to the warden. I'm afraid we've made a terrible mistake. I want Alex to come home.'

'Ma'am, as I explained to you last week, the warden isn't here. He's had root canal surgery. There've been complications. He's in hospital, half-dead with appendicitis.'

'*Appendicitis?* I thought he was having dental work done.'

Stacey located the piece of paper the warden had given her. 'I meant to say he had an abscess that caused septicaemia. He's a very ill man.' That part was certainly true; he was sick in the head. 'He'll be in touch as soon as he's recovered, Mrs Pritchard.'

'And there's no one else who can help me?'

'No, ma'am. Warden Cartwright likes to speak to all parents personally. But you shouldn't worry. Alex is doing just fine. Every mom feels the way you do now, but one day you'll look back and laugh about this. Alex loves the nature at Camp Renew. I can email you a photo right now.'

As instructed, she pressed Send on the only picture the academy had of a smiling Alex – taken after a wilderness walk.

Hanging up, Stacey felt queasy. It sickened her to lie on behalf of the warden. He'd not updated her on the current crisis, but the walls were thin and she'd heard every word.

Anything could have happened to poor Alex. People were abducted, murdered, bitten by poisonous snakes or attacked by bears every day. She could be lying in a ditch with a fractured leg, too weak to call for help. Yet instead of admitting they'd lost her and getting the cops involved, Strike and his minions were wasting precious time by planning to hunt her down like a wild animal.

So distressed was Stacey that, while cleaning the warden's office, she swept the sawdust off the floor and gazed absently at the nail jutting out of the board above it without connecting the two. Vigorously, she buffed the great head. There were few things the warden abhorred more than a dusty elk.

18

Day 7, Bridger Trail, Wyoming

Death by a thousand cuts. That's what it felt like. The wind sliced Alex's face, buffeted her from all sides, screamed, moaned and tried to shove her off the steep trail. The mountain, over five thousand four hundred feet of it, caused her thighs to burn as if they were being seared with a branding iron. The rocks in her path seemed to have been put there for the sole purpose of twisting her ankles. It even hurt to breathe.

She laboured upwards, leading Scout, until she could stand the torment no longer. Her legs hurt so much tears began to stream down her cheeks. She urged Scout past and held fast to his tail. He pulled her after him, puffing and snorting, his rose-gold quarters bunching with effort. The first couple of times she'd tried it he'd nearly kicked her head off. But he was keenly smart and soon understood that dragging her up was a whole lot easier than carrying her.

Still, she felt guilty about every extraneous item she'd put in his Snugpax or tied to the saddle. Glory rules dictated that all riders without private crews had to pack water bottles, energy bars, nuts, ready-cooked rice and beans, and condensed milk sachets, plus maps, directions, vet certificates and their rider registration card.

To get her through the next twenty-four hours, Alex also had waterproofs, spare socks and underwear, waterproof trousers, polo shirt and jeans, tent, groundsheet, sleeping bag, camping stove, survival blanket, torch, matches, first aid kit, a Swiss Army knife, Scout's Polarfleece blanket, a dry saddle pad, glo-sticks for night riding, a hoof pick, a sponge on a string, a heart rate monitor, lent to her by Gill, Vaseline, electrolytes and ice gel. Scout was wearing his Easyboots to protect his feet from the rocks.

In case of emergencies, Alex carried two portions of horse feed, a complex mix of extruded corn, soya oil, salt, vitamins E and B, selenium and soya bean hulls. Plus a dog-eared novel: *Roughing It* by Mark Twain.

She did not have a phone.

How Scout found the energy to keep going with all that weight on his back, Alex could not comprehend. For her, simply crawling out of her sleeping bag required a monumental effort of will. This morning she'd hobbled to the shower as if she was ninety.

She had so many raw patches on her legs and bum that she resembled the 'before' photo in a dermatologist's handbook. Mercifully, she hadn't contracted boils like some of the riders she'd seen staggering from the medical tent. Nor had she fallen. But her saddle sores were so excruciating that, had it not been for Gill, who'd kindly given her both chamois cream to prevent chafing and rashes, and cortisone to reduce inflammation and heal, also in her bags, Alex would have been tempted to quit the race on the fifth evening.

Every time her nerve failed her, Scout's relentless drive swept them on. At the vet gates, his CRI stats were at least as good as top Arabians like Little Dove and the Carling Brothers' fantastical Akhal-Tekes. Other horses were crashing out left, right and centre. Only ninety-two had made it through the three hundred mile vet check. But Scout burned with some insatiable inner fire.

He was not, she'd come to realise, a pet. His wildness was undiminished. Despite everything they'd gone through together, he distrusted her. Any sudden movement would send him rearing back, terror in his eyes. He hadn't thrown her or tried to trample her like he had the warden but that, she suspected, was only because they had a common goal. He was consumed with the urge to return to some distant Wyoming homeland. She happened to be heading the same way.

Yet somehow his wariness made every small gain all the sweeter. Only this morning she could have sworn that he looked pleased to see her as she approached him with the tub of Vaseline to prevent cracks on his pasterns.

And he ate. That was critical. Many riders had a nightmare trying to persuade stressed, anxious horses to eat and drink away from familiar surroundings. Scout had a wild mustang's understanding that food meant survival and water was not optional.

Fuelled, he brimmed with a yearning to move, move, move. Today, for instance, Alex would gladly have spent an extra twenty-four hours close to hot food and showers. Snow was forecast and being snuggled in her sleeping bag was much more appealing than trying to win a race. But a volunteer had come to rouse her from her tent. Scout was causing havoc in the corral, trying to break out, wanting to go.

There was a shortcut being talked about in the camp. An 1864 trail forged by Jim Bridger, a legendary mountain man charged with finding safe passage for settlers' wagon trains journeying from Wyoming to the Montana goldfields. Few traces remained of it but a couple of locals swore by it. The majority of the competitors, Gill and Verity included, would be taking the main race route via Shoshoni and Wind River Canyon – a less risky option.

With severe weather moving in, the race organisers had issued stern warnings about travelling alone. The riders taking the shortcut turned out to be a group of rough-looking men unafraid of tackling the mountains in hostile conditions. Alex had screwed up her courage and approached Verity to ask if she could ride with her and Gill as far as the fifty-mile vet gates near Thermopolis. She'd have preferred to speak to lovely Gill, but the American woman was deep in conversation with one of the officials.

'I hope this is not going to become a habit, Sarah,' Verity had said tartly. 'Gill's a professional, you know. She's a champion with a race to win. And I'm aiming to finish in the top ten. We can't nanny less experienced riders.'

After Alex had assured her that this would be the very last time she'd impose on them, Verity gave an exaggerated sigh. 'Well, I *suppose* it would be all right, but in the future you might want to call on your parents' friends – the *owners* of your mustang – for support. You can come with us today if you're ready to go right now. We're riding against the clock.'

'I can be ready in about thirty minutes,' Alex said. 'I still need to give Scout his electrolytes and get some supplies together and . . . '

Verity had looked at her as if she was mentally defective.

'You do understand that we can't possibly wait?'

It was then that Alex decided she'd rather take her chances with the vagabonds riding the shortcut than spend another minute on the road with Verity and her condescending manner and loaded questions.

'*Soooo, Sarah, where does your father live now? Has he remarried?*'

'My dad,' Alex had told her, 'is dead.'

And so here she was, on a wind-blasted mountain like something out of *Pale Rider*. Shale, scrub and giant boulders – the black mouth of a cave yawning from one. Any minute now Clint Eastwood would come riding over the horizon in his long brown coat and preacher's dog collar, snowflakes settling on the flanks of his dapple grey. He'd be ambushed by an evil outlaw gang. Clint's Remington revolver would flash and the outlaws would be no more.

Those were the kind of flights of fancy she used to occupy her mind during the long days on the trail. They stopped her from dwelling on whether or not her mum was having a nervous breakdown thinking she'd been kidnapped, or if her mug shot was on Fox News.

'Troubled teen Alexandra Blakewood, a British student at therapeutic boarding school Camp Renew, was last seen over a week ago when she was sent on a wilderness retreat . . . '

Unfortunately, cowboy films tended to remind her of her dad, who had a new family and no longer wanted her, and that always made her angry.

Scout gave a final heave and they crested the rise. Alex's leg muscles were killing her, but the exhilaration and sense of achievement she felt was worth every scrap of pain. They were on the roof of the world – pinpricks in a vast sea of emptiness. Below them was a flat basin of scorched earth, peppered with sagebrush and wispy grass. It stretched into infinity, interrupted only by a twisting river and the Big Horn Mountains, which rose in creased blue splendour above the plains.

In England, the sky seemed barely high enough to accommodate the trees. Out in the country, clouds bumped along the hedgerows or skated across fields low enough to brush the pollen from daffodils. In towns, they draped themselves over the office blocks and houses like wet cotton wool, causing claustrophobia.

Wyoming was the universe magnified, its scale overwhelming. The dome of sky seemed high enough to contain several galaxies, and the landscape was no different. The Big Horn basin alone looked large enough to contain all the earth's inhabitants. Gazing at it, Alex felt a rush of euphoria tinged with melancholy.

The stories Gill had told had brought the Old West to life so evocatively that, as they'd ridden, they'd unfolded before her as if the ghosts of the past still lived and breathed. Gazing down on the valley, she could almost see the furry bison that had once grazed these plains in such epic numbers that in the early 1800s a man could ride from dawn to dusk without reaching the end of a single herd. For centuries an estimated sixty million of them had been the lifeblood of the American Indians, providing meat, milk, shelter and clothing.

Then the white fur trappers arrived. After decimating the beaver populations of every river in the land, they started on the bison. Hunting the American buffalo was a lucrative business, and a crack marksman could fell a hundred in a day.

Gill had described a white mountain of sun-bleached bison skulls that had piled up until it eventually numbered thirty-one million and had to be carted away to California to be ground into fertiliser. So effective was the shooters' work that, within a few decades, less than five hundred bison remained on the entire continent – with devastating consequences for the tribes who depended on them.

The US government barely noticed. They were too busy seducing emigrants from as far afield as Scotland and Russia with promises of shining mountains and golden prairies: 'Your own farm for $3 an acre!'

There was only one problem. The land wasn't the government's to give away. It was the home of the Sioux, the Navajo, the Shawnee, the Apaches and other tribes, and had been the home of the Paleo-Indians before them as long as 47,000 years ago.

To begin with, Gill said, many tribes were willing to share their land and the bison that grazed on it. They signed one peace treaty after another. Again and again they were betrayed, herded into far-flung or barren reservations, their sacred hunting grounds decimated, their homes, families and way of life destroyed.

In Colorado, the peace-loving Cheyenne chief, Black Kettle, was massacred along with his family and hundreds of women, children and unarmed braves by General Custer and his soldiers, while innocently encamped in a small, bleak reservation given to them by the government. Afterwards, it was said that Custer ordered some 680 Indian ponies to be shot. So movingly did Gill recount this tragic tale that tears had streamed down Alex's cheeks as she told it.

Meanwhile, the European settlers continued to pour across the West in their wagon trains, buoyed by dreams of sun, wheat, gold and freedom. Instead they were met by 'savage' Indians and natural events on a Biblical scale: floods, droughts, plagues of locusts, wildfires so diabolical that they singed the wings of the birds in the air, hailstones the size of turkeys and dust storms capable of hurling fully grown mules into the next county.

Once more, the icy wind attempted to launch Alex into oblivion. As she picked up Scout's lead rope, she glanced back the way they'd come. A shiver went through her. The camp at Badwater Creek had been erased by a curtain of white. As she tried to take in the implications of what she was seeing, a couple of snowflakes floated down like rose petals and settled in Scout's mane.

For the first time since she'd started the race, Alex felt real terror. If the storm was headed her way, she was in trouble. Shielding her eyes from the glare of the weak noonday sun that still held sway on the other side of the mountain, she desperately scanned the valley for signs of life. At last she spotted five or six riders moving along a creek. If she hurried, she could travel with them or close to them as far as the fifty-mile camp near Thermopolis. That way, she'd have company if the weather got really rotten.

But what if it was already too late?

A week's hard experience had taught her that distance was near impossible to judge in this terrain. Objects that seemed far were often near and those that seemed close frequently turned out to be three-blister journeys. What if it started to snow in earnest before she reached the other riders? What if she got lost?

She had the sense that she was about to cross a divide. That she could turn back and hope for the best, or go forward and trust that it would work out okay. Either way, she'd never be the same again. Scout made the decision for her, tugging impatiently at his lead rope. Alex took a deep breath and stepped off the precipice.

The blizzard hit as they were negotiating the last tricky slope. Within seconds, Alex barely knew which way was up and which was down. Beneath her, Scout snorted, stumbled and shook snow from his ears and mane.

Once on level ground, she oriented herself by the mountain. As long as it was at her back, she was heading northwest. But when the snow began to pile up in drifts, a compass heading was no longer enough. Scores of gulches, ridges and creeks lay between her and the place where she'd last seen the other riders. Even a minor fall or injury could lead to death in these conditions.

To make matters worse, Scout kept veering to the right. Eventually, she let him have his way. He was a mustang. This was his home ground. If any horse was capable of getting them out of this situation alive, it was him.

As soon as she gave him his head he started to trot in the direction of the Big Horn Mountains. When Alex tried to slow him and steer him to the left, he bucked violently and accelerated. Terrified of falling so far from help, she loosened her reins and prayed. She kept up a steady stream of chatter and stroked him constantly, just to remind him that she was with him and they were a team. She told him that if either of them panicked, they were done for.

The phrase that kept coming into her mind was 'Moon of Cold Exploding Trees'. That was the name given to an apocalyptic day in January 1886 when the Great Blizzard, a tornado of frozen dust, had raged and screamed across Wyoming, Montana, Kansas and Dakota for seventy-two hours. Whole families froze to death as their flimsy cabins were buried up to their chimneys in snow, cowboys pushed their ponies through hat-high drifts and bloodthirsty wolves and starving cows rampaged through the towns. Tens of thousands of cattle were frozen solid where they stood.

It was this last image that haunted Alex most. What frightened her was that, if she and Scout didn't find shelter soon, becoming an ice statue was definitely on the cards.

The wind was close to gale force and it was coming right at them. When Scout floundered in a snowdrift, Alex was able to slow him to a walk. She made the decision to pitch her tent and wait out the storm.

It seemed an interminable age before she saw a pile of boulders topped by a dead tree. They were the height of Scout's ears and no more, but they offered some relief from the driving snow and wind.

As she struggled to put up her tent, she thanked her lucky stars that Glen at the Easy Rider stall had insisted she bought one that stood firm in high winds. Before retreating inside it, Alex unzipped her sleeping bag and draped it over Scout. She wasn't convinced that his Polarfleece rug was enough.

The mustang's ears were pinned to his head and he was shivering. He looked as wretched as she felt. She pressed her face to his, rubbing his neck, trying to get his circulation going.

'You're my best and only friend in this whole entire world,' she told him as he screwed up his eyes against the swirling wind and snow. 'Don't even think about getting pneumonia. If I didn't have you, I don't know how I'd cope.'

She debated whether to hobble him but was concerned that he might get even colder if his movement was restricted. In the absence of anything better, she used a tent stake as a hitching post. The last thing she did before retreating into her orange cocoon was give him water and food. The water froze almost before he could get to it but she hoped a feed would warm him up.

Inside her tent she couldn't stop shaking. A block of ice seemed to have lodged in her chest. It took all the willpower she possessed merely to remove her jacket so she could put on an extra polo shirt and a dry pair of jeans and socks. For extra measure, she added her waterproof trousers.

Curled into a ball on her groundsheet, head resting on Scout's saddle, she tried to take her mind off her plight by picturing her ex-classmates. They'd be filing into double maths around now. Gemma and Izzy and their mates would be gossiping about reality shows, fashion and boy band members with spiffy haircuts. She wondered what they'd say if they could see her huddled in a freezing tent in a Wyoming snowstorm – a boot camp fugitive on the run with a stolen horse. Doubtless, they'd think her a total crackpot. It would cement her status as an outsider and a failure.

Alex realised that she didn't care. Regardless of what happened next, she'd never regret the past week. Thanks largely to Scout and Jonas Ellington, they'd been the best days of her life.

If she had her time over, there were only two things she'd go back and change:

The first was a secret. So secret that she didn't even want to admit it to herself.

Number two on the list was getting to know Will Greyton. At the three hundred mile camp at Badwater Creek, he'd caught her eye across the dining area. She'd smiled and waved but turned away before he attempted to speak to her. She'd bitterly regretted dropping her guard in Medicine Bow Forest and had been determined it wouldn't happen again. She'd worried that a distraction like him could ruin everything.

Now she wished he was there. She wanted to know everything about him: Where he'd got his unusual grey mare and his sexy Southern drawl, and why he was risking life and limb in this race. She wondered what his home life was like and whether he had one parent or two, and whether or not he had a girlfriend. Most of all, she wished he was physically there. His smile alone lit a fire in her.

She wished her mum was there too. A hug would have been most welcome. Did her mum still love her or did she, like Alex, have so many confused emotions – some of them hateful – that she no longer knew what she felt? How would she react if she knew that her daughter was lost in a blizzard? Would she blame herself for sending Alex to a boot camp, or would she blame Alex for the decisions that had led to her being camped in sub-zero temperatures in the middle of nowhere?

Outside in the storm, Scout let out a primal whinny. The tent swayed on its moorings. Alex sat up in terror. Wolves! Were there still wolves in Wyoming?

Grabbing her Swiss Army knife, she lifted the tent flap. The wind had reached such a pitch that she felt, rather than heard, distant thunder. It intensified by the moment. Out of the whirling white came a herd of wild mustangs, snow spraying up around them like sea foam, nostrils blowing steam. Scout wrenched free of his tether, causing the tent to collapse. Alex dived for his lead rope but her gloves were too clumsy to hang on to it. Knocking her aside, the palomino raced ecstatically to meet his friends.

The howling gale drowned out her yells. As if by some prearranged signal, the herd swerved in concert and was gone. Alex's tears turned to ice on her cheeks.

There were a million ways to die in the West. Being alone in a blizzard without a horse, phone or sleeping bag was among them.

19

No Water Creek Ranch, Wyoming

'Dad, forget what you've seen on the news,' said Will. 'You know how reporters exaggerate. I'm in a warm bunkhouse, not out in the snow. There's a fire and everything. Stop worrying! Didn't we agree that there's no point in me trying out for this job in Colorado to help pay our bills if you're going to fret? I promise I'm not about to die of hypothermia. The cooking's an improvement on mine too. Right before I called I had two huge bowls of vegetarian chilli. With all the trimmings.'

It was one of the few semi-truthful phone conversations he'd had with his dad since leaving Chattanooga. When the blizzard had blown in earlier that day, The Glory organisers appealed to locals to help provide accommodation close to the fifty-mile vet gates south of Thermopolis. A local rancher had opened his bunkhouses to twenty race competitors.

Much to Will's relief, Zach and the Carlings were staying elsewhere. Ever since he'd stopped Zach from strolling off into the night with Slim Jim's Morgan stallion, he'd been the target of a petty vendetta. He now knew to double-check his cinch, saddle and bridle before he rode, but he couldn't police everything. Any time he turned his back, Shiraz's water bucket was upended, or he'd return from breakfast to find his spare jeans dangling from a high branch, or maple syrup in his saddlebags.

At No Water Creek Ranch, the men's bunkhouse was shabby and had mice but it was free of thugs and very cosy. That, to Will, was worth all the luxury in all the five-star resorts in the US.

Not that he'd ever stayed in any.

When he'd finished cleaning his boots and tack and putting anything washable in the machine, he took a long shower. Water was scarce in Wyoming, but he stood under the jet with steam rising in clouds from his skin until his bones and muscles thawed.

Afterwards, he checked on Shiraz. She was blissed out in a hay-filled barn. Unlike him, she was suffering no ill effects from the journey. Her eyes were bright, her legs free from swelling. Her appetite had never been better. It was as if she'd been born to do this. That day's ride had been one part sheer, unadulterated misery, nine parts hell, but Shiraz had leaned into the wind and got on with it. If anything, the big freeze incentivised her to move faster. Nothing Will did persuaded her to slow down.

Already unsettled by the depressed air of the Wind River Indian Reservation town, Shoshoni, with its boarded-up motels and casino-advertising billboards ('800 Gaming Machines!'), Will had dreaded the trip through the canyon itself. He hadn't anticipated the immensity of it. Riding into the teeth of the blizzard, with the tawny-yellow, rust-streaked walls of rock towering above him and soapy green rapids roaring below him, had been bleakly thrilling. Trotting through the whirling snow, Will had been reminded of his skin-crawlingly dull but non-life-threatening job at the Bigger Burger.

Was there something masochistic in his nature that he preferred dicing with death in Wyoming?

In the No Water Creek ranch house, Will sat beside the crackling fire. It was almost five p.m. The other riders were watching *The Good, The Bad and The Ugly* on an enormous flat-screen TV. Will was a fan of the movie, but he couldn't relax. By chance, he'd seen Alex's name – her official name, that is, Sarah Wood – on the accommodation list for the No Water Creek Ranch. After she'd snubbed him at the last camp, he'd made up his mind to have nothing further to do with her. Clearly she had issues. Or she didn't like him. Or both. In any case, he wanted her gone from his head. She was an unwelcome distraction.

Nonetheless, she'd saved him from the psychotic moose. They were sort of friends. Unfriendly friends, but still . . . He kept watching the door. Any minute now she'd come waltzing through it, pushing her tangled caramel hair from her face and looking quite ridiculously beautiful as usual. She'd be shattered and frozen to the core like all of them, but she'd be fine. Her palomino mustang would have got her through the snowstorm. That's what mustangs did. They survived blizzards.

If she could just do that one thing for him – walk through the door – he wouldn't care if she was rude to him or ignored him. He wouldn't care about anything so long as he knew she was safe.

Just then, the door creaked open.

Will reached it in two bounds. In came Gill Redmond, the champion endurance rider, followed by a short, bristly woman in a maroon anorak. They were wind-burned and plastered with mud and melting snow, swaying with weariness.

'Have you seen Alex?' Will blurted out. Fortuitously, his question coincided with a shootout in the film, because as soon as the words left his lips he remembered her telling him not to confuse people by mentioning that name.

Verity ducked around him, making a beeline for the table of coffee and pecan pie. 'Who?' she asked over her shoulder. Gill had been intercepted by the rancher.

'Sarah Wood.' Will tried to keep the impatience out of

his voice. 'I saw you riding with her the other day. Were you with her again today?'

'We're not a crèche,' Verity responded tartly as she helped herself to two slices of pie and a generous serving of cream. She had a British accent. 'Gill has a race to win and I'm aiming to finish well myself. Did you know that after today's snow fiasco, there are only fifty-three riders left in the game? *fifty-three!*'

'Did you at least see Sarah this morning? Do you know what route she was planning to take?'

Verity fixed him with a laser stare. 'Are you a friend of Sarah's? What was it you called her? Does Sarah have a different name – a nickname maybe?'

Will wanted to shake her.

'Apologies, ma'am, I should have introduced myself.' He gave her his best Bigger Burger smile. 'I'm Will Greyton. And you are . . . ?'

'Verity Morden. From Surrey, England – same place as Sarah.'

'Well, Miss Verity, let's just say I'm a concerned party. Sarah's a long way from home, as you've just pointed out. Even by British standards, I think you'll agree that the conditions outside are pretty bad. There were severe weather warnings at the Badwater Creek camp and a notice up advising riders not to attempt to travel to Thermopolis alone. I'm wondering why Sarah didn't try to join you and Mrs Redmond.'

Gill came over and poured herself a coffee. 'What's this about Sarah? Is she here yet? I've been fretting about her all day. I wish we'd asked her to come with us. She's a fantastic rider but if I were her mom I'd be having some sleepless nights thinking of her out in this weather.'

'She's missing,' said Will, though he wasn't yet sure if that was the case. He turned again to Verity. 'Do you know what time she left? Did you speak to her this morning?'

'Why are you both looking at me like that?' Verity said sulkily. 'Am I her nursemaid? If she's lost in the snow blame her parents, not me. If you must know, she did turn up just as we were leaving. But the girl wasn't ready. It was going to take her at least another forty minutes to sort out her horse – which, by the way, is not her horse. There's something weird about that whole set-up.'

Gill went very still. 'Verity, what did you say to her?'

'What difference does it make? This is not my fault.'

'Verity, I'm asking you for the last time. What did you say?'

Verity's mouth pursed as if she'd sucked on a lemon. 'All I said was, "You understand we can't wait for you." She didn't seem that bothered. She muttered something about how it didn't matter and that in any case she'd be better off going over the mountains.'

'*Over the mountains* . . . She's sixteen years old. Have you any idea what you've done?' Gill turned on her heel and marched away.

Will's fists clenched at his sides. 'If anything has

happened to Sarah, if one hair on her head is harmed, I'm holding *you* personally responsible.'

He strode to the door and snatched his coat and hat off the hook.

Verity's voice rose shrilly. 'She's not who she's pretending to be, your girlfriend. She's a liar and a fraud and I'm going to prove it. If you know what's good for you, you'll stay away from her.'

Snow forced its way into Will's eyes, nose and mouth. It blinded, suffocated and choked him. The constant screaming of the wind had long since rendered him deaf. He was scarcely capable of hearing his own thoughts. Despite the layers of protective clothing he wore, he was growing colder by the minute. It was as if the cheerful fire and steaming shower had never happened.

Had it not been for the quarter horse lent to him by the rancher, he might have had to admit defeat. A record amount of snow had fallen and he had no idea what lay underneath it. That's why Ed Barrett had given him Chinook. Even in darkness, the cow pony knew every rock and crevice between Buffalo Creek and the Big Horn Mountains. Accustomed to rounding up cattle in all weathers, he plodded on stoically by the light of Will's torch, making detours as he saw fit.

There were only three people out searching for Alex – four, if you counted Gill, who was phoning local hospitals, ranches and mines in case anyone had seen her. The emergency services had been notified but they were stretched to capacity and not prepared to endanger further lives by initiating a search before sunrise. Nor were The Glory organisers. Too dangerous, they said. At first light, a mountain rescue team would be dispatched. A couple of race volunteers would drive back to Badwater Creek in the hope of finding Alex along the way.

Until then it was two wranglers and Will. The cowboys, who knew the terrain, were searching the foothills of the nearby mountains and along the creek. Will was sticking to the flat. He was more exhausted than he'd ever been in his life, but he kept going in spite of the voice in his head that told him he had more chance of locating a pin in an avalanche than he did of finding Alex.

With the aid of the GPS on his phone, he'd travelled much further north-east than he intended, reluctant to admit defeat. He was about to turn back when his pony shied violently.

Struggling to right himself in the saddle, he saw what had startled Chinook. It was an olive-green sleeping bag. Will's heart did a hopeful skip. If it belonged to Alex, maybe he was close to finding her.

He jumped off his horse to take a closer look. The sleeping bag was soaking wet. It was then that he noticed that the ground had been churned up by the hooves of many horses. Most had been obscured by powdery new

215

snow, but there were enough to tell him that a herd had passed this way.

Fear lent Will energy. The palomino was a mustang. It was entirely possible that he'd seen a herd of fellow mustangs and bolted away to join them, throwing Alex or wrenching away from her. If she was lying in the snow, bleeding or unconscious . . .

He intensified his search, riding in wide circles around the spot where he found the sleeping bag. It was agonising work. The snowstorm was relentless. His pony battled valiantly on but it, too, was flagging.

In the end, it was nothing short of a miracle that a random sweep of his torch revealed a red bandana tied to a dead tree. Will urged his pony nearer. There, on the leeward side of a stack of boulders, was a tent so covered in snow it resembled an igloo.

He leapt off his horse and raced towards it. The temperature beneath the canvas was no different to that outside in the blizzard. Wrapped in a foil survival blanket, Alex was perfectly still. He was sure she was dead. In the white glow of his torch she looked like a pale blue angel.

Will lifted her into his arms and pressed his face to hers. Her skin was as chilly as marble. He hadn't cried since he was twelve and broke his collarbone falling off his bike, but he wept now.

'Lions, tigers and bears . . . ' she murmured.

'Alex! Oh, thank God, you're alive. Alex, listen to me. You have to hold on. You have a race to win, remember?

We're going to have a showdown, you and I. A proper duel.'

Laying her down gently, he rushed to collect blankets, hand warmers and a flask of coffee from his saddlebags. He climbed under the blankets with her, holding her close in a bid to pass on his meagre body warmth.

It seemed to take forever for her to come round, but at last she began to ramble, making no sense. Her eyes flickered open. Tenderly, she touched his cheek. 'I wished for you, Will Greyton, and you came.'

Will didn't trust himself to respond. He sat up. 'Don't try to talk. You need to get some of this coffee into you.'

Her eyelids slid shut. She drifted out of consciousness again. He shook her awake and coaxed her into drinking the steaming sweet brew. After swallowing a cupful, she revived noticeably, sitting up unaided, but when he offered her more she turned her head away.

'Alex, you need to drink as much as you can. You've got hypothermia. You could have died.'

To his astonishment, she turned on him. 'So what? What difference would it have made?' Her voice shook with fury. 'Why did you have to interfere? Why couldn't you have left me alone? It would have been better for everyone if you'd just left me out here in the snow.'

'You don't mean that.'

'Yes, I do. You don't know how much. If I'd gone to sleep in the snow, no one would have missed me – not even Scout, my horse. He was my only friend and he showed me that he, more than anybody, doesn't care. He knocked me into the dirt and galloped away.'

'*I* care,' Will said.

She gave a bitter laugh. 'That's only because you don't know me. You don't have the first clue about me. Want the truth? I entered this race on a stolen horse, using a fictitious name. I ran away from a boot camp for "troubled teens". Can you believe that? My mum and stepfather who supposedly love me sent to a boot camp on the other side of the world. I did trash our home but, you know, they could have grounded me for a year or two. But, no, I had to be frog-marched across the Atlantic to a teenage prison in Colorado. "Camp Renew", they call it in the glossy brochure. It's a "corrective boarding school" slash labour camp. My real dad either hasn't been told or is too busy playing happy families in the Australian sun to bother.

'So I absconded with Scout – that's the real name of my mustang, not Goldie. Only he's not *my* mustang. He belongs to Warden Cartwright, a sadist who's planning to send him to the slaughterhouse for misbehaving. I wanted to save him. I thought that I could set him free in the wild after I'd proved to everyone that I could do something good and special with my life by winning The Glory. Naturally, I failed at that, like I fail at everything else. Now he's gone, and who can blame him? Everything I touch is a disaster.'

Will gazed steadily at her. 'Are you done with the pity party?'

Alex was taken aback. She picked up the coffee mug with an unsteady hand and took a couple of swallows. 'Yeah, I'm done.'

'Because when you're finished with the "Loser of the Month" speech you've prepared, you might want to consider that I and two wranglers who don't know you from Eve left a warm fire, a hot dinner and a comfortable bunk to drag ourselves halfway across Wyoming on the most pig-awful, hell-freezing-over night I've ever had the misfortune to experience. Why the heck would we do that if we didn't care? Sounds as if your mom and your stepfather love you enough to try to help you too, even if they have a pretty poor way of showing it.'

Alex opened her mouth and shut it again.

'And while we're on the subject, there's someone else who'd like to show you how much they appreciate you.'

He pushed back the tent flap. Standing beside his pony, as innocent as fresh-fallen snow, was the palomino.

20

Dolphin House, Waratah Avenue, Perth, Australia

Sam Blakewood awoke with a start, gasping for air, like a free diver bursting from the ocean after too long without oxygen. Between the blind and the windowsill the sky was an intense blue. Glittering pools of early morning sunshine promised another baking day in paradise.

Shortly, his three-year-old twins and sixteen-year-old stepdaughter would fly in and demand that he take them to the beach. Miranda, his second wife, would make her famous barbecue sauce and they'd spend the day by the ocean making sandcastles, body-surfing and eating chargrilled seafood. It was everything he'd hoped for when he left his grey office job in the UK.

There was only one thing missing: Alex.

For a long time Sam had been able to live with the lies he told himself. That Alex would come out to Australia for summer holidays and Christmas breaks and it would be brilliant. The distance meant that they'd see each other less often, but when they did it would be 'quality time' – an improvement on the harried evenings and weekends they'd experienced when he was always tired and irritable from work.

In Australia, they'd prioritise fun. He pictured himself teaching Alex to surf and taking her horse riding in the Blue Mountains. They'd watch cowboy films, like they used to. Alex and his stepdaughter, Allison, would bond over pop stars, and Miranda would win Alex round with her Anzac biscuits. They'd be one big happy family.

Somehow, it hadn't worked out that way. In four years, Alex hadn't visited once. When he'd first moved to Perth, it had hurt Sam so much to call and hear the disappointment in Alex's voice that he'd begun to avoid it. Before he knew it, whole months were going by without them speaking. Eventually, he'd only called on birthdays and at Christmas.

Unable to bear not talking to his daughter, Sam started writing her emails. He'd describe the birds and flowers he encountered on his morning walks, films he watched, horses he knew she'd love. He'd tell her how he missed her so much that he was convinced there was an actual hole in his heart, growing larger by the day.

Those emails were on his iPad. There were close to five hundred. One day he'd be brave enough to press Send.

A month earlier, Sam had woken in the dead of night with a panicky conviction that Alex needed him. He'd rung the house in Surrey. The answer machine informed him that the 'Pritchard' family was away in Paris. Sam didn't try again. Alex was doing fabulously without him. She didn't need him at all.

But last night's dream had shaken him. It was about Alex. When she was little, she'd gone through a phase of being terrified of the dark. She'd refused to sleep in her own room. So Sam had come up with a game. He'd turn off the lights in her room, hold her hand and together they'd rename the monsters of her imagination.

The bogeyman under the bed was christened Engelbert Poodle Brain. The giant tarantula that lurked in the cupboard, waiting to pounce under the veil of darkness, was a cousin of kindly barn spider Charlotte in the E.B. White novel and really very nice. And the ghouls and ghosts that terrorised her could be transformed at a stroke into cuddly lions, tigers and bears.

Pretty soon Alex was the most fearless six-year-old Sam and Natalie knew. He could still remember Alex giggling as he turned off the light each evening. Together they'd chorus: 'Lions, tigers and bears! Oh, yeah!'

But in his dream his daughter had not been a six-year-old, afraid of the dark. She'd been a teenager lost in a storm. The shapes she was renaming were snow monsters.

Sam flung off the duvet, causing Miranda to grumble in her sleep. Something was wrong. He could feel it in his gut.

In the kitchen, he dialled Alex's mobile. It went

straight to voicemail. Next, he dialled the Pritchard house. The number was engaged. Over the next hour he called again and again, but it was permanently busy. With each failed call the tight feeling in his chest grew worse.

Allison came bounding into the kitchen in her tennis outfit. 'Ohmigod, you're still in your PJs. Did you forget I have a tennis tournament this morning?'

Sam hung up, repressing a groan. He'd try again tomorrow. It was silly to attach so much importance to a dream.

'The Beeches,' Virginia Water, Surrey, England

Natalie turned off the BBC news and tried not to have a nervous breakdown. Colorado and the surrounding states had been hit by record snowfalls, blizzards and gales. Amateur video footage made it look like Armageddon. All she wanted to do was speak to Alex, but Camp Renew was as impenetrable as the White House. Trying to reach a person on the telephone was like dialling the Oval Office and expecting to have a chat with President Obama.

Jeremy kept reminding her that Camp Renew's policy on phone conversations was there for a reason. 'How is Alex supposed to settle in and make friends if she's constantly reminded of home? The entire point of sending her there was to encourage her to take responsibility and make meaningful changes. How's that going to happen if we keep clinging to her?'

By *we* he meant Natalie. If *you* keep clinging to her.

Natalie stared out the window at the acer tree that Alex, aged eleven, had given her for Mother's Day. She loved it. Sam had paid for it, but it had been Alex's idea. He'd told her afterwards how Alex had made him drive from nursery to nursery in search of the perfect one.

Funny how, now that Alex was gone, all Natalie could remember was the good things about her daughter. Her compassion for any suffering person or animal; her incredible warm smile; the simple joy she found in nature, old films and horses.

At the thought of horses, Natalie's anxiety returned. Something was wrong, she was sure of it. She had to pluck up the courage to call Sam. She'd been meaning to do it ever since Jeremy had convinced her to send Alex to Camp Renew, but somehow she hadn't found the right time or words. Now it was going to sound so much worse. 'I'm sure Alex is doing well at her correctional boarding school in Colorado, but since they haven't allowed me to speak to her in weeks, I'm a little concerned. What do you suggest I/we do about it?'

She dialled her ex-husband's mobile in Australia, where it was early morning, but it went straight to voicemail. For the best part of an hour she tried his landline again and again, but it was constantly busy.

Jeremy came blinking into the room in his pin-striped pyjamas, wondering if she was coming to bed.

Unable to contain her frustration, Natalie banged the phone back into its cradle. On the kitchen counter was the wilderness photo of a smiling Alex sent by Stacey at Camp Renew, plus another of her covered in flour during a cooking class.

Perhaps Jeremy was right. She was giving herself an ulcer for nothing.

'War Office', Camp Renew, Colorado

Stacey had always prided herself on the welcome she gave Warden Cartwright's visitors, but nothing in her St Petersburg College 'Advanced Skills for Today's PA' diploma course had prepared her for the man currently prowling around her office. He'd been sitting in her chair when she arrived at 8 a.m., perusing a hunting catalogue.

It was not, she felt, a coincidence, that he'd left the catalogue lying open on her desk. Page 54 featured a man in camouflage trousers and a fluorescent orange vest, beaming with a .22 calibre semi-automatic 'Takedown' rifle.

'Tell me again where old Strike is,' said Dirk Bowery, pausing at a motivational poster of a sepia-toned Abraham Lincoln: 'WE CAN COMPLAIN BECAUSE ROSE BUSHES HAVE THORNS, OR REJOICE BECAUSE THORN BUSHES HAVE ROSES.'

Stacey shifted in her chair. 'Sir, I don't mean to be rude

but I've told you three times that Warden Cartwright is—'

'At death's door. Yeah, so you keep saying. I don't believe I've ever heard of a man sufferin' so many afflictions in such a short period of time. Root canal, hospital superbugs, abscesses. Why, at this rate I'm wonderin' if he'll even notice if he loses a finger or two.'

'Excuse me?'

'You're not going to tell me which hospital he's in, are you, darlin'?' drawled Bowery, testing the door of the warden's office. It was unlocked.

'Hey, that's private!' cried Stacey, but the visitor was already letting himself in. 'What is it that you do for Horizon Investments?'

Bowery grinned at the elk and gave it a hearty punch, causing it to judder on its moorings. A puff of sawdust drifted to the floor. 'I'm what you might call an enforcer.'

The warden was an ex-military man, so there was not much to be gleaned from his immaculate office. The only oddity, Bowery decided, was a moth-eaten teddy bear sitting on top of a filing cabinet.

'What's this?'

'That's Pluto. He belongs to . . . one of our students. The warden is keeping him safe.'

The thug tapped a calloused finger on the desktop planner. '"Craters of the Moon?" What's that? Old Strike doing a science project?'

Stacey approached the desk with caution. 'Craters of

226

the Moon is a National Monument in Idaho, not in outer space.'

'A National Monument, you say? Well, isn't that dandy. I was just thinkin' of taking me a vacation.'

As Bowery followed Stacey from the office, he scooped Pluto into his bag with a practised hand. Instinct told him there was something suspicious about the toy. Or valuable. Why else would Strike Cartwright be keeping it 'safe'?

The instant he left, Stacey made up her mind to call the cops and/or FBI about Alex's disappearance. She didn't care if it got her fired. She'd had enough. God alone knew what had happened to that poor girl. Stacey's conscience would not allow her to tell one more lie to her mother.

She was reaching for the phone when Chase Miller burst in. 'We've found her! The British girl, Alexandra – the warden's found her.'

'What! *How?* Where's she been? When's she coming back?'

Miller looked uncomfortable. 'It's not that easy.'

'What do you mean? Is she sick or injured? Her mom's going out of her mind.'

'Stace, the reputation of the academy is at stake. The girl's got herself mixed up in something crazy dangerous – a horse race – and it's not going to be a picnic extracting her. Not without attracting unwanted attention. But Warden Cartwright says not to worry. You've got to trust him. He has a plan.'

21

Day 11, Le Grizzly Campsite, Washakie Wilderness, Wyoming

'Hey, Alex, are you awake? Want to see something amazing?'

Alex was snuggled in her sleeping bag in a cosy daze, delaying the moment when she exposed her limbs to the day's sharp chill. At the sound of Will's voice her mouth curved into a smile. She poked her head out of her tent. 'How many more amazing things can there be in one country?'

'Loads. We're not even halfway through the race.'

It was true. They were around four hundred and twelve miles from Boulder and eight hundred from Hood River, Oregon, give or take fifty miles. It all depended on the routes they chose.

'Give me a minute.' Alex wriggled into her fleece and

gloves and crawled out into the crisp morning. 'What's up?'

'Nature's jewellery.'

And then she saw it. Every blade of grass was encased in its own teardrop of ice, transforming an ordinary patch of lawn into a glittering carpet. But it wasn't only the grass. In the forested wilderness surrounding them, every leaf and pine needle was sheathed in a frozen stalactite, through which the sunrise shot its rose-gold rays. The overall effect was dazzling.

'Better than Tiffany's,' remarked Will with a grin.

Alex breathed a happy sigh. 'Better than all the diamonds in the world.'

Breakfast was a charred piece of campfire toast spread with peanut butter and strawberry jelly and washed down with weak coffee. They were the first riders up, so the only sound was birdsong. As she savoured her humble repast and pored over a Wyoming map with Will, Alex was conscious of watching herself from a distance. Not one cell of her bore any resemblance to the girl who'd organised the Facebook party.

For most of her life, she'd taken the accessories of her privileged life for granted. She'd grown up believing them indispensable. Her iPhone, laptop, CDs and DVDs, potions and lotions, holidays in Devon and Tuscany, and clothes for every season, sport and whim – every one of them had seemed as vital as breathing. But it didn't end there. Running out of her favourite breakfast cereal had been enough to ruin her day.

The race had changed that at a stroke. The key to successful endurance riding was learning how to do more with less. Alex started with an advantage because she and her hat, boots, saddle, numnah and breastplate together made up the minimum rider weight of seventy-five kg almost exactly. Even so, every gram she could shed from her Snugpax was a gram less for Scout to carry. She'd even considered throwing away *Roughing It*, the Mark Twain book that had saved her sanity when she was alone in the blizzard, until Will told her it was he who'd left it for her to find at the Badwater Creek camp.

And then there was Will. Should she shed Will?

Wasn't that how she'd thought of him as little as three days ago, as an intriguing but unwanted distraction?

These were the things she knew about the boy who'd saved her life.

His favourite books were *Riders of the Purple Sage*, *To Kill A Mockingbird*, anything by Carl Hiassen and *Black's Veterinary Dictionary*.

He liked scratchy old blues and bluegrass records by musicians she'd never heard of, college rock and Dolly Parton.

'You're kidding me, right?' said Alex. 'About Dolly Parton, I mean.'

'Actually, I'm not. She's a song-writing legend.'

Then he did this shy-smile, fringe-flopping-over-his-face thing, which made her stomach feel as if it was free-falling from the 102nd floor of the Empire State Building.

He'd been a vegetarian since the age of five after deciding that he didn't want to eat his friends. That, he told her, had been the worst part of flipping outsize patties at the Bigger Burger. Frying flesh. Well, that and the uniform.

Alex learned most from the things he didn't say.

For instance, he was fascinated by all things veterinary and questioned the race vets and No Water Creek rancher, Ed Barrett, closely about the most minuscule details relating to animal health. Yet when she asked whether he'd ever considered becoming a vet, the shutters came down in his grey-green eyes and he started talking about the weather.

Just as she'd changed the subject when he tried to ask her about her father.

His own dad was recovering from a cardiac arrest. Alex had overheard Will on the phone to Len, telling some fantastical story about taking care of cattle in the snow on a ranch in Colorado. When he realised she'd caught some of the conversation, he'd flushed scarlet.

'Dad doesn't know about the race. I-I didn't want to worry him.'

Any boy who'd ride fifty miles in sub-zero temperatures then think nothing of venturing out into a snowstorm on a fresh horse to save the life of a girl he barely knew and, at the time, didn't particularly like, was not the type of boy to abandon the gravely ill father he adored to ride a month-long race that put him in mortal danger. Not without extremely good cause.

When the same boy wore threadbare clothes and saddled his horse with a mismatched selection of cobbled-together tack, it didn't take a brain surgeon to put two and two together.

Over the past couple of days, she and Will had talked non-stop, as if they'd been saving up conversations for half their lives. But they no longer joked about beating one another in the race. Neither of them wanted to know what would happen if they found themselves going head to head for The Glory.

As soon as she'd finished breakfast, Alex practically sprinted to the main corral to prepare Scout for the day's ride to the Grand Teton National Park. She couldn't wait to see him. Ever since he'd returned of his own accord in the blizzard, something had changed between them. Will teased her that Scout had come back because he'd become addicted to the mints and sugar cubes Alex used to pep him up in between electrolyte doses on rides, but they both knew that it was about something much deeper.

Following Will's dramatic rescue, Alex had been assessed by a volunteer paramedic from Thermopolis. Thanks to the efforts of Ed's courageous young wranglers, she, Will, Scout and the cow pony, Chinook, had been transported back to the ranch at the height of the blizzard. Had it not been for them and, of course, for

Will finding her in the first place, Alex knew that the outcome would have been very bad. As it was, she was mainly suffering from dehydration and exhaustion. The paramedic gave her a couple of vitamin shots and put her on a drip.

Alex remembered almost nothing about the next twenty-four hours. When she finally woke on the ninth day of the race, the ranch house at No Water Creek was deserted. Will was nowhere to be seen. She'd panicked that the race had continued without her, until she remembered that Days eight and nine were compulsory rest days and a third layover day had been added to prevent riders putting themselves or their horses at risk in the aftermath of the blizzard.

She'd been on her way out to the barn to see Scout when the rancher stopped her in her tracks.

'Oh, no you don't, young lady. As your host, I'm banning you from going anywhere near your trouble-causing mustang today, 'less it's for a quick hello. I don't mind telling you, he's a handful. The farrier worked on his feet yesterday – put on super-light aluminium shoes – and my wranglers will look after the rest of him today. He'll keep them on their toes, but it'll be good for them. You're to take it easy today – my wife's orders. If you've recovered and are in the mood for a miniature vacation tomorrow, I thought I might show you and Will around our little neighbourhood. There's someone I'd like you to meet.'

Next day, he took them for a slap-up Mexican brunch

of *huevos rancheros* in Cody, a cute rodeo town tucked in among the mountains. Every other shop sold cowboy boots, stylish Western shirts, Stetsons and hot sauce. Alex looked longingly at a pair of boots in the window of one store. Right now she couldn't afford so much as a stick of gum, but if by some miracle she won the race she planned to come back for them.

Next on the agenda was the Buffalo Bill Museum, an evocative record of the history of the West. For Alex, the highlights were the Plains Indians and gunfighters exhibitions and the Deadwood stagecoach, which she'd last seen in *Calamity Jane*.

Passengers of the stage needed strong hearts. A dime novel excerpt described its frenzied midnight journey from Cheyenne. Six 'plunging, snarling' horses flew through a 'wild tortuous canyon, fringed by tall spectral pines', urged on by a driver who managed his charges like a circus ringmaster, his long-lashed whip resounding like a pistol shot in the darkness.

Afterwards, Ed drove Alex and Will to the Hideout Ranch in Shell, near the Big Horn Mountains. Perhaps because she'd stared death in the face and lived to tell the tale, Alex's senses seemed super-powered that day. Sunshine lit the lemon-yellow leaves of the white-trunked aspen trees that stood out in vibrant relief against the frosted mountains and azure sky. A glassy black lake in an emerald pasture mirrored the scene.

At the ranch, Ed introduced her to Kyra, who specialised in working with rescued wild mustangs never before touched by a human hand. Kyra was fine-boned and small yet, using the techniques of natural horsemanship, she demonstrated in a round pen how a horse weighing close to a ton could be gentled, backed and persuaded into a trailer or over any number of scary obstacles using nothing more than eye contact, a plastic bag on a stick (not to hurt the horse, but as a positive aid to helping him overcome his fears) and the gentlest fingertip pressure.

'For me, the biggest difference between a domestic horse and a wild mustang is that mustangs are free in their minds,' Kyra told Alex. 'Horses that grow up being treated like pets and friends can be messed up, be greedy, be disrespectful. You know that thing some horses do when they rub their heads against you when you're petting them or tacking them up, and almost knock you off your feet? That's not cute or funny. That's a sign of disrespect. They're basically saying, "Hey, I'm bigger than you. Any time I want to push you around, I will."'

Mustangs, Kyra told her, had no emotional baggage – not if they were kindly treated. Kyra said their centuries-old battle to survive had unexpected benefits in ordinary stable yards. For example, they avoided laminitis instinctively by eating green grass only for a short time. They needed no stabling. And as long as the snow was not much deeper than their knees, they could find grazing by digging for it.

Alex loved the idea that Scout's mind was as pure and

unblemished as his big heart, but that wasn't the only reason her day out with Ed and Will was one of the best of her life. Since she'd recovered faster than any of them had expected and the weather was good, the three of them borrowed quarter horses and rode through Trapper Creek Canyon, shadowed by cliffs of pink granite dusted with snow. The iron- and bentonite-rich soil was a burnt umber hue so intense that the horses' muddy hooves stained the creek red as they crisscrossed its rocky bed. Mule deer with big almond-shaped ears watched shyly from the crags above.

Alex breathed in the scent of juniper berries, laughing with shock when a bump from her helmet caused the snow-laden foliage to dump its freezing load down her neck. The contrast of the sparkling snow against the scarlet leaves of the canyon trees was so pretty it was hard to believe it was real. Alex felt as if she was riding through a Christmas card.

Ed showed them ancient Native American engravings known as petroglyphs, set in sandstone and interspersed with cowboy graffiti. In the afternoon they drove the horses into the Big Horn Mountains and rode up to Devil's Peak. They dismounted at the top and stood looking out at the adjacent snowy range and red cliffs and bluffs. A valley of snow-tipped sagebrush lay far below.

Alex felt the way she had on top of Bridger Mountain, as if something inside her was unfurling and taking wing. Will glanced over at her and their eyes met and held. It was Alex who dropped her gaze first. This boy

236

she hardly knew made her feel the way the wide open spaces of Wyoming did – terrified and exhilarated. And few things frightened her more than the knowledge that some day soon all of this would have to end.

They were sad to say goodbye to Ed and move on. Alex had the impression that in Will the rancher saw the son he'd never had. He told them that it was years since he'd met such courageous, motivated young people and that, if they ever cared to become wranglers, they had a job on his ranch any time they wanted it. On the morning they left, he presented them each with a parcel containing cowboy boots, a Western shirt and thermal socks. Alex was so overwhelmed by his kindness that she burst into tears.

'If you knew me, you'd know I don't deserve any of this,' she started to say, but he hushed her up.

'I'll admit I don't know a great deal about your background, *Ms* Sarah Wood, and to tell you the truth I don't care to. We all have a past and it's open to interpretation. What I do believe is that you can tell an awful lot about a person by how they deal with adversity and how they treat their horses. On both counts you score off the charts. That makes you more than okay in my eyes.'

A day and fifty miles later, Alex felt a rush of happiness as she recalled his words. She was still smiling when she noticed Desert King, Jack Carling's platinum-coloured stallion, wandering listlessly across the next corral. There was something odd about the way he was walking. He wasn't lame but he was moving stiffly, as if he were arthritic. Most race mornings she felt the same way, but then she wasn't an Akhal-Teke, bred to endure.

The camp buzzed with riders hurrying to shower or wolf down breakfast, but the corral area was temporarily deserted. Will had gone to fetch Shiraz. Alex debated whether to take a closer look at Desert King. Since the race began, she'd been fascinated by the Carling Brothers' magical horses. The brothers were such celebrities and their aura so intimidating that she'd never dared get too near to the Akhal-Tekes. Now she had a good reason.

Tethering Scout to a hitching post, she climbed through the railings and crunched across the frozen ground to the stallion. He showed the whites of his eyes and snapped his teeth as she approached. Alex had dealt with a couple of difficult stallions at Dovecote Equestrian Centre, so he didn't scare her. Keeping her body language confident but non-threatening, she let him sniff her hand before attempting to stroke his neck.

'What's going on with you, handsome?' she asked softly. 'Feeling under the weather?'

He snorted loudly in response. Alex was marvelling at the silkiness of his metallic coat and it took her a minute to notice that the frosted grass around his forefeet was speckled with blood. Before she could react, a rough hand grabbed her left shoulder and spun her round.

She found herself up close and personal with an unshaven Jack Carling. 'What do you think you're doing, little girl? The King ain't some prissy pony wanting to be petted. Trying get yourself killed?'

'I thought . . . I was only . . . He was walking funny.'

A groom shoved past her and snapped a lead rope on the stallion's head collar.

'Walking funny?' Carling bristled with menace. 'Not half as hilariously as you'll be walking when I report you for horse nobbling. Know what that is? It's when jealous rivals try to harm other people's rides to prevent them from winning.'

Alex was stunned at how quickly he'd turned the tables. 'I'd rather die than hurt a horse—'

Out of the corner of her eye, she saw the race clerk heading their way. He was an officious little man who gave her the creeps. Wayne Turnbull was rumoured to favour the riders he liked and pitilessly punish or expel riders who so much as looked at him the wrong way. She'd been careful not to do anything to draw his attention.

Jack was suddenly charm personified. He patted Alex on the arm as if she was his favourite dog. 'I'm sure you wouldn't harm him, doll. Sorry if I came on a bit strong. If anything happened to the King, I'd be as mad as all get out. *You'd* be the same if someone messed with *your* horse, wouldn't you? Gotta run. Good luck today. No hard feelings, huh?'

He was gone before Alex could get a word in edgeways,

shaking the clerk's hand in greeting and leading him away.

The groom smirked at Alex. 'That's Jack. Lives life at a million miles an hour.'

Alex stared at the stallion. His head was up and he looked alert and ready to go, his legs springy. The transformation was uncanny.

'You might want to tell Jack to slow down enough to have a vet look over Desert King before he rides out this morning. His horse is sneezing blood.'

She got a sneer in response. 'I don't know what your agenda is, kid, but you're talking out of your hat. The King has never been in better form. He and Wyatt's horse, Zephyr, are favourites to win this race. You wanna make those kind of accusations, you better be a hundred and ten per cent sure. What blood? Prove it to me. *Show* me.'

But the ground was scuffed, either by accident or on purpose, and the crimson specks erased.

The groom put his grizzled face close to hers. 'You saw nothing, do you hear that? *Nothing.*'

'But I did see it,' Alex told Will as they set out in the direction of the Grand Teton National Park. 'It wasn't my imagination. There *were* spots of blood in the ice and they came from Desert King. Not that anyone would ever believe me.'

Will's expression was grim. 'I believe you. The only question is, what are we going to do about it?'

22

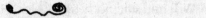

Day 12, Grand Teton National Park, Wyoming

For most of that day, Will rode looking over his shoulder. He had a creeping sense that he and Alex were being stalked. Not just followed, but hunted – though whether their pursuer was animal or human, it was difficult to say.

He tried to pinpoint when the feeling had started. On the plains and in the mountains, anyone or anything with malicious intentions would have been visible for miles. At the ranch they'd mostly been out or asleep. In the end he fixed on Cody as the place he'd first had the sensation that they were being watched. Using store window reflections he'd studied passers-by, but try as he might he'd not been able to identify a watcher.

In the snow-coated wilderness the feeling returned. Twice he was sure he saw a mountain lion stealing after them through the ghostly trunks of the aspens, the knots of the bark themselves eerily like eyes. Another time, he was positive he'd heard the ring of horseshoe on rock. When, a short time later, a black shape had darted across his peripheral vision, he'd whirled in the saddle. Using the excuse of a dropped glove, he'd loped back to investigate, braced for a man or black bear. But as far as he could tell they were alone.

Will had said nothing to Alex. He didn't want to worry her. She knew as well as he did that between them they'd gathered an impressive selection of enemies. Verity had quit the race after a row with Gill, but the forty-one remaining riders included the Carling Brothers and Zach and Axel, the would-be horse thieves from the overflow camp. The race clerk too was always on the prowl.

Will did not underestimate the dark motives of any of those men, but he doubted they'd waste energy playing mind games in snowy forests. That left an unknown quantity. And if the hunter wasn't after him, they had to be after Alex.

From the moment she'd told him her story, Will had been as mystified as Alex was about the deafening silence from Camp Renew. Most days, he listened to the news. If a British teenager had been reported missing at any time since the race began, he'd know about it.

Delighted as Alex was that she had yet to be caught, he knew that to her the lack of pursuit was final proof that her parents didn't love her. If they cared, she was sure they'd be using every available news outlet and social media platform to scream about her disappearance. There'd be detectives, forensic scientists and bloodhounds involved. Camp Renew would be undergoing a brutal trial by media.

That, Will told her, was why he was convinced that something sinister was going on. A cover-up. A game.

'Think about it. This Strike Cartwright is obviously a fully paid-up psychopath. He's not going to let a British teenager ride out of his boot camp on his own horse. It would be a crushing blow to his ego and the authorities would probably shut the place down. My theory is, he'll prioritise damage limitation. Under the rules, you were only allowed to call home a couple of times a month. If you spoke to your mom the day before you left she wouldn't have expected another call for a week or two. Unless the warden has told them you've vanished, how would your parents even know? Cartwright might be using this time to search frantically for you. It's around now that he'll be beginning to sweat. Sooner or later, your mom's going to insist on speaking to you. Then all hell will break loose.'

It was not only Alex who lived with the ever-present threat of discovery. On the phone the previous night, Will's dad had cheerfully informed him that his latest obsession was The Glory.

'Heard about it, son? You must have. It's this long-distance horse race that began in Colorado and goes all the way to Hood River, Oregon. Surely the wranglers on your ranch have been talking about it? CNN did a special on it. I've been hooked ever since. It's causing a ton of controversy because there are riders catching hypothermia in blizzards and falling into frozen rivers and all kinds of disasters. Personally, I think it's fantastic. A challenge worthy of the name. There are some real characters in the race, too. They interviewed these two Wyoming brothers who ride these fancy shiny horses from Turkmenistan. Good-looking devils – the brothers, that is – but too full of themselves for my liking. My money's on an outsider. Someone completely unexpected.'

Will could stand it no longer. 'Dad, I have to go. The credit's about to run out on my phone. It might be a while before I can ring again.'

'No problem, son. We can chat about it next time you call. Try to catch up with the latest on this race on TV. It's the kind of thing that would appeal to you and Shiraz. That said, I'm mighty glad you didn't know about it. You'd have been tempted to enter and that would have given me another heart attack for sure.'

As soon as Len hung up, Will texted Tom and told him to go over to the house and find a way to disable the television. *Get rid of every newspaper while you're at it,* he added. *Leave nothing but the Nashville Scene.*

In the initial stages of the ride these dark thoughts had crowded Will's mind and caused a headache to hover, but he couldn't hold on to them. The scenery was too mesmerising. Every breath, every step was a privilege.

Red and purple grasses rippled like wildfire against silvery creek beds. They passed a cracked, dry lake-bed pooled with mirages of water long since evaporated. And mid-afternoon, they dismounted and gazed in wonder at a golden plain densely covered in bison, the animals' hooked horns, quarterback shoulders and thickly furred coats living echoes of the past.

For Will, who'd always thought that nothing could top camping alone in the mountains with Shiraz, the best part was being able to share the experience with someone, especially when that someone was a tangle-haired girl, headstrong, horse-mad and ridiculously brave.

The image that kept coming into his head was of a salt-timer. The grains of sand were rushing through it and he only had these hours and this race to learn everything there was to know about her. But because he was in denial and didn't want to believe that some day soon they'd be rivals again, he rationed the number of questions he asked and savoured her responses.

For instance, he now knew, definitively, that her favourite movies were *Singin' in the Rain*, *Rear Window* and *The Fault in Our Stars*.

Her favourite books were *Thunderhead*, *Charlotte's Web*, *To Kill A Mockingbird* and *Wuthering Heights*.

About her taste in music, the less said the better.

He also knew that when she rode she became part of Scout, an impression enhanced by the similarity of their colouring. When they were galloping, she'd lean forward, English-style, and her honeyed hair would entwine with his flaxen mane.

Earlier that day, Shiraz and the palomino had spontaneously started racing. Chunks of snow and mud were flying up around them and the sky was an electric blue. The wind in their lungs was as bracing as a mountain stream. As they swept across the valley Alex turned to him, laughing, and the sun lit her brown eyes with violet.

The feeling that had come over him the day she danced to charm the moose in Medicine Bow National Forest made his heart contract again. It was a dangerous emotion, especially because it was combined with a powerful attraction, and he immediately set about damping it down. He reminded himself angrily that they were friends and would never be, *could never be*, anything more. Starting tomorrow, he'd go back to riding alone.

But a voice in his head countered with the argument that together he and Alex were stronger. That if she was the one being hunted – perhaps by someone sent by the sadistic warden at Camp Renew – she needed a protector. Of course, if he and Alex found the proof they needed and turned Jack Carling in for doping his horse, they'd both be in need of bodyguards, but until then Will intended to watch over her. In the meantime, wouldn't it be good for everyone – humans as well as horses – if he and Alex enjoyed the adventure along the way? If they were a little less lonely?

And so he relaxed and watched Alex watch the snowy peaks of the Tetons darken against the sunset. The bushy black trees that clung to their outer slopes were silhouetted against the cherry-pink sky, like bison descending.

By the time he and Alex rode into the Grand Teton camp, the stars were as bright as headlights. The first thing they noticed was that the atmosphere seemed muted. The usual pre-barbecue chatter, where people licked their wounds or told tall stories about their day, was absent, and not purely because their numbers had thinned. Clusters of whispering riders broke apart as they passed. Zach shot Will a glance of pure poison. It was a look that said: *If you think I've forgotten we have a score or two to settle, you're mistaken.*

'Is it just me, or are people staring at us as if we're foxes that have been at the chickens?' murmured Alex.

Mike Berry hurried up to them, leading Dietrich Anders's powerful Arabian. 'You'll never guess what's happened . . . '

Will grabbed a bucket and a sponge. 'Don't tell me. The Yellowstone super-volcano is about to erupt.'

'Something even worse. Jack Carling is gone.'

Alex put down Scout's saddle. 'Gone where?'

'He's out. Disqualified. Caught red-handed plying Desert King with bicarb, bute and synthetic corticosteroids. The whole shebang. That wonderful stallion was so lame he could barely crawl without drugs. Tragically, he's now likely to have laminitis for life.

247

Folks say that Jack became so obsessed with winning he persuaded himself that he could fix Desert King when the race was done.

'Wyatt's convinced that either you or young Will here reported his brother. Did you? Better watch your back, kids. Jack has a lot of fans. They'll be gunning for you.'

Snake River Grill, Jackson Hole, Wyoming

Strike Cartwright speared the last morsel of rare dry-aged Black Angus rib-eye steak and sat back to flick through a pile of newspaper cuttings with his right hand. His left forearm was bandaged. Midnight Magic had inexplicably savaged him while being unloaded from his trailer near Thermopolis. Cartwright had already instructed Chase Miller to dispatch the beast to the slaughterhouse the instant the hunt was over and Alexandra Blakewood was safely back at Camp Renew.

Across the country, the media were reporting that the race was a fiasco. With typical glee, newspapers and TV channels had amassed dramatic photographs of riders being hauled out of snowdrifts or displaying gruesome wounds or frostbitten fingers. One competitor had launched a $20 million lawsuit after being bitten by a dog during a rest stop. Banner headlines variously branded the race a GRAND FOLLY or GLORIOUS DISASTER.

The warden found it amusing. At the same time, he hoped the race wasn't cancelled. Apart from his trip to ER for a tetanus jab and a couple of stitches, he was enjoying himself. The panic he'd experienced when Ken and Sue-Ellen returned from Boulder having found no trace of Alexandra had subsided. Once again, his instincts had triumphed. He'd been so convinced that the girl had found some way to enter The Glory that he'd spent an age scrutinising the start list procured by Chase Miller.

To begin with, nothing had rung a bell. It was only when Sue-Ellen spotted a line in the *Denver Post* saying that the youngest contestant was a sixteen-year-old girl, a last-minute entry, that the warden suspected the trail was growing hotter.

In Thermopolis, he'd been gifted with a stupendous piece of good fortune. While enjoying a cocktail in the bar of the Best Western Plus Plaza, he'd struck up a conversation with an Englishwoman drowning her sorrows. For the price of two mojitos he'd extracted her tale. She'd been a proud contestant in The Glory until she'd fallen out with a friend over a teenage rider, a fellow Brit, who'd been irresponsible enough to get herself lost in the blizzard.

'You can't imagine what a hard time I've been given by everyone,' she whined. 'Anybody would have thought I was her paid nursemaid and had dumped her in a snowdrift myself.'

Verity took a consoling swig from her glass. 'My

ex-friend, Gill, was so upset about it that she said she no longer felt comfortable allowing me to ride the Arab horse she'd loaned to me for the race. Quite obviously, that made it impossible for me to continue. She's offered to fly me back to the UK, first class, but I'm considering legal action. Then the rancher followed suit and said he'd prefer it if I stayed in a hotel. And after all that, the wretched girl was completely fine. Not a scratch on her. A bit cold, but aren't we all?'

'Indeed we are,' agreed the warden. 'And what was the girl's name?'

'She claims it's Sarah Wood, but I believe her real name is Alex. Alexandra. She's a runaway or a fraudster, I'm utterly convinced of it. And it wouldn't surprise me to learn that she's stolen her palomino mustang. I'm not a fan of mustangs myself, but he's a fine horse.'

At the mention of the horse that had trampled him, the warden's face darkened. 'Sounds as if she could do with a spell at Camp Renew. That's my academy in Colorado. We're a corrective boarding school. Our wilderness therapy works wonders with monstrous teens.'

Verity glowered. 'Yes, but instead she's having the time of her life swanning across America on someone else's horse. Goodness knows what her parents are thinking. I'm thinking of contacting a policewoman friend of mine in the UK and asking her to do some investigating.'

Cartwright almost had a heart attack. God forbid the policewoman's enquiries led her to the door of

Alexandra's mother and stepfather. He immediately invested in another mojito for Verity and placed a consoling hand on her arm.

'Madam, if you'd allow me, perhaps I could be of service to you. I'd be delighted to make a few discreet enquiries for you, especially since I'm going to be following the race myself.'

Recalling the conversation now, he glowed with satisfaction at his successful crisis management. As thrilling as it had been to use some of his old Special Forces techniques to track Alexandra through the streets of Cody and the Grand Teton National Park, the time had come to pounce. Summoning the waiter, he paid the bill and leapt in his car. It was being driven when necessary by Chase's friend, Gap, who was out of the race and volunteering as a marshal. By tomorrow morning, he and the girl would be back at the academy. He'd get Stacey to bill her parents for all expenses, including the mojitos. Plus the $50,000 for the year ahead.

At The Glory camp, most people had already turned in. Teenagers being what they were, Strike was worried that Alexandra and the boy would be sharing the same sleeping bag, but Gap informed him that they were camping side by side at the far end of the site.

Equipping himself with a bottle of chloroform and a couple of plastic wrist ties, the warden set off down the dark forest path. The pair were standing beside the open flap of one of the tents, deep in conversation. A torch lit the tent's orange interior.

In order to hear what they were saying, Cartwright had to wriggle through the icy wet undergrowth on his belly. It was an unpleasant experience. His bitten arm throbbed and he had to crawl perilously close to a gully of uncertain depth. Halfway there, a chunk of earth gave way and he was almost catapulted into oblivion. But it was worth it. Soon he was so close to the tents he could have reached out and touched them.

'They're not going to try anything,' Alexandra was saying. 'They wouldn't dare. There are too many witnesses.'

'Don't be too sure,' said the boy. 'In Boulder, Jack Carling threatened to put a rattlesnake in my sleeping bag if I didn't mind my own business.'

'That's rather worrying, because I think I just saw something wriggle in it.'

'Ha ha.'

'No, I'm deadly serious.'

The boy crouched to investigate. There was a muffled curse. Alex leapt back with a scream as he hauled the sleeping bag from the tent and lifted it gingerly.

On the brink of being discovered, Cartwright dived into a bush on the edge of the precipice. With an almost human sigh, the bank crumbled beneath him. He plummeted into the blackness. Lying winded in the gully, he watched helplessly as the sleeping bag was shaken out above him. A fat, twisting shape sailed into the moonlit sky. There was no mistaking the rattle of an enraged snake. The warden covered his eyes in horror. Of all the laws in the universe, one was immutable.

What went up inevitably came down.

23

Day 16, Snake River Plain, Idaho

Some nights Alex woke in a cold sweat, unable to decide which terrified her most: being found and torn away from everything she considered precious – Scout, Will, the race and the freedom of the big skies and cinematic landscapes – or *not* being found, because of the lack of love that implied.

Or rattlesnakes taking naps in her sleeping bag.

For better or worse, the road had become her home. It was liberating to get up and go each day, needing nothing but her hat, horse and tent. She and Will had reached Idaho and that in itself was a milestone. They were closer to the finish line than the start!

Before leaving Wyoming, they'd used one of their compulsory rest days to join Gill and a couple of other riders on a tour of Yellowstone National Park. There, sweeping forests parted to reveal a turquoise lake ringed with stony white beaches and snow-topped mountains. It was if someone had Photoshopped the Caribbean and the Swiss Alps into one surreal whole.

Here, too, the West's beauty was only skin deep. Everywhere you turned, there was something that could kill you. In among the cutesy gift shop postcards and calendars of frolicking bear cubs and moody black and white mountains Alex found a book entitled *Death in Yellowstone*. It documented the many visitors who'd been gored by bison and elk, mowed down by forest fires and avalanches, or ripped from limb to limb by grizzlies. Others had drowned or simply been boiled alive in beguiling aquamarine hot springs topping 200 degrees Fahrenheit.

Hardly surprising that Jim Bridger, the old mountain man, had called Yellowstone the 'place where hell bubbles up'.

Alex navigated the wooden walkways with trepidation, the rattlesnake incident still fresh in her mind. There was something eerie about the place. The artist's palette hues of the bubbling mudpots and pools were wonders of nature, but it was hard to forget the people and animals they'd swallowed. She was inclined to see the steam-belching hot springs and sky-searing geysers the way the local tribes once had, as duelling spirits of good and evil.

Like a backdrop descending in a theatre production, the weather and scenery changed as they crossed the state line. Idaho was sun-baked prairies, quaint shacks and haystacks, golden fields so neat they might have been combed. Red barns presided over pastures dotted with picturesque horses. In one, six chestnuts played a game of chase with a donkey, their flaming manes vivid against the blue sky.

Day by day, mile by mile, atom by atom, Alex was transforming, as if the very landscape was imprinting itself on her soul. She had a new body, taut with muscle, and new skin. When she looked in the mirror, she barely recognised the sun- and wind-tanned stranger who gazed back at her. Even her riding had changed. At Dovecote she'd had tons of enthusiasm and a modicum of talent, but her impetuousness had led her to take outrageous risks. She'd also prided herself on her ability to master horses no one else wanted to ride.

With Scout everything was different. Thanks to a tip from Gill, she rode with longer stirrups, which were easier on her knees and made her feel more connected to him. She had no desire to conquer him, nor could she. They were a team. He'd never love her the way Shiraz loved Will, because he wasn't built that way, but he trusted her, whickered with pleasure when he saw her each morning and, most tellingly, he felt a duty of care towards her, just as she did him.

Periodically, other riders joined them on the road. That morning they'd spent several enjoyable hours with Slim Jim, the ebullient Texan on his Morgan stallion. Jim worshipped Will.

'He saved my horse from a terrible fate,' he confided in Alex. 'Never got to the bottom of what it was exactly. He said it was a mountain lion, but I suspect there was more to it. The rogues in our camp were real sore about something the next day. Point is, he's one in a million, Will.'

More often than not, though, she and Will were alone, which was the way Alex liked it. Unfortunately, it also meant she spent far too much time in her own head. Her brain ceaselessly returned to the same questions: *Why weren't her parents looking for her? Didn't they care that she was missing? Had she been such a terrible daughter that they no longer loved her?*

On the night of the snowstorm, Will had shocked her into thinking differently about her mum. She'd had a sudden mental image of her past with her mother cut out of it. It was like looking at a book filled with black ink drawings, with all of the colour, flowers, beauty and imagination chopped out of it. Because, before her mother had been battered by life, it was she who'd encouraged Alex to dream.

So she'd forgiven her mum and, by extension, Jeremy. But she hadn't forgiven herself. Because the secret that she carried in her heart like a burning burr was that she was the reason her father had gone to Australia and never come back. It was *her* fault.

She'd never forgotten the day he came to tell her that he and her mum were getting divorced. Like some clichéd dad in a soap opera, he'd 'fallen' for his Australian secretary, a woman Alex had always mistrusted because she was way too familiar and sickly-sweet with Alex and way too touchy-feely with her father. A week of rows had preceded this announcement. The half-moons of purple-black exhaustion beneath his eyes made her dad look as if he'd been punched. Alex wished he had.

'We're moving to Perth in Australia,' he'd informed her. 'Miranda, me and Allison, Miranda's daughter. Right away, probably. Well, you know, Allison is starting at a new school and we have lots to organise. You'd like her. She's as gifted at tennis as you are at riding. In time I hope you'll become friends.'

He held up his hands to defend himself against Alex's laser beam glare.

'Okay, okay, maybe it'll take a while. Anyway, you'll always be my number-one girl. Try not to take all this to heart, honey. It's stupid grown-up stuff. Your mum and I love you. That'll never change. We might not be living under the same roof any more, but I'll FaceTime lots and you can come out to Australia in the school holidays for some sun and sea.'

A balloon of pain and anger swelled to bursting point inside Alex. Perth was about as far from Surrey as he could possibly go without moving planets. 'Don't you understand that I. Hate. You?' she said, enunciating each word precisely, like an actress in a stage play. 'I'll *never* forgive you. Never ever. I hope you die. And you can forget about me coming to Australia. I wouldn't waste my time. If a shark ate you tomorrow, I wouldn't shed a tear.'

The blood drained from her father's face. 'You can't mean that, Alex. All the great times we've had together . . . I-I thought we were friends.'

'You thought wrong,' she raged. 'I loathe and detest those boring old films.' Another lie. 'As long as I live, I never want to see you again.' Lie No. 3.

As soon as the words left her mouth Alex wanted to snatch them back. Out loud, they were like bullets. Her dad reeled under the impact of them.

'Be careful what you wish for,' was all he said.

Four years had gone by since then, during which the sunshine had gone from Alex's life. It had gone to Perth, which seemed unfair when the Australians already had it in abundance.

The moment her father had exited the room she'd wanted to run after him, tell him she didn't mean it. Tell him that she didn't hate him, could never hate one cell of him, because he'd saved her from the monsters all those years ago, and because, once upon a time, sitting beside him on the sofa with a big bowl of hot salty popcorn, watching films, beat every kind of entertainment going, apart from riding.

But, of course, she hadn't chased after him. She'd stayed where she was as if her feet were superglued to the floor. She hadn't taken the terrible words back. She'd let her dad go to the other side of the world believing that she never wanted to see him again. And, whether by fate or circumstance, her wish was granted. The promised beach holiday never materialised. There was always some excuse why it couldn't happen. She supposed he was too busy polishing the silverware of popular, goody-two-shoes Allison as she wowed Australia with her backhand.

A year after leaving, her dad had called her mum to say that he was flying to the UK on business and it would be nice to spend time with his daughter. Just as Alex was getting used to the idea, Sam's new wife, Miranda, discovered she was pregnant. The trip was postponed indefinitely. The rare phone calls Alex received from her dad were becoming ever more awkward and stilted. Soon they'd peter out altogether.

On long days in the saddle, these thoughts taunted her. The leather squeaked rhythmically: *I hate you, I love you, I hate you, I love you* . . .

Towards evening, they crossed a burnished gold field bisected by a creek the colour of sapphires. Will was riding a little way ahead. He sat tall in the saddle, swaying easily with Shiraz. They belonged together, he and his mysterious grey mare, a willowy creature who looked as if she'd been poorly sculpted from leftovers – over-long racehorse legs, shapely but large ears that almost touched in the middle, huge black eyes and ironing-board flanks. Her faith in Will was absolute. She'd carry him to the four corners of the earth if he asked her to.

At the creek, they stopped to let the horses drink and rest. When Alex sponged Scout down, the mirrored powder-blue mountains and streaked vermillion sky rippled in the water like an Impressionist painting. When he lifted his head and let out a long, contented sigh, she ran a hand over his damp muzzle and felt his warm breath on her skin. One of the greatest joys of the journey was thinking up small ways to make him happy.

Afterwards, she sat on the bank and made a picnic of crackers, pickles, cheese and root beer. Will examined the horses. His sensitive hands ran over their legs, checking for pain or swelling. He rewarded them with apples, laughing at their expressions of ecstasy. Alex was conscious of taking a mental snapshot of the scene. These were the memories she wanted to hold on to. Right now, they felt as fragile as gossamer.

Back in the saddle, she and Will took advantage of the flat, cushioned going, loping fast towards Pioneer Mountain to make up time. Armies of electricity pylons marched alien-like into the purple-orange twilight.

When the horses eased up, breathing hard, Will came to ride beside her. She tried to ignore the tingle that went through her any time she allowed her gaze to linger on the Wrangler jeans and fringed brown leather chaps that hugged his thighs. She absolutely DID NOT fancy him.

'Mind if I ask you a question?' he said.

Can I kiss you?

Alex started guiltily at the thought. She gave herself a

261

mental slap. The sooner she and Will went back to being rivals, the better.

'Go ahead. Ask me anything.'

He looked at her curiously. 'Are you okay?'

'That's what you wanted to ask me?'

'No, it's not. It's just . . .'

'What?'

'Nothing. When I found you in the blizzard, you were delirious. You were mumbling about people, places – I didn't really catch any of it.'

She gave a nervous giggle. 'That's a relief.'

'Except one phrase. You said it as though it was a mantra or a prayer. "Lions, tigers and bears." You kept saying it over and over. "Lions, tigers and bears." Does that mean something significant to you?'

A knife twisted inside Alex. She turned away quickly, relieved that her expression was hidden by the sweeping violet shadows. 'Did I really say that? How funny. Maybe I was channelling *The Wizard of Oz*.'

They rode in silence after that. Night fell like a blanket. Alex put her hand on Scout's neck, glad of his warmth. An ill wind had begun to blow.

Her sense of apprehension grew. The further she got from Colorado, the safer she should have felt, but it wasn't working out that way at all. The rattlesnake had freaked her out. After Will had flung it into the gully, they'd heard a weird, inhuman cry. They'd peered into the black hole but there'd been no further movement or sound.

Lying awake later, it had occurred to Alex that she and Will had automatically assumed that the reptile had been put there by a Jack Carling fan or family member aggrieved that their hero had been thrown out of the race. But what if it hadn't? What if Strike Cartwright or one of his creepy goons was tracking her, plotting her capture or demise?

The first thing we ask at Camp Renew is compliance. What happened to students who didn't comply? Did they end up like the elk?

Ever since that day in Cody she'd been unable to shake the feeling she was being watched. She'd said nothing to Will, not wanting him to think her paranoid, but it was there all the time, this sixth sense that she was prey.

On and on they rode, silhouetted in miniature against the boundless sagebrush steppe grasslands and inky sky. It was around 9 p.m. when they reached the turbulent burnt ocean that was the Craters of the Moon lava fields. Glancing upwards at the chocolate-chip slopes of Pioneer Mountain, Alex noticed the nose of a dark car parked in a viewing spot. It was partially concealed by a clump of sagebrush.

Even as she registered it, Will gestured in a different direction: 'It could be my imagination, but I'm sure someone's watching us from those rocks over there. I saw something glint – maybe a night-vision scope. Probably just a hunter on the lookout for some dinner, but it might be a good idea for us to get out of here.'

Alex was in full agreement. Only thirty-eight riders

remained in the race. Every one of them was desperate to win. Just *how* desperate remained to be seen. Between here and the next camp was a long stretch of wild and lonely road. If anything happened to her and Will, there'd be no one around to witness it.

Up on the hill Strike Cartwright, nauseous from anti-venom and painkillers and as mad as the rattlesnake that had almost cost him his left hand, was thinking exactly the same thing.

24

Craters of the Moon, Idaho

Dirk Bowery set down his Yukon Ranger night-vision binoculars and sipped his gas station coffee. It tasted like strained mud. That was the worst of these jobs, being away from his freshly ground Celinga Ethiopia coffee brewed with reverse osmosis water. It was especially difficult when night drew in and he was required to spend many tedious hours in one spot, watching for his quarry. He hoped he didn't nod off at a crucial moment.

Picking up the glasses again, he peered into the darkness. The binoculars lent the cinder cones and charred, chunky waves of the lava fields a greenish tint, causing them to resemble a storm-tossed lunar sea in a science-fiction film. The visitor centre brochure had informed him they were at least fifteen thousand years old. Once the Northern Shoshone had hunted elk, bison, cougar and bighorn sheep on the trails they'd cut around the lava fields. Wagon trains, too, had congregated here on the way to the goldfields in Salmon River. Bowery was ready to testify that nothing moved here now. The Craters of the Moon Monument was the last word in desolate.

Stifling another yawn, he suddenly remembered the teddy bear he'd found in the warden's office. He'd shoved it into his bag as he'd sped away from Camp Renew and had forgotten all about it. Retrieving Pluto now, he examined him carefully. What secret did the bear conceal?

It was a loose thread that alerted him to the possibility of a pouch. An attempt had been made to sew up the teddy's side seam. All the more suspicious. It took Bowery less than two seconds to rip open the bear's stomach. Inside was a bulging plastic bag. He was sufficiently intrigued to risk turning on his torch. When he saw the contents he laughed so hard the car shook.

Headlights swung into the visitor centre below, reminding him of the task at hand. He placed Pluto on the dashboard. 'Well, well, well,' he mocked. 'You have been a naughty bear.'

Focusing the night-vision glasses, he was delighted to see a green-tinged Strike Cartwright step out of the vehicle. With his bulging muscles, he looked like the Incredible Hulk. Why the man was visiting a tourist attraction in the dead of night Bowery couldn't begin to imagine, unless it had something to do with the horse race everyone was talking about. Perhaps he had a financial interest in it – a bet.

Over the past eight hours, Bowery had seen many competitors go by, some energetically, most in an advanced state of exhaustion. One man had toppled from his mount right outside the visitor centre. Not long afterwards, an ambulance and trailer had arrived to take them away.

The warden crossed the road and began to climb the mountain. His left hand was wrapped in a bandage the size of a boxing glove. He also appeared to have a bandaged bicep. However, Bowery was alarmed to see that in his right hand he carried a camouflage gun slip.

Concealing himself behind some rocks, Cartwright scanned the horizon with a night-vision scope. Bowery turned his own binoculars in the same direction. Two riders were crossing the plain at speed. As they slowed and came into clear view, he saw that they were teenagers – a boy and a girl.

The warden unzipped the slip. To Bowery's horror he took out a tranquilliser dart gun and aimed it at the riders. As his intentions became clear, Bowery moved into action with the swiftness that had made him one of the greatest enforcers in the business. If the idiot warden tranquillised one or more of the teenagers, it would compromise Bowery's entire mission. There'd be cops crawling all over the place. In no time at all, they'd spot his number plate on CCTV. He'd have to go into hiding. It would be a nightmare.

Pausing only to pop a can of pepper spray in his pocket, Bowery slipped from the car and moved as noiselessly as a panther down the mountain, using the sagebrush and boulders as cover. It helped that the swirling cloud had almost blacked out the stars.

He was closing in on the warden's position when some instinct caused Cartwright to glance round. When he caught sight of Horizon Investments' enforcer, his entire body convulsed. The last thing Bowery saw before the moon's white glow was extinguished was the tranquilliser gun swinging to target him.

The hunter had become the hunted.

Clawing his way up the slope in double time, Bowery threw himself into his car. He was so busy trying to recover his breath and grab a more effective weapon from his bag that he failed to see a patrol car come up behind him until its blue light strobed across his windscreen. There was nowhere to run. Even if he escaped the cops, that Camp Renew moron might shoot him in the rump with a tranquilliser dart. Better to brazen it out.

He wound down his window. 'Good evening, officer,' he said. 'How ya doin'?'

'Would you step out of your vehicle, sir?'

'Is there a problem?'

'We've had reports that a vehicle with your licence plate has been seen acting suspiciously in the Craters of the Moon area.'

Bowery was in the midst of his carefully rehearsed speech about being an amateur geologist when a second cop climbed out of the patrol car, this one with a German shepherd. If Bowery had a heart, it would have sunk. The dog started out keen and went into overdrive as it approached the driver's seat. With a joyous bark, it sprang at the dashboard and sank its teeth into Pluto. From then on, the situation was only ever going to end one way.

'How many times do I have to tell you that the drugs aren't mine?' Bowery protested as he was handcuffed and read his rights. 'They've been planted in my sweet little niece's teddy bear. The gent you need to be lookin' for was right over there not ten minutes ago. Strike Cartwright. He's armed and dangerous. Send your dog after him. He can't have got far. You've gotta believe me. He's a warden at one of those camps for delinquent teens in Colorado.'

Marvelling at the self-delusion of criminals, the second cop tucked the plump sachet of white powder into an evidence bag and tossed the deflated teddy bear onto a nearby bench. The first tourist to visit Craters of the Moon the following morning would recover the bear, wash him and give him to his three-year-old daughter, who'd be crying because she'd lost her fluffy rabbit. He'd be so preoccupied with this delicate operation that he'd fail to notice Warden Cartwright snoring in a nearby hollow after accidentally shooting himself in the thigh with his own tranquilliser gun.

Cleaned and re-stuffed, Pluto would continue his US road trip, this time on the Oregon Trail.

25

Day 18, Coyote Point Trail Riding Center, Idaho

The rain came across the plains like a tsunami, arriving at The Glory camp late afternoon on a rest day in a freezing wall of iron-scented fury. Within seconds, Alex and Will were soaked, their tents swimming on their moorings. The horses fared rather better. The camp was based at an out-of-season trail riding centre, east of the Boise National Forest, where the emphasis was on equine comfort. While their riders shivered, Shiraz and Scout were snug in a red barn, munching on corn and hay.

'We could move in with them,' joked Alex, but they'd already hinted at that in Wayne Turnbull's hearing and the chief clerk had vetoed it on the grounds of health and safety.

Will's loathing of the man intensified. 'Health and

safety? What planet is the man on? That just shows you he's been living it up at the Best Western while the rest of us have been wallowing in the mud and snow like hogs. Has he seen the injury statistics of the two hundred and sixty-nine riders who've been eliminated? What does he think is going to happen to us in the barn? Are we going to sue Green Power if we trip over a floorboard?'

Alex laughed. 'Don't let him get to you. He isn't worth the energy. Anyway, you should be celebrating. You're lying tenth in the race after close to eight hundred and fifty miles. Have you any idea how phenomenal that is? Don't get complacent because you think I'm eighteen whole places behind. I'm still planning to win.'

He grinned at her. 'I'm glad to hear it. I was worrying that you were going soft on me.'

'Not a chance,' said Alex, but she flushed at the remark. Did that mean he'd noticed that her feelings for him had crossed the line from pure friendship? Was he warning her off?

Well, if he was he needn't bother. She warned herself off every single day. Nothing good could come of falling for him. He had to win The Glory to save his father and pay for his operation. She had no choice but to do everything in her power to finish first. If her parents still hadn't bothered to search for her by the time the race was over, she'd have to assume she was out on her own and would need every penny she could get.

But it was hard staying on the right side of the attraction line. She and Will were together all day and every day, longer if they were riding through the night. They needed each other, depended on each other, watched each other's backs. After the peculiar incident at Craters of the Moon, where they'd seen what appeared to be hunters hunting one another on the lower slopes of Pioneer Mountain, they'd ridden so close together they were almost touching.

Almost being the operative word. Since the night of the blizzard, Alex had taken very good care never to come into actual physical contact with Will. She had a feeling that if he ever laid a hand on her, either intentionally or by accident, she might go up in flames.

Right now any sparks had been well and truly doused by the storm. Ducking away from the rain's stinging arrows, the pair joined the other crewless riders in the large tepee known fancifully as the Green Room. 'Clueless' was the nickname given to them by those horsemen with support teams, despite the fact that their ranks included endurance champions like their friend Gill and the UK's Manny Wilder. Sadly, Slim Jim and his Morgan were out of the race.

The tepee was carpeted in sisal matting and a fraying Persian rug. A selection of beanbags, a book swap corner and a table loaded with coffee and cookies completed the look. On wintry days, frozen, saddle-sore riders nearly came to blows in their bid to claim the beanbags nearest the electric heater, but today even the heater had given up the ghost.

'Do you want the bad news or the worst news?' asked

Robbie, a diminutive former jockey who was in charge of rider logistics for the Clueless. His wizened brown visage was nearly always creased into a smile.

'Let's get the worst over with,' said Manny.

'The Weather Underground is predicting fierce storms and rain for the next couple of days. Be prepared and be careful.'

There was a chorus of groans from the wet, exhausted horsemen.

'Go on, hit us with the bad news,' said Camila, a tough, wiry Hispanic woman from New Mexico.

'I don't know how to tell you this . . . '

'Get it over with,' barked Zach with a scowl.

Robbie grinned. 'Just messing with you. There *is* no bad news. The good news is that the best fondue restaurant in Boise is offering meals on the house to every Glory rider still in the race. Anyone interested in taking them up on it, see me for transportation. And that's not all. A local launderette has volunteered to take away your soaking, stinking, festering clothes and sleeping bags and return them before you go to sleep tonight, fragrant and dry. How's that for an act of charity?'

Cheers greeted this announcement, turning to teasing boos when he followed up by saying: 'Don't thank me, thank the town of Boise. You guys are heroes around here. Well, either that or freaks of nature.'

Boise was a hip college town full of right-on coffee shops and bare brick galleries. Even at night, with the rain turning the tree-lined streets to rivers and making watercolour splotches of the neon lights, it was irresistible.

Sitting at a black-lacquered table dipping bread into a pot of bubbling cheese with Will and a couple of Canadian riders, Alex had to pinch herself. If it weren't for the hollow feeling she got every time she thought of her parents, and the fear of discovery that nagged at her like toothache, it would have been a perfect evening.

It was around 11 p.m., late for the weary, aching riders, when the bus dropped them back at the camp. The rain slowed to a trickle long enough for them to collect their clean laundry and get it to their tents, but started again soon afterwards.

'We should check on the horses before we turn in,' said Alex without enthusiasm.

'I'll do it. You look done in. Tuck yourself up in your sleeping bag.'

Alex protested, but Will was insistent. 'There's no point in both of us slogging through the mud to the barn. The lane will be like an assault course after all this rain. Get some shut-eye. I'll be back in ten minutes.'

'Will?'

'Yeah?'

'We need to talk about when we're going to be rivals again. We can't keep dodging the issue.'

Something akin to anger flashed across his face

but was gone so quickly that she wasn't sure if she'd imagined it. 'Sure thing. Whenever you like.'

Then he was gone, erased by a curtain of black rain.

Alex burrowed into her sweet-smelling sleeping bag, but as dog-tired as she was she couldn't doze off. She kept listening out for Will. Just knowing that he was in the tent near hers usually made her sleep more soundly.

Usually.

Not counting those hours when she'd tossed and turned thinking about him for reasons that had nothing to do with feeling safe . . .

Twenty minutes went by. Then thirty. Thunder ripped through the heavens like a rifle shot, frightening Alex into full wakefulness. The rain pelted down with a disturbing fury. Where was Will? She tried to console herself with the thought that he was probably fussing over Shiraz. There wasn't another rider in the race who took better care of their horse. He was totally devoted to her.

Over the roar of the rain she heard the gunning of an engine. Wriggling out of her sleeping bag, she peeked through the tent flap in time to see blurry red tail-lights disappearing down the drive. A deep sense of unease came over her. Will should have been back by now.

She pulled on her boots and jacket and braced herself for the onslaught. The rain was a living, breathing thing, slamming into her, trying to drown her. Halfway along the track, she slipped and fell into a puddle. As she forced herself on, she had visions of Will sitting happily in the admin office, chatting to one of the vets. When he returned and found her looking like the survivor of a mud-wrestling contest, he'd think of her as helpless again.

The barn was dark and silent, the race security guard nowhere to be seen. Alex pushed open the heavy wooden door. 'Will?' she called. 'Will, are you in here?'

No answer. As she'd thought, he was back at the main camp. Before leaving, she plucked up to courage to walk into the hay- and horse-scented gloom to say goodnight to the horses. Unable to find the light switch, she left the barn door open. The arc of yellow cast by the bulb outside barely illuminated the entrance. Scout and Shiraz were at the far end. The dark end. Frequent shivers of lightning and the pounding of the rain on the roof made the barn feel creepier still. Hardly surprising that Dietrich's Arab was wild-eyed and pacing.

As she approached the liver chestnut to attempt to calm him, she tripped over something in the shadows. She glanced down. Lightning popped like a flashbulb. In its momentary fluorescent glare, Alex saw Will's outstretched body. He'd been battered almost beyond recognition. His jacket was sticky with blood.

She dropped to her knees with a cry, fumbling for a pulse on his cold wrist. Either he was unconscious or he was . . . dead.

26

Day 19, Race Headquarters, Hood River, Oregon

'So let me get this straight,' said Natalie Pritchard. 'A teenage girl comes to you the night before the start of a horse race that crosses some of the most lethal and isolated territory in the United States. She's British, claims that all her money has been stolen, has no ID and a story that even you admit sounds improbable, and you not only let her enter, you sponsor her, no questions asked?'

Jonas regarded her calmly from the sofa. He'd been reading a novel about huskies racing the Iditarod when Natalie had come in from the rain with two husbands (current and ex) and an FBI agent, a square-headed man amusingly named Con. Jonas had stood up to introduce himself but, after attempting to shake their hands (declined) and offer them hot drinks (declined) and/or chairs (declined), he'd returned to his seat on the cracked leather sofa.

'That's not quite correct. I asked Sarah – that's what she told me her name was – what made her think she was tough enough, strong enough or brave enough not to quit at the first hurdle.'

The husband, dressed in ironed jeans, shiny black shoes and a formal black coat, laughed rudely. 'Alex always quits at the first hurdle. It's her default setting.'

'Don't you dare you talk about my daughter that way!' intervened Sam. In contrast to Jeremy, he was tanned and rugged. 'Alex does not—'

'Shut up, both of you,' snapped Natalie. Her eyes were shadowed with worry and exhaustion. 'Go on, Mr Ellington. What did she say?'

'Please call me Jonas. She said she was none of those things. Not tough, strong or brave. She told me she had a long history of screwing up and hurting and disappointing people. She blamed herself. Unlike every other competitor, she didn't seem interested in the money or fame. I think she wanted to prove to herself that she could do something meaningful with her life.'

'*Meaningful* is studying hard in school, passing exams and going to university,' said Jeremy. '*Meaningful* is not destroying the home of the people who've given you everything with a Facebook party, or running away from a luxurious academy designed to transform young lives—'

'It's not the luxurious academy you promised me it was at all,' retorted Natalie. 'It's a money-grubbing boot camp, one that saw no reason to notify us that my daughter had been missing for weeks. Not hours. Not days. Weeks! And after losing my child, the warden has the nerve to go on vacation. If I get my hands on that man before the police do, I'll give him root canal surgery myself. Without an anaesthetic.'

Jeremy continued as if she hadn't spoken. 'It doesn't alter the fact that Alex's latest caper is going to cost a king's ransom in airfares, hotel bills and lost work time. Added to which, she's committed a felony by stealing Warden Cartwright's horse . . . '

Jonas gave a snort of laughter. 'Is that where the mustang came from? I did wonder.'

'Oh, this is funny to you, is it?' demanded Sam. 'My daughter could be jailed or sent to a young offenders' institute for horse theft, and you find that amusing?'

'First off, she won't get a minute of jail time.'

The FBI agent was indignant. 'Now, sir, you can't guarantee—'

'I believe I can,' said Jonas. 'When the race is over I'll call Camp Renew – yes, I'm familiar with the boot camp you're referring to; I've employed young people who've been traumatised there. I'll offer their lead wrangler two or three times what the horse is worth. Trust me, he'll take it. Then the mustang won't be a stolen horse at all. He'll be my horse and Alex will have my full permission to ride him. If that fails, I'll pay for a lawyer myself to get her off on a technicality.'

Hopping up, he went over to a promotional poster of a grinning Jack Carling and his Perlino Akhal-Teke and ripped it from the wall. It distressed him that he'd misjudged the man so badly. He crumpled Jack into a ball and tossed him into a recycling bin.

'Look, I get it,' he said. 'You're her parents and you've had a bad scare. If it was me, I'd also be off my head with worry. But with respect, y'all are looking at this upside down and back to front. It's a simple matter of perspective.'

'Perspective!' spluttered Jeremy. 'We're going to sue you for everything you've got and ever will have. We're going to grind you and Green Power into the dust. Let's see you put a positive spin on that.'

Natalie pressed her hands to her temples. 'What are you saying exactly, Mr Ellington?'

'Jonas, please. The way you see it, most of Alex's actions over the past few weeks are consistent with her past pattern of rebelling then apologising, failing then saying she'll try harder, letting you down then telling you she'll never do it again. Am I right?'

Jeremy: 'One hundred per cent.'

Natalie, reluctantly: 'There is some of that, yes.'

Sam: 'It's not entirely her fault. Perhaps the divorce . . . '

Jonas studied them in sad disbelief.

'Hundreds of teenagers have been through Camp

Renew's programme, detesting it and being crushed by it. Have you any idea how much courage and initiative it took for Alex to escape into the unknown and to rescue a condemned horse while she was at it? Warden Cartwright is notorious. Understandably, she did not want to remain and be tormented by him. She somehow got herself to Boulder, around fifty miles away, where the only money she had in the world was stolen. She must have been terrified. Yet, rather than collapsing in a heap and calling you collect to come bail her out of the mess, she had the ingenuity and sheer guts to come to our Boulder office and convince me that she had what it took to enter a twelve hundred mile race on the cusp of winter.'

He smiled at the memory. 'I did everything I could to put her off, but she was determined to do it so that she could save the mustang and return him to the wild. You know what she told me? "If you trust me with this chance, I'll give it everything I have. My whole heart." And she has. Three hundred and three riders entered The Glory. Thirty-one remain. Your daughter is among them. So far she's ridden close to nine hundred miles.

'I'm not sure about you, but if she was mine I'd proud enough to pop.'

At the end of this speech, even Jeremy was stunned into silence. Rain played percussion on the cabin roof. Sam roused himself first.

'For a minute there, Jonas, you almost had me convinced. But you forget one thing. Our daughter is only sixteen. At any point during those nine hundred miles she could have died, lost a limb or ended up in a coma. Before I knew she'd got caught up in this lunatic race, I read an article about it on the plane from Australia. The journalist documented the staggering number of fractures, wounds, bites, frostbitten fingers, rashes and boils sustained by riders in such grisly detail they're actually seared on my brain. One woman almost died after hitting her head on a rock when her horse threw her into a freezing creek. I thought to myself, why would anyone put themselves through that? But they at least were responsible adults.'

He threw Jeremy a contemptuous glance. 'So I'm in agreement with my ex-wife's new husband, something I never thought I'd hear myself say. We're suing you for endangering the life of a minor, for false advertising, for criminal neglect, for . . . for—'

'We're going to throw the legal book at you,' summarised Jeremy.

Jonas sighed. 'Fair enough.'

'Folks, we've wasted enough time,' said the FBI agent. 'The clock's ticking. If this joker can pinpoint the approximate location where we might find your daughter, we can dispatch a unit to pick her up. The sooner we get her home safe, the easier everyone will sleep.'

Jonas picked up a map and marked a couple of crosses on it. 'Unless they've taken a shortcut, they're likely to be between here and here.'

'*They?*' exclaimed Sam. 'She's travelling with someone? What a relief it'll be if she's found a couple of older, sensible women to take her under their wing.'

'Her companion's a teenage boy. Will Greyton.'

'A *boy!*'

'All the more reason for us to find her as soon as possible,' said Jeremy. 'Come along, Con, let's talk to your colleagues. Try not to worry, Nat. With a bit of luck, Alex will be safe and sound by lunchtime.'

With a smart snap of his umbrella, he stepped out into the downpour, followed by Sam and Con.

Natalie was the last to leave. She threw Jonas a freezing glare from the doorway. 'Goodbye, Mr Ellington. You'll be hearing from our lawyers.'

He said quietly, 'Natalie, how well do you know your daughter?'

She rounded on him furiously. 'Better than I know myself. Judging from your earlier comments, you have no children, *Jonas*, because if you did you'd know that they become part of you, as if you breathe the same breath. From the moment of their birth, you'd face down lions for them. And, yes, I'm aware that not every parent feels that way, but I do. Until a month ago, Alex had never spent a single night away from home. I can't claim to always understand her, but, yes, I know her. More importantly, I love her.'

'In that case, I think there's something you ought to see.'

'That's not my daughter,' said Natalie categorically.

'Is that really my little girl?' Sam said in awe. 'I always knew that those Westerns we watched would come in handy. Can you believe how she negotiated that creek? You'd never know she'd grown up in the English Home Counties. It's as if she was born to race a mustang across the West.'

He and Natalie sat on either side of Jonas on the old sofa, watching on his laptop footage of key moments of Alex's ride. Jeremy had disappeared into the rain with Con to organise what he privately viewed as her 'capture'.

'I don't understand how you've filmed this,' said Natalie. 'Did Alex give her permission? If we'd seen these pictures on the news weeks ago, we could have rescued her immediately and saved ourselves a lot of heartache.'

Jonas did his best to conceal his frustration. After everything she'd seen, she still didn't get it.

'Before the start of the race, every rider had to sign a photography release contract. It's standard practice in any public event these days. Means people can't sue you later if their image turns up on social media. From the outset, I was determined that the race was not going to be a media circus. I gave the print and television media restricted access only to the celebrity and professional riders, on the understanding that my team would release exclusive footage of the other riders on the day the race ends. Alex knew there was a chance her image would be beamed across the world at the end of October. What she didn't – doesn't – know is that we've set up hidden cameras at treacherous or telegenic spots throughout the race.'

He pressed play on the video. Alex was labouring up a mountain in a gale. She looked as if she was in agony. At one stage she almost fell and tears started pouring down her cheeks.

'Stop!' cried Natalie. 'I can't stand another minute of this. It's like some hideous reality show.'

Jonas pressed pause. 'Hardly. Again, it's all a matter of perspective. Personally, I see it as a triumph of the human spirit, but I won't show you any more if it distresses you.'

'Go on,' Natalie said weakly. 'You might as well play it. I don't think I'm capable of feeling any worse.'

'We are going to sue you,' Sam warned Jonas. 'Don't think we're not.'

They watched Alex and Scout crest the mountain. Girl and mustang stood side by side on the summit, gazing out across the vast mountain wilderness of Wyoming. There wasn't another rider in sight. It was so cold that Alex's breath emerged in smoky puffs and yet she lingered there for several long minutes. Her caramel hair and the palomino's creamy mane entangled in the wind until they seemed joined.

Natalie wiped her eyes with a tissue. 'She looks so happy. Exhilarated. She's far too thin, but she looks so peaceful and free.'

There was a catch in Sam's voice. 'She looks as if she belongs in all that wide open space; like she's come home.'

The door crashed open. Jeremy said importantly, 'The FBI want to know if you can narrow the search area?'

Jonas picked up his phone. 'I'll call Wayne Turnbull, the chief clerk. Find out when they left the last vet check.'

When he hung up, a change had come over him. 'They're still at our camp near Boise, Idaho. Apparently, Will, her friend, is . . . ' He chose his words carefully. 'Under the weather.'

'Great,' said Jeremy. 'I'll tell Con to pick Alex up.'

Natalie stood. 'Wait.'

She turned to Jonas. 'What would you do if you were me or Sam? Would you stop her or let her ride?'

Jonas got to his feet. 'I'm not the best person to ask.'

'He most certainly is not,' agreed Jeremy.

Natalie ignored him. 'Jonas, would you let her finish? If she was your daughter?'

Jonas cleared his throat. 'On reflection, it might be sensible to take her out of the race. You're right. She's very young and the rivalry between riders is likely to get more intense as the race nears the finish. There are still over three hundred and sixty miles of rain, snow and wilderness to go. It's better that you stop her now in case . . . in case . . .'

'In case what?' demanded Natalie. 'In case she experiences more blissful moments, like the one on the

286

summit of the mountain? Do you know, I've only just realised how much I hate the word *sensible*. I've spent half my life being prudent, boring and conventional. It's suffocating. No wonder Alex was going crazy cooped up at her over-regulated school and in our safe, over-insured house—'

Jeremy was affronted. 'I beg your pardon. If it weren't for me, you'd have paid twenty-five per cent extra on your premiums.'

'—in the suburbs. It's a very nice life for someone who enjoys comfort and matching furniture but it doesn't have the thrill of galloping a mustang across the Wyoming wilderness.'

'So what are you suggesting?' asked Sam.

'I'm suggesting that we change our point of view and consider looking at life the way Jonas, Alex and this boy Will do. Frankly, I think there's a lot we can learn from them. We should trust our daughter to do this thing that means so much to her and we should believe in her. I'm proud of her and I want her to be proud of herself.'

Sam laughed in amazement. 'We're going to let her finish?'

Jeremy said, 'You can't seriously be thinking of rewarding Alexandra for her outrageous, irresponsible behaviour?'

'Shut up, Jeremy!' cried Natalie and Sam together.

'I think we should let her finish the race on her own terms,' Natalie went on, 'whether that's today or in three hundred and sixty miles. On one condition.'

Jonas had to restrain himself from cheering. 'What's that?'

'I want you to get a message to her. I need her to know that I love her.'

27

Day 19, Coyote Point Trail Riding Centre, Idaho

Reluctantly, excruciatingly, Will stirred into consciousness. He heard the rain before he saw it, drumming on the roof like a heartbeat. His initial attempt to open his eyes was a failure. Three ghosts hovered above him. His second try was better. Alex, Robbie, the former jockey in charge of rider logistics, and an earnest man with white hair emerged from a pea-soup fog. So did pale blue walls and a painting of wild ducks flying over a wheat field. Alex's face was tear-stained and blotchy. She looked as if she hadn't slept.

Will wished that the other people would go away so he could surrender to a long-held desire to kiss her, but before he could dwell on the thought any further the man with white hair, evidently a doctor, said, 'Don't try to move or speak.'

Will immediately made an effort to do both things, with disastrous results. Wave after wave of searing agony went through him. It was like being torched by a flame-thrower.

He sank into the pillows. The events of the previous night came back to him in a series of jumbled flashbacks. The mud on the track; the storm battering at him; two figures looming out of the dark barn, sheet lightning making ghouls of them and their black masks. *This'll teach you to mind your own business*. He'd landed a couple of good punches before one man kicked him in the kidneys and the other came at him with a knife, but he'd gone down fighting.

'Shiraz!' he said hoarsely. 'Alex, they were doping her with something. I tried to stop them. Is she okay?'

Alex gave him a reassuring smile. 'Don't worry. She's doing well. Thanks to you, they didn't get to give her the full dose. We found the half-empty syringe in her stall. She was pole-axed last night, but she's slept it off. It certainly didn't put her off her breakfast. Anyway, none of that matters. The only thing that matters is that you're alive. You didn't look it when I found you.'

The chair beside the bed creaked as Robbie leaned forward. 'Did you recognise them, Will? Anyone we know?'

Will had a flashback of the hunting knife, its wicked blade flashing as it thrust at him. Even if it was Zach's he'd never be able to prove it. 'I don't suppose there were any witnesses?'

'Afraid not. No CCTV at the barn either, although given the conditions I doubt it would have done much good. The cops have taken fingerprints. I wouldn't get your hopes up.'

Robbie twisted his hat in his hands. 'I'm sorry, Will. You were doing so well. To be lying tenth after close to nine hundred miles is no mean achievement. Having it end like this is outrageously unfair. For Sarah too. You were both doing so well. If I could get my hands on the boys that did this to you, I'd be tempted to give them a kicking myself.'

'What are you talking about?' Will wanted to rub his eyes to clear his vision, but his arms wouldn't work. 'My race isn't ending. What time is it? I have to get up and get Shiraz ready.'

'It's after ten and you're not going anywhere,' said the doctor. 'If you hadn't been wearing so many layers, you'd likely have died last night. As it is, you've got a nasty gash and the most arresting spectrum of bruises outside the Northern Lights. I've given you a couple of shots for tetanus and pain, and Sarah here has been tending to you with an ice pack. The best thing you can do now is rest. The couple who own this place are devastated that you were attacked on their land. They're insisting that you rest in their spare room for as long as you need to. Do yourself a favour and take them up on it. My advice, stay off your horse and avoid all strenuous activity for at least a month.'

Robbie warned: 'Will, don't do anything stupid. This

is a one-prize race. You'll never catch Wyatt Carling and the leaders now. They left at three a.m. No point in killing yourself when you've already lost.'

After they'd gone, Will turned his head towards the window, too depressed to speak. Nickel-coloured rivulets of rain coursed down the panes. His fractured reflection reminded him of Frankenstein's monster. Ridiculous that his first thought on regaining consciousness had been about kissing Alex. Not a lot of chance of that ever.

Alex broke the silence. 'Will, your dad rang while you were unconscious.'

The full horror of the situation hit him. He'd gambled with the last of his father's savings and lost. When Len found out, the shock would put him in hospital and it would be Will's fault entirely.

'I need to call him.' He struggled into a sitting position, sweating with pain. A gauze dressing was taped over the little knife wound on his bare stomach, just below his ribcage. The bruises the doctor had described covered his upper body in such profusion he looked as if he'd been tattooed. Dimly he wondered who'd undressed him.

Alex handed him a glass of water. 'I've already spoken to him. I told him you're okay.'

Will immediately spilled half the water on the sheets. 'You talked to him! What? *How?* You shouldn't have done that. The stress of this could kill him.'

Alex grabbed a towel and mopped the bed. 'Calm down, Will. Your phone was ringing and I answered it. I thought it would be worse if he didn't hear from you.

I told him the truth but not the whole truth. Basically, I explained that I was a friend who sometimes rode with you and that you were still asleep after a very long, very exhausting day in the saddle. He seemed quite relieved. He asked me if I thought you were enjoying yourself, if you were happy. I said that with the snow, rain and gales it could be pretty tough but, as far as I could tell, as long as you were with Shiraz and out in nature, you were in heaven.'

Will exhaled. 'What did he say?'

'He thanked me profusely. After that, there was this long pause. The line was crackling and I thought we'd been cut off. Eventually, he said, "Tell Will I'm thinking of him and that if I could be there with him, riding alongside him, I would. Tell him I'm proud of him and that, no matter what happens, he shouldn't let anything stop him."'

Her brow creased. 'Will . . . do you think your dad's guessed that you're riding in The Glory?'

'Definitely not!' he said vehemently. 'No way.'

Then, despairingly, 'God, maybe he has.'

By contrast, Alex's face was suddenly alight. She'd shrugged off tiredness like an old cloak and was fired up again. 'Will, listen to me. I have a plan. Now that I know you're all right I'm going to carry on with the race. I know it's a long shot but I'm going to give it everything I have. I'm packed and ready. As soon as I've saddled Scout, I'll hit the road.'

He felt the blow in his solar plexus, but told himself

off for being so selfish. It was because she'd stayed to care for him that she was so far behind.

'Absolutely, you should go. Thanks for everything and especially for saving me last night. I didn't mean for it to become a habit – you rescuing me. Good luck. Hope you catch them.'

'Oh, I intend to,' she said with conviction. 'Scout and I are going to do everything in our power to win this race for your dad. I know it's a long shot but, hey, the tortoise beat the hare. I've thought it through. All I need is enough money to set Scout free in Wyoming. Possibly not even that. A mustang charity might help me. Provided I can do that, I give you my word that if a miracle happens and I win, I'll give you every penny so that you can get Shiraz back to Tennessee and your father can have his operation.'

'You'd do that for me?'

'Will, you saved my life. It's the least I can do.'

'But what about you?' Will said. 'You need the money too.'

Her smile didn't quite reach her eyes. 'I'll be fine. I'll call home and face the music.'

'*No*,' said Will. 'You're amazing and I'll never forget this, but no.'

'*No?*' She sounded hurt.

'A hundred per cent no.'

'But—'

'No buts. If you win The Glory, I want you to win it for yourself and Scout. You've come too far and fought too hard to do anything less. If I can make it out of this bed, I'm going to attempt to do the same.'

Alex gasped. 'Will, you're not capable of riding anywhere. You heard what the doctor said.'

'I did, and I'm choosing to ignore it. My father's life is a whole lot more important than a few bruises. Look, as it stands now, you and I are effectively out of the race. It's hard to admit, but it's true. Robbie's right. We're hours behind Wyatt Carling, Manny and the other leaders. But if we give up now, they've won – Zach, Verity, your warden, the Carlings or whoever. If we roll over onto our backs like Labrador puppies, we're basically telling them that it pays to brutalise and threaten people. I'm sorry, but I'm not prepared to do that.'

Alex perched on the edge of his bed again. 'I agree, but maybe there's another way. Will, you look as if you've been run over by a cement truck. Riding as far as the end of the street would not be a good idea.'

'Oh, it's a terrible idea. But if we ride together – if you help me and I help you – at least for the next twenty-four hours, it just might work. First, though, we're going to have to get creative with a map. To have any chance at all, we need a radical shortcut.'

28

Day 20, Snake River, Idaho state line

'Well, it was short and it is radical,' said Alex.

She and Will stood on the riverbank, gazing across at Oregon. They might as well have contemplated swimming the Atlantic. Below them was a foaming jade chasm. They'd chosen the narrowest section of Snake River in the belief that they might be able to wade across, but the relentless rain had swelled it to an oceanic torrent. Even the horses were goggle-eyed at the sight of it.

Alex was so frustrated she could have wept, but she made light of it for Will's sake. It had almost killed him to come this far. He claimed that the pain was lessening as the hours passed and was nothing compared to the torture of the previous day when he'd climbed out of his sick bed and ridden fifty miles, but she didn't believe him. He was constantly hot when he should have been cold and cold when he should have been hot. She worried he was running a fever.

'At least we can say we tried,' she told Will. 'It was worth taking a chance. What's our Plan B?'

'We don't have one. Our only other option is to ride west for fifteen miles and cross on the bridge, but that would mean losing a lot of the ground we've gained. In that case we might as well quit now.'

Alex loosened Scout's girth and gave him his electrolytes. The palomino licked his lips and pulled a face. 'I can't believe that we've ridden nearly a thousand miles, only to be defeated by a river.'

Will sank to the ground and leaned against a rock. Despite the chill, there were beads of sweat on his forehead. 'It's not like we're the first.'

Alex joined him, unwrapping an energy bar and handing him half. 'What do you mean?'

'The Snake isn't just any old river. The reason it's been given so many names – Mad River, Lewis River, Shoshone River, Saptin River – by so many different explorers is because it has so many faces, a lot of them treacherous. See how the terrain gets wilder and more mountainous to the east of us? That's Hells Canyon. In the nineteenth century the pioneers on the Oregon Trail to California used to battle their way over the Salmon River and Blue Mountains and down the steep sides of the gorge, only to have their hopes or lives wrecked by the rapids on Snake River. Before it was dammed there were hundreds of them. Get caught in them and it was like doing three rounds in a spin cycle.'

The rain had ceased for the first time in two days. Earlier, Will had joked that if it continued much longer they'd be growing fins, the horses included. How he'd managed to raise a smile when every step was agony for him, Alex couldn't imagine, but he did, keeping fatigue and depression at bay with stories about two of his heroes, Captain Meriwether Lewis and William Clark.

Cocooned in her jacket, peering through the porthole of her hood as the driving rain made a watercolour painting of the valleys and hills they passed through, Alex found that Will's Southern accent had a meditative quality. His narrative of the expedition that had made American icons of Lewis and Clark unfolded before her like a film.

Hunched wearily over Scout's sodden withers, she'd learned how in 1903 President Thomas Jefferson charged Captain Lewis with finding and mapping the most direct waterway across the West before the British, French and Spanish moved in to claim it. Lewis asked his friend William Clark to be second in command. Their adventures and those of the thirty unruly Corps of Discovery soldiers who accompanied them across mountains, cataracts and canyons over the next couple of years, were about the most romantic, terrifying tales Alex had ever heard.

Along the way, Lewis and Clark had to foster relations and broker peace with the Indian tribes they encountered, a task made easier by their Lemni Shoshone interpreter, Sacagawea. Some tribes drove them to the point of madness with their thieving, violent savagery; others became dear, trusted friends, saving their lives time and time again by guiding, feeding and sheltering them.

Will vividly described a stand-off between the white men and the Sioux in South Dakota over what the chiefs perceived as a lack of gifts. As the braves readied their bows and pulled arrows from their quivers, Lewis ordered his men to cock their weapons and held a lighted taper over his own swivel gun. Clark had his sword in his hand and was ready to fight to the death before the Sioux chief, Black Buffalo, called on his warriors to stand down.

'The thing I've had in the back of my head every time Shiraz and I have had a difficult descent on this trip is how one of their packhorses slipped as the expedition was winding its way down this perilous narrow precipice,' said Will. 'It fell hundreds of feet. They were all devastated. When they reached the bottom they went to collect what was left of his load, expecting to find the poor horse in bits. Incredibly, he barely had a scratch.'

He nodded towards Snake River. 'Hard to believe that they sailed right where we're sitting – Lewis and Clark. They had these heavy wooden dugouts and when they reached the Columbia River, where we're headed, they made it across a Class 5 rapid. That's the most deadly there is. The Sioux were lining the banks in their hundreds, quite sure that these idiot Americans were going to drown. They couldn't believe their eyes. Lewis's journals are full of descriptions of "horrid" swelling water, "boiling and whorling in every direction".

'So what would *they* do?' Alex asked. 'If Lewis and Clark found themselves in our situation, what would they do?'

Will laughed. 'They wouldn't let a little thing like Snake River stop them. Actually, that's not quite true. It did defeat them once, but they came up with a Plan B.'

'We should too,' said Alex, even though the thought of going anywhere near the swirling water scared the living daylights out of her.

Will sobered. 'Alex, crossing a river this size in the best of conditions is dangerous. Crossing it in temperatures this low when it's running hard could be suicide. We can do a few things to minimise the risk, but it's still massive. You need to be aware of that.'

'I'm not turning back.'

Will grinned. 'Didn't think so. How are your raft-building skills? Fancy trying your hand at making a doughnut?'

Midway across the river, the *Discovery Doughnut*, as they'd named their round raft, hit a rock, tipping Alex into the torrent. The shock of the freezing water was so great that she thought her heart might stop then and there.

'Will!' she screamed as the current tore at her. She

went under, spinning like a top. She'd always thought of herself as a strong swimmer, but the cold sapped her strength in seconds. She floundered hopelessly.

Dizzily, she tried to figure out which way was up. Her lungs screamed for oxygen. A tremendous tiredness came over her. All at once it didn't matter. Any of it. She was too exhausted to fight any more. Snapshots of love flickered through her mind. Her mum smiling through her tears when Alex presented her with an acer tree for Mother's Day. Her dad lifting her onto a seaside donkey on Brighton beach when she was five. Scout coming towards her through the swirling snow. Will's heart pressed against hers in the frozen tent, warming her, reviving her, bringing her back to life.

It was Will's hands that found hers now, pulling her powerfully to safety. She fairly flew to the surface. Disoriented, she struck out for the bank they'd just left, coughing up foul water.

'Use the current, don't fight it,' panted Will as he trod water, keeping a firm grip on her while tugging at the rope secured to the raft. 'Whatever you do, don't panic. Grab hold of the doughnut. We're going to attempt to get across the river at a forty-five degree angle. Watch how the horses are swimming. They're huffing and puffing and scared witless but they aren't wasting energy. They're just inching towards the bank when they can. Do the same and we'll be absolutely fine.'

Throughout the crossing he talked to her in the same calm, confident tone he used with Shiraz if she was

301

frightened. His powerful arms and shoulders bunched and strained as he pushed the gear-loaded raft across the river, kicking strongly. The horses followed, snorting in disgust, blowing bubbles. When the current did finally sweep their riders to the opposite bank, it did so with such force that the raft disintegrated. Fortunately, by then it was shallow enough to stand. Alex and Will rushed to snatch their gear before it sank without trace.

It wasn't until Will had hauled their saddles to a dry, sheltered spot close to a stand of trees, and ensured that Alex and the horses were uninjured, that he stopped. The effort had cost him dearly. His face was ghastly white, the purple bruises standing out in sharp relief. As he untied their tents with shaking hands, Alex saw that his knife wound had reopened. Blood seeped through his white vest.

She was at his side in a second. 'Will, stop what you're doing and sit down.'

Taking the rope from his unresisting fingers, she led him to the groundsheet she'd spread. He didn't so much sit as topple over.

Dangerously chilled herself, she found it difficult to focus on what to do next to help him. Oddly, it was the survival instruction she'd received at Camp Renew that came to her aid. She could still remember Bud Baxter's drill instructor roar. Recalling it galvanised her into putting up her tent in record time. The horses were hungry after their exertions in the river but they'd have to wait.

Will was so weak that it was difficult just to get him into the tent. Ignoring his protests, she peeled off his wet vest and jeans and dried his bare chest and back with her spare polo shirt. The wound below his ribcage seeped watery blood and pus. It was as if the life was leaking out of him. She cleaned it with bottled water and taped a gauze dressing over it.

'Alex . . . so sorry . . . I'll be better in a bit. Don't know why I'm s-so cold . . . The horses . . . wait . . . will help you . . . '

'Shhh . . . Get into the sleeping bag. I'm going to leave your dry jeans and boxers here. Take off your wet ones if you can. I'll be right back.'

Outside, she changed out of her own soaking clothes. Her priority was lighting a fire. The damage wreaked by the storm meant that there was no shortage of fallen branches, but most of them were wet. The best she could do was break pieces from the crumbling middle of a rotten tree.

With the aid of a chunk of firelighter and the kindling she'd got into the habit of stuffing into her coat pockets – feathers, twigs and small pinecones – it flared and took hold. The only thing she didn't relinquish was a piece of bark from a cascara sagrada tree. The name of the tree meant 'sacred bark' in Spanish, a rather poetic name for something that Will had told her was one of the most efficient laxatives known to man.

'Six minutes to lift-off. I've never seen it in action, but one of the cheerleaders at my school put it in the sports drink of a football player who'd said vile things about her on Facebook and apparently the effects were quite spectacular. He drank it right before he went out on the pitch for the biggest game of the season, so you can imagine.'

Alex had preferred not to imagine, but she'd slipped the bark into her pocket for future consideration. Before the race ended, she planned to put it to good use.

After she'd found Will unconscious in the barn, she'd run to Wayne Turnbull for help. The way the chief clerk had dragged his heels and prevaricated before calling the race medic, and the way he'd tried to weasel his way out of calling the cops by insisting that Will must have fallen and hit his head, had left her in no doubt that he knew or had his suspicions about who was behind the attack.

She could never have proved that so there was no point in pursuing it, but if the opportunity ever presented itself she did intend to make him reflect on the way he'd treated people during the course of the race.

The fire she'd made was not exactly the bonfire she'd hoped for, but it was big enough to help thaw out her limbs. She'd built it as close as she dared to the tent, hoping that the ambient heat would reach Will. When it came to making hot chocolate, it was easier to use the miniature gas stove.

While it was warming up, she fed the horses and checked their legs and flanks. Aside from a scratch on Scout's shoulder, they were no worse for wear. Shiraz even whickered when Alex came over with her special mix, a show of affection and appreciation she usually reserved for Will alone. After everything they'd been through, it was astonishing to Alex that, though increasingly tired, the horses still actively looked forward to the surprises of each new dawn. They were great friends too. The thought that, within hours, they'd be separated forever was unbearable.

Hot drinks made, she took her pocketknife and cut a square of sphagnum moss from a fallen tree trunk, as Bud Baxter had taught her. Back in the tent, Will's condition had worsened. His eyes were shut. Violent shudders wracked his body. She managed to rouse him enough for him to swallow a few sips of hot chocolate and a couple of paracetamol, but he lay down again almost immediately, mumbling apologies.

Brown liquid oozed through the gauze on his abdomen. Tenderly, Alex removed the dressing and cleaned the wound for a second time. Then she pressed the green, fluffy moss against the pink cut. According to Baxter, sphagnum moss had been widely used by the Indians and medics in the First World War to treat battle wounds. Few products were more absorbent, and it was said to have antibiotic properties. As Alex covered it with a square of gauze and taped it into place, it struck her that it would be the height of irony if Camp Renew's advice saved Will.

Unzipping the sleeping bag, she climbed in with him. He was running a high fever. Chills rippled through him. She put her arms around his waist and pulled him close, trying to warm him as he had once warmed her.

He stirred but didn't open his eyes. 'Alex,' he mumbled. 'You . . . and Scout . . . should . . . go . . . The . . . race . . . Wasting time . . . My fault . . . '

She said drily, 'Yes, of course I'm going to abandon you to freeze to death in some lonely wilderness in . . . Where are we now? Oregon?'

After that she held him tighter than ever. His breathing became more laboured and she started to panic that, having survived the attack, the river had killed him.

Three times she picked up his phone to call the race emergency line. Twice she put it away. If he had to be evacuated to hospital, he'd be out of the race. When she picked it up for a third time, there was no signal. For better or worse, he would not be seeing the inside of the local A&E department.

She settled on talking as a way of keeping him going. After all, it worked for coma patients. 'That day in Idaho, you asked me if the phrase "lions, tigers and bears" meant anything to me. I lied and said no. But it does. It's something my dad used to say when I was a little girl and scared of the dark. Every night I used to cry and scream if they tried to make me sleep in my own bed. Then Dad had this notion that we should rename all my monsters. Said it would give me power over them. We came up with silly nicknames like Engelbert Poodle Brain or turned them into lions, tigers and bears. Pretty

306

soon I couldn't wait for it to be night so I could conjure up my animal friends.

'After that, it was a trick I used any time I was frightened. I turned every monster into something cuddly. Gave it a cute face. Didn't matter if it was an exam, a bully or if I was jumping a difficult fence. I did it right up until I was twelve and Dad told me he was divorcing Mum and moving to Australia. The thing that hurt the most was that I didn't see it coming. I thought our family was invincible. As a kid you never expect a monster to come in the shape of one of your parents and I had no defence against it. It was as if my dad had ripped off my superpower cape. It made me think that love wasn't real. That it was a lie. We had this horrific argument. I said things, unforgivable things, and he went away and never came back.

'From then on, my monsters just got bigger and bigger and I had to make myself badder and badder to fight them off. I began to think that one day I'd just explode like a nuclear bomb. But on the night of the blizzard, when I thought I might die of fear as well as cold, summoning up the lions, tigers and bears was the only thing that got me through the endless hours. And you. The thought of you kept me going. *You* kept me alive, Will Greyton.'

It was only then she realised that he'd stopped shivering and was sleeping, his eyelashes fanned across his tanned cheek. A wry smile tugged the corner of her mouth. She'd finally plucked up the courage to tell Will the truth about her dad and how she was to blame for him never coming back, and he hadn't heard a word. In a way, she was relieved. God knew what he'd think of her.

She rolled onto her side and looked at him, causing the top of the sleeping bag to slip aside. Now that he was out of immediate danger, it seemed illicit to be pressed up against his hard muscled body, especially since he was wearing nothing but black boxer briefs. Every contour of him was visible in the dim beam of the torch she'd clipped to the tent roof.

A wave of longing rippled through Alex and she snuggled up to him again, running her hands over his strong smooth back. 'Typical,' she murmured. 'I finally get close to the sexiest boy on earth and he's unconscious.'

Moments later she was asleep herself. Her last thought was that it might be wise to relocate to the other tent. Sometime after midnight she awoke with no clue where she was. It was the warmth of Will's skin that brought it all back to her. What kind of nurse was she – falling asleep when he was gravely ill?

The torch had either gone off or been turned off. The silvery light of a full moon shone through a parting in the tent flap. As her eyes adjusted, she suddenly became aware that Will was propped up on one elbow, studying her.

Embarrassed, she shifted as far from him as was feasible in the confined space of the tent. 'This is a bit

308

awkward, isn't it? Sorry. You were so feverish that I was worried that if I didn't warm you up you'd get pneumonia or something. Don't move. I'll sleep in the other tent. How are you feeling? Can I get you some water?'

He grinned. 'Relax, Alex. I feel better than I have for days.' He touched the gauze dressing on his abdomen. 'Moss? I'm very impressed. The pain's almost gone.'

She lay down wordlessly, heart pounding. Really, it was imperative that she remove herself from all physical contact with him as quickly as possible, but an intoxicating sensation was stealing through her limbs and she felt quite incapable of going anywhere.

Will murmured: 'You were you saying something about wishing I was conscious?'

Her face burned. 'That's not fair. You were supposed to be asleep.'

He smiled. 'I heard you in my dreams.'

Slowly, languorously, he leaned forward and kissed her cheeks, then her eyelids, then her earlobes and neck.

Alex tried to get it together to form a coherent sentence. 'Will, we can't. We definitely should not . . . Well, maybe . . . '

He slid a hand beneath her T-shirt and moved it upwards. A moan escaped her. 'Oh, no . . . '

He pulled away. 'No?'

'Will, we can't,' said Alex more firmly. 'Remember what we agreed? For your dad's sake, it's critical that you win this race. We're a long way behind. To have any chance at all, you're going to have to push yourself and

Shiraz to the limits of endurance and beyond. I'm going to be doing the same with Scout, but if we fail I don't want be the one to hold you up. Or vice versa.

'Besides,' she added, 'you're injured.'

'Yes, but I'm recovering fast! I know I'm still a little banged up and not exactly an oil painting but—'

'Will, I'm being serious. Tonight we're friends, but tomorrow we're going our separate ways. In order for that to work, we have to be clinical about it. No riding together, no chatting in camp, no looking out for one another. We'll be arch competitors and nothing more. Win or lose, it's time to face facts. In less than a week this'll be over. You'll return to Tennessee and I'll either beg my parents to fly me home to the UK or be arrested and dragged screaming to Camp Renew. Let's be realistic. We're never going to see each other again. The sooner we part company, the easier it'll be.'

The words seemed to come from someone who wasn't her, someone sensible, someone who wasn't about to walk away from the love of her life. She wanted so much for him to tell her that she was mistaken, that he cared too much to let her go and that the bond they'd formed could never be broken, but all he said was, 'You're right. We can't. We're already too close. Getting any closer would be a huge mistake. Sorry I crossed the line. Tomorrow we'll be rivals again. As soon as it's light, I'll pack up my stuff and go.'

Alex sat up, hugging herself defensively. She tried to focus on the sliver of moonlight and not on the boy beside her. As the silence lengthened, his words hung in the air like a veil of steel. *We're already too close. Getting any closer would be a huge mistake.* Not merely a mistake but a huge one. If she had any pride at all she'd go, but the instant she left the connection between them would be severed. He'd be lost to her forever.

'There is one thing we need to consider,' she said.

'What's that?'

Involuntarily, she glanced at him and instantly regretted it because his eyes were smoky with desire and she couldn't tear her gaze from his mouth. More than victory in The Glory, more than all the money in all the banks in America, she wanted to kiss him.

'What?' Will asked softly. 'What should we consider?'

'Well,' she said, 'what if tomorrow never comes . . . ?'

29

Day 29, Race Headquarters, Hood River, Oregon

At 9.25 p.m. on a blustery Friday night, Wayne Turnbull sat contemplating the black leather briefcase on his desk. He was so delirious with excitement he could barely breathe. When, earlier that day, the bank manager had lifted the lid and displayed its contents, Turnbull had been overwhelmed with the urge to fling the whole lot up into the air and have a quarter of a million brand spanking new dollar bills rain down on him.

'Monopoly money!' he'd joked to hide his elation. The manager laughed politely, as if it was the first time anyone had ever said that to him. He'd handed Wayne the briefcase and a white envelope with his name on it. Approximately four minutes later the chief clerk was driving down the highway with enough cash to flee the country and start a new life on the beaches of Brazil.

He'd been tempted to keep going to Seattle, where he'd booked a 6 a.m. flight to Rio in the name of John Davey Wallace, but if he went missing before he'd completed his evening race duties his absence would be noted. The cops would be on his trail faster than a dog on steak. Better to stick it out until the riders were safely tucked up in their tents before hitting the road with their prize money.

It was a smart decision. No sooner had he deposited the briefcase in his office safe than all hell broke loose. With fifty miles and less than twenty-four hours to go, two of the best-performing competitors, Kaamil Nader and a little-known wrangler from San Antonio, had crashed out of The Glory. Kaamil's Arabian had torn a ligament and the wrangler had shattered his right leg in three places after falling over a ball during an impromptu football match with the grooms.

As if that wasn't enough, Wayne had returned to his office to find Sarah Wood stealing one of his Dragon Fuel energy drinks. The sheer nerve of the girl blew his mind. She'd apologised with a cheeky grin and left the bottle on his desk, but she hadn't looked remotely remorseful. He'd sent her on her way with the threat of disqualification ringing in her ears. The least she deserved was a sleepless night.

Thinking about her and Will Greyton made his blood boil. Wayne took several large gulps of the Dragon Fuel in an attempt to simmer down. He'd never forgiven Will for foiling the theft of the Morgan stallion on the second night of the race, doing him out of an easy $10,000 – his cut of the deal.

But what Sarah had done was, in a way, worse. Her heated exchanges with Jack Carling and his groom had been witnessed by the brother of one of the race vets. It turned out that the vet already had his suspicions about Desert King. An operation to trap the rodeo rider was launched within the hour. Before he reached the next vet gate, the stallion had failed a drug test and Jack had been arrested.

While it wasn't Sarah's fault that he'd been disqualified, Wayne did blame her for triggering the chain of events that followed. The eviction of Jack from the race was particularly infuriating because he and Wayne had had a deal. Wayne had turned a blind eye to certain goings-on in return for Jack cutting him in on the weekly takings of his betting syndicate – a syndicate that also included Zach.

Wayne took another angry swig of the Dragon Fuel. Between them, Will and Sarah had cost him and the others a small fortune. It rankled that the combined efforts of Jack Carling's villainous friends, Zach and crew, plus the full fury of the West's winter weather, had done little to slow their progress. When the boy was laid low after a savage beating in Idaho, Wayne had been optimistic that his endurance racing career was at an end.

Not that he condoned violence. Whatever else he'd done in his chequered past, it wasn't that. But he hadn't exactly called a halt to it either. Nor had he mentioned to Wyatt and Zach that it hadn't been Will or Sarah who'd shopped Jack Carling; it had been one of the race volunteers.

In the end it didn't matter because the teenagers had proved unstoppable. Will had somehow dragged himself off his sick bed, aided and abetted by the girl. Unbelievably, they'd made up so much ground that Will now had a genuine shot at the title and the girl wasn't far off. His only small comfort was that they'd fallen out or broken up or something. Having previously been as thick as thieves, they now actively avoided each other. Hardly surprising, when so much money was at stake.

Wayne smiled to himself when he imagined the chaotic scenes that would greet the news that, after twelve hundred miles of rain, snow and suffering, the fortune the winner was expecting had gone AWOL. Things could get ugly. Wayne was unconcerned. By then, he and the $250,000 would be halfway to Brazil.

Opening the briefcase, he breathed in the inky scent of the money. If there was a better perfume, it hadn't been invented. It still astounded him that his plan had gone so smoothly. He almost pitied Jonas. Gloria, the boss's PA, had never made any secret of her distrust of Wayne. Fiercely protective of Jonas, she'd tried in vain to counsel him against allowing the race clerk to go alone to collect the money.

'Jonas, hon, have you lost your mind?' she'd demanded

bluntly. 'You might as well send a lion to bring you a lamb. Can't you give the winner a big cardboard cheque like they do on the lottery? Or if you're insistin' on cold hard cash, let me go fetch it for you with Hank from security.'

She'd stared pointedly at Wayne. 'We'll keep it out of the hands of any unscrupulous persons, don't you worry 'bout that.'

But Jonas would not be swayed. It had to be cash and it had to be his clerk who collected it.

Wayne chuckled at the memory. It just went to show that a Harvard education was no use at all if you were a romantic, perpetually dreaming of saving not just the planet but every waif and stray on it.

He was finishing off the Dragon Fuel when he remembered the envelope the bank manager had handed him. He'd assumed it was some sort of receipt, but now he recognised his boss's handwriting on the front. As he opened it, he was suddenly assailed by stomach cramps. They ripped through his abdomen with hurricane force, bringing tears to his eyes.

Dear God, that was all he needed – food poisoning when he had to drive hundreds of miles to Seattle with his precious cargo. The cramps subsided in under a minute but he was unnerved by their viciousness. It occurred to him that the British girl might have tampered with his Dragon Fuel, but he couldn't think of any good reason why she would do such a thing. It had to be the barbecued pork he'd eaten at lunch.

Sweating, he turned his attention to the envelope. His black eyes scanned the enclosed sheet of paper in growing disbelief.

Dear Wayne,

If you're reading this letter, you've collected the $250,000 intended for the winner of The Glory. You have two choices. You can either ensure that the rider who deserves it receives it safely at the prize-giving ceremony tomorrow afternoon, or you can abscond with it. Don't tell me that the second option – running off to some South American country and drinking cocktails on the beach for the rest of your days – hasn't crossed your mind.

Shocked? Don't be. I've always known about the jewellery store robbery and your vacation in Colorado State Penitentiary. However, as you're well aware I'm a big believer in redemption. I gave you the most important position in this race, that means so much to me, in the hope that you would seize with both hands the opportunity to be a better man. Over the past month I'll admit there've been aspects of your behaviour that have disappointed me. Attempted horse theft? Bullying? Gambling? Really, Wayne, if you're going to remain a career criminal you might at least show a bit more imagination.

Right now you still have options. Consider them carefully. 1) Bring the money to the prize-giving ceremony tomorrow afternoon. 2) Take it and have it always on your conscience that you repaid with your worst impulses a rider who, if I'm not mistaken, will have given the very best of themselves in

order to triumph in the harshest, most extreme conditions
any horseman could be expected to endure.
Yours in hope,
J.

Wayne laughed out loud when he read the last paragraph. The naivety of the man was extraordinary. He honestly imagined that his bleeding heart liberalism would see his chief clerk trotting off obediently to the prize-giving, reformed and contrite, smiling for the cameras. It was high time that Jonas learned a valuable lesson: the world didn't work that way.

With a last gleeful glance at the crisp banknotes, Wayne shut the lid of the briefcase and picked it up. It was time to hit the road. But as he shrugged into his jacket, the stomach cramps attacked again. It was a measure of their intensity that Wayne gave no thought to the security of the cash as he flung the briefcase onto the desk, wrenched open the door and bolted out into the night.

Nor did he see the tall, bald man who had been poised to knock when the race clerk tore past him. Raising his eyebrows at the explosions emitting from the staff bathroom, Strike Cartwright let himself into Wayne Turnbull's office.

All in all it had been a terrible month. He'd had a middle finger amputated after the rattlesnake bite turned nasty, been chomped and kicked by Midnight Magic, and accidentally shot himself in the thigh with his own tranquilliser gun in his desperation to escape from Horizon Investments' psychotic enforcer. Now he had a streaming cold. Worse still, the cops and FBI had been crawling all over Camp Renew, asking difficult questions.

The most confusing news from Helga at the academy was that Alexandra Blakewood had been 'found safe and well' by her parents and the FBI. Knowing full well that the only place 'Sarah Wood' could have been discovered was riding her stolen mustang in The Glory, Cartwright had fully expected her to be whisked back to Britain or returned to Camp Renew. But nothing of the kind had happened. According to Gap, who was still spying for him, she'd simply continued on her way.

Perhaps the girl's parents had foolishly decided to let her finish without informing race officials that she was a fraud. It was an omission Cartwright intended to correct. If nothing else, he wanted the satisfaction of dragging her back to Camp Renew kicking and screaming, and having her charged with horse theft. Once he had her at the academy, there was still a chance that he could pressure her parents into paying the $50,000 for her future fees in exchange for him not calling the police over the stolen palomino.

He'd also stuffed her teddy bear with cocaine and intended to use that as leverage. Proof positive that Alexandra was bad to the bone. As far as he knew, Pluto had been overlooked by the authorities and was still on his desk. One small mercy amid the sea of depressing news.

319

The orchestral cacophony of the clerk's bowels carried through the office wall. Cartwright winced in sympathy. As he paced the office, alternately blowing his nose and sucking on a throat lozenge, he couldn't help but notice the passport and e-ticket on the desk. Curiosity got the better of him. He was most intrigued that a man bearing an uncanny resemblance to Wayne Turnbull, only with a different name, was scheduled to fly to Rio the next morning.

Idly, he flipped open the briefcase. It didn't take a brain surgeon to deduce that he was looking at the race winner's cash.

Strike Cartwright had heard about people having epiphanies, but he'd never experienced one. Until now. It took him less than twenty seconds to arrive at a decision. Running Camp Renew had been entertaining, but it certainly wasn't worth losing digits to snakes and enforcers. What he really needed was a fresh start. With a quarter of a million dollars to fund it, the possibilities were infinite.

Pausing only to ensure that the chief clerk was still occupied, he picked up the briefcase and hurried into the night. The race headquarters were situated quite some distance from the camp. At this hour they were mostly deserted. There were no CCTV cameras. Nobody had seen the warden come. Nobody saw him go.

30

30th October, Oregon Trail, Columbia Gorge, Oregon

After a month of clobbering the horsemen with every weapon in its arsenal, the weather made amends on the final day of the race. A late-night gale blasted the clouds over the horizon and laid a dazzling carpet of scarlet and lemon leaves on the forest trails. Dawn arrived in a scattering of gold glitter. It lent a warm glow to the low red-brick buildings and converted warehouses that housed the cafes, yoga studios and bohemian boutiques of downtown Hood River where, fuelled by espresso, volunteers were already hard at work hanging banners welcoming 'Glory Fans' and the 'Fearless Riders of the Snowy Sage'.

As the sun rose, it crept up the powder-blue flanks of Mount Hood, passing the Timberline Lodge and creating a halo above the snowy summit. It was that which gave

Will the sense of being suspended between heaven and hell. Heaven because it was the final day of the race and the scenery that Shiraz trotted through was nothing short of spectacular. Red barns were set against forests that blazed with wildfire colour, a paddle-steamer lumbered along the mighty Columbia River and Mount Hood rose like a beacon against the sky.

Hell, he'd discovered, came in many forms. It was the chafing and aching, the bruises and blisters, the cumulative exhaustion that infected every cell and fibre of his being. It was the list of worries that multiplied as the finish line loomed. What happened if he lost? How on earth was he going to get himself and Shiraz back to Tennessee with only $12.20 in his pocket? How would he break the news to his dad that he'd blown their savings? That he'd done nothing but lie for a month? That he'd failed in his bid to find a way to pay for a heart operation? Where was he going to keep Shiraz if he did get her home? Would he have to sell her? Would the Bigger Burger give him back his old job?

For the umpteenth time, he checked his phone. For the past twenty-four hours he'd not been able to raise either his father or his friend Tom. Before leaving the camp, he'd messaged Tyler, asking him to drive round to the house to check that everything was okay. Tyler had promised to swing by later that afternoon.

Will tucked his phone away and closed his eyes, trusting Shiraz to find the way. He wanted to empty his mind but Alex kept finding her way into it. Heaven took many shapes too. When he wasn't admiring the view, the memory of her soft, strong body pressed against his played over and over in his head.

Hell was getting up and leaving her without saying goodbye. It was every hour since. It was going to great lengths to avoid her in camp, and turning away without a smile or a word when he once rounded a corner and almost collided with her. She'd tried to say something to him but he'd pretended not to hear. He'd even flirted with a girl groom when he knew Alex was likely to see him.

He'd tried to tell himself that it was for her own good. That as much as he wanted victory for himself, he wanted it for her too and if behaving like an utter bastard helped them both achieve what they needed to achieve, then it would be worth it. It wasn't as if she had any deep feelings for him. They weren't even friends. She'd made it crystal clear to him that everything ended that night. *Let's be realistic. We're never going to see each other again.*

Even before what had happened happened, her words had cut him to the quick.

So he'd done what he could to protect himself, throwing up high walls topped with razor wire. The way he saw it, he didn't have a choice. Unless he won The Glory, he had nothing to offer her. They lived on different continents, for one thing. Why on earth would someone as gorgeous and altogether wonderful as Alex want to be with an out-of-work burger flipper?

The irony was that now if he did win the race and was in the position where he could afford to buy her dinner, or even fly to the UK to see her, she'd want nothing to do with him.

The twenty-mile marker flashed by. Will snapped into life, banishing Alex from his thoughts. He had no chance of fixing anything with anyone if he didn't win. Starting out that day, he'd been seventh on the leader board after being given an unexpected boost by the elimination of Kaamil and a wrangler from San Antonio – ten spots ahead of Alex. Five hours on, he'd slipped to eighteenth.

It was a calculated gamble. Throughout the morning, he'd nursed Shiraz along, practically carrying her in an effort to conserve the last of her energy. He made frequent water, electrolytes and rest breaks. Competitor after competitor had passed them. As tired as she was, the mare had fought to go after them. Now Will gave Shiraz her head.

She responded as she had for over 1,180 miles, stretching out, ears pricked, her great heart powering them forward. Within minutes, they'd passed four riders. Will pushed aside every thought that wasn't about racing.

He tried channelling the spirit of the 'pony riders' of the nineteenth century, feather-light men of steel who'd carried letters nineteen hundred miles across the continent in eight days, come hail, sleet or hurricane. Unarmed and unstoppable, they'd streaked across the landscape for fifty miles at a stretch, changing horses every ten miles, then flying onward, Mark Twain said, 'like a belated fragment of a storm'.

Then there was Frank T. Hopkins and his 'Longest Ride'. Will had wanted so much to believe that Frank and his mustang had cruised from Galveston to Vermont with such little effort that they'd covered eighteen hundred miles in thirty-one days with no rest, but having ridden over a thousand miles himself he now knew it for the myth it was. Still, there was something about the spirit of Hopkins, if not his audacious claims (*Joe and I were in Rutland thirteen days before the next horse and rider arrived . . .*), that was inspiring.

With twelve miles to go, Will took another gamble. He stopped at a stream, untacked Shiraz and sponged her down. He put Vaseline on her pasterns, allowed her a small feed and rested her as long as he dared, knowing that if he miscalculated what he thought she was capable of by even a minute, he'd have lost the race right then and there. Last, he checked her heart rate. If he pushed her too hard, they'd be disqualified and everything would have been for nothing.

Back in the saddle, he ran his hand along Shiraz's neck and implored her to give him everything that remained in her tank. Sensing his urgency, the mare increased her speed by increments. For the most part, she preferred trotting to loping but the rest break had given her the extra boost she needed. Big ears flopping, black eyes shining, she flew past Manny Wilder and two Argentinians, her silvery Arab tail lifted high behind her.

As they sped past a vineyard and along a sandy track through a forest, Wyatt Carling came into view, weaving through the shadows. This time Shiraz needed no encouragement. She accelerated after Zephyr with a ferocity that suggested she had some grievance with the stallion every bit as personal as Will's with his rider. Wyatt glanced over his shoulder and dug his spurs into Zephyr's foam-streaked flanks, drawing blood.

Will had never thought of Shiraz as particularly fast, but she barely touched the ground as she fought to close the gap. Will lay low on the mare's neck, her mane stinging his face. By his calculations, there was only one rider ahead of Wyatt and that was Gill on Laughing Dove Esmeralda. The American woman's champion Arab was in a class of her own but she, like every other horse in the race, was bone-weary. If Will could overtake the Akhal-Teke, he had as good a shot at the title as anyone.

Shiraz's neck was wet with sweat, but she showed no sign of flagging. She drew level with Zephyr and began to overtake him. Without warning, Wyatt spurred his horse sideways, grabbed Will's jacket and gave it a vicious wrench. Caught off guard, Will lost a stirrup and was almost pulled from the saddle. He tipped so far down that the fingers of his right hand grazed the dirt, but Shiraz stayed steady long enough for him to claw his way upright.

'If you think I'm going to let you win after what you did to my brother, you can think again,' spat Carling, his breath coming in gasps. He drove the stallion after

Shiraz, his face contorted with exhaustion and rage.

Will knew Shiraz could not keep up such a furious pace. Nor did he want her to. He had to let Zephyr pass.

Shiraz had other ideas. The more he tried to stop her, the faster she flew. As Wyatt lunged at him again, Will saw that they were rapidly approaching a split in the trail. Feigning that he was going to go left, he used a cowboy manoeuvre to check Shiraz enough to let Zephyr's rump cross in front of her, before whisking her to the right around a great twisted tree.

Carling vanished from view. There was a crack, a high-pitched neigh and a thud. For an instant, Will was conscious of nothing but the muffled beat of Shiraz's slowing hooves. He steeled himself to turn in the saddle. Zephyr was bolting riderless through the forest in the other direction.

As Shiraz came to an uneven halt, Will looked longingly at the trail that led to Hood River. He thought he saw Little Dove's dappled grey hide moving swiftly through the trees. Shiraz could catch her, he was certain she could. The $250,000 was within his reach. If Wyatt Carling was injured, he'd brought it upon himself. No one would blame Will if he left the man lying on the track for a marshal or some other rider to deal with – a rider who didn't have a father with a heart condition.

Except, Will knew, his dad. His dad would never forgive him if he abandoned an injured rider – even, and perhaps especially, if it was for his sake. More importantly, he'd never be able to live with himself.

Sick with disappointment, Will turned a reluctant Shiraz just as Manny Wilder, pursued by the Argentinians, came hurtling through the forest. Will's heart leapt. Maybe they would stop to help Wyatt, letting him off the hook.

But the riders didn't break stride.

'Is Wyatt hurt?' yelled Will as they passed, but if any of them heard they gave no indication of it.

Wyatt was lying collapsed against a tree, clutching his forearm. It was not until Will had leapt off Shiraz and rushed to his side that he realised that the rodeo rider had nicked an artery. His shirt and jeans were sticky with blood.

'I need to get up, need to find Zephyr,' Wyatt said weakly. 'And you, you need to go. Finish the race.'

Will paid no attention. He cut away Wyatt's sleeve, raised the rider's arm above his heart. After applying a tourniquet and firm pressure to the wound, he reached into his pocket for his phone. It was gone. Presumably, it had fallen from his pocket during the struggle with Wyatt. Now if his dad fell ill or desperately needed him, he'd never know.

'Have you any idea how much trouble you've caused?' he said furiously after reviving his patient with a protein drink that he'd planned to use himself.

Wyatt sat up, grimacing. 'I have a fair idea. Thanks for coming back. No way do I deserve it.'

Another competitor trotted past. He paused long enough for Will to appeal to him to call a marshal or the race emergency line, but his mumbled response was unintelligible.

Wyatt ran a grimy hand across his eyes, leaving a smear of blood on his cheek. 'Man, I don't know what to say. Sorry seems inadequate. I'm getting the sinking feeling that I've read you all wrong.' He gritted his teeth as Will closed the wound with Steri-strips, covered it with a gauze dressing and swathed it in bandages. 'It wasn't you, was it?'

'If you mean did I report your brother to the authorities for doping his horse, the answer is no. But that's only because I didn't have proof.'

Wyatt said, 'I'm not gonna excuse what I did', 'because it's inexcusable, but if you want an explanation, it's that old habits die hard. I've been looking out for my little bro my whole life. Maybe it's time I retired and let him clean up his own messes. Gutted as I am that I've destroyed my own chances, it's nothing compared to how I feel about ending yours. I'm going to make it up to you, Will. You can take that to the bank.'

'You think you can make up for putting a rattlesnake in my sleeping bag?'

'You found a rattler in your sleeping bag? Oh, Lord, wait till I get my hands on my brother. I'll wring his neck.'

'Forget it,' Will said gruffly. 'Drink some water.'

Out of the greeny shadows loped Scout, Alex leading Zephyr. She was off the mustang before he'd plunged to a stop. 'What happened? Can I do anything to help?'

329

'It's my own fault,' Wyatt told her. 'I behaved like an ass and I got my dues. Zephyr stumbled on a root and I went over his head like a beginner. His hoof caught me as he tried to recover his balance. Will, here, patched me up when he'd have been well within his rights to punch me. Neither of us have a phone so here we are.'

Alex glanced coolly at Will, avoiding his gaze. 'I'll stay with Wyatt. You need to hurry. You have a race to win, remember?'

'So do you.'

She shook her head. 'Will, nothing is more important than your dad's operation. Get on Shiraz and go.'

'It's too late.'

'Maybe, maybe not. If you don't try, you'll never forgive yourself.'

He willed her to look at him but she was busy pouring Scout some water and getting ready to take over with Wyatt. His heart felt as if it was dying in his chest. Only the thought that he might still be able to achieve what he had come for kept him breathing. 'You're sure?'

'Positive. Now get going.'

'I'll go on one condition. If I win, will you have dinner with me? It can be anywhere you choose. Paris, if you like.'

'Will, you're wasting time.'

'Alex, please.'

A ghost of a smile touched her mouth. 'Let's talk about it when you win.'

And with that he had to be satisfied.

'Paris?' said Wyatt. 'A guy offers you dinner in Paris and you have to think about it? See, this is why I don't understand women. Although, come to think of it, he didn't specify whether he meant Paris, Texas or Paris, France. You want to plump for France.'

'I don't want to talk about it,' said Alex, doing her best to keep pressure on his bandaged arm, which had begun to bleed again. 'Especially not to you. Have you any clue what a nightmare we've been through, thanks to you and your beastly brother?'

'So I've heard. I'm very sorry. If it helps, I'm paying for it now. This hurts like the blazes.'

There was a pause. 'What's with you and Will anyway? Can't you see he's one of the good guys?'

'I thought he was, but it turns out he's just like every other boy.'

Alex couldn't keep the bitterness from her tone, even though she knew that she had no right to be angry with Will. It was she who'd insisted that they'd only succeed at being rivals if they were coldly clinical about each other. It was she who'd said blithely, *Let's be realistic. We're never going to see each other again.* She'd told him that because it was true. Whether they liked it or not, they lived poles apart.

But that was before he'd kissed her. Before what happened happened Before she knew she loved him.

When she'd awoken to find him gone without a word

or a sign, she'd almost quit the race then and there. Two things had kept her going even when Will had smashed her heart into tiny little pieces by blanking her at every camp: her promise to Jonas and money, or lack of it. As long as she was competing, she had access to showers, road supplies and food for both her and Scout. Once The Glory was over – barely a couple of hours from now – she and the mustang were on their own. A month had gone by without a single person trying to find her. Even the warden had given up.

Nobody cared. It was that simple.

Wyatt handed her a surprisingly clean bandana to wipe away her tears. 'What's your story?'

Alex shrugged. She might as well be honest. None of it mattered any more. 'Teenage runaway from the UK, stolen horse.'

Wyatt whistled through his teeth. 'I've gotta hand it to you, girl. You've got guts.'

They were alerted to an approaching vehicle by the horses. It hurtled through the trees and skidded to a stop. Robbie and a paramedic jumped out.

'We got here as fast as we could,' said Robbie. 'A French rider phoned it in.' He smiled wryly at Alex. 'Are you attracted to trouble or is trouble attracted to you?'

'Don't you dare give her a hard time,' Wyatt scolded. 'Without her and Will, I probably wouldn't be here.'

As the paramedic knelt and took a blood pressure cuff from his medical bag, Wyatt looked up at Alex. 'What

332

are you still doing here? I mean, I'm grateful and all, but haven't you got a race to finish?'

Alex didn't move. 'I've lost. There's not a lot of point in hurrying anywhere. It's not as if anyone will notice if I don't turn up.'

'Are you kidding me?' cried Robbie. 'Half the country is lining the streets of Hood River, cheering for every last one of you riders. There's precious few of you and you can't let them down. You and your horses are famous.'

He delved into his pocket and took out a small black velvet box. 'Jonas gave this to a marshal friend of his to give to you, but the man was called away on a family emergency and he made the mistake of entrusting it to the chief clerk. Like a lot of other things, it slipped Wayne's mind and we only found it this morning when . . . Well, let's just say that Wayne has caused us something of a headache. Actually, a migraine might be more accurate.'

Alex took the box from him with a puzzled frown. It looked familiar. When she saw the exquisite gold locket it contained, she almost dropped it. Her mum had given her the necklace for her eleventh birthday. Inside were two tiny photos of her parents.

'It was delivered to Jonas – in person,' Robbie said with a smile. 'Your mom and dad, well, they want you to know that they love you.'

31

The Glory Closing Ceremony, Hood River, Oregon

The winner's cheque was the size of a door, its cardboard backing so flimsy and unwieldy that it almost blew into the Columbia River when Gloria gave it to Jonas.

'Aren't you going to say I told you so?' he asked with a grin.

'Not today I ain't, honey, because for once the weather's being kind to us and I don't want to rain on your parade. Besides, if you didn't do half the crazy things you do, you wouldn't be you and we wouldn't be here and I, for one, am glad about that.'

She leaned closer. 'Aren't you just a bit curious to know who put the cascara sagrada in Turnbull's energy drink? That's what the medics reckon it was.'

'Is that so?' Jonas said non-committally.

'Uh huh. Kind of funny to think that if someone

hadn't decided to play a prank or take revenge on him at that particular moment, your cash might be on its way to Brazil about now. What do you call that?'

'A coincidence?'

'Karma is what it is. What goes around in this world has a habit of coming around, although on occasion it takes its sweet time.'

'It doesn't alter the fact that the money is still missing. Just because we've caught one thief doesn't mean we'll catch the other one.'

Gloria shook her head. 'Sure we will. It was an opportunistic theft, not a planned one. That means there's plenty of margin for disaster.'

She glanced over at the area reserved for riders and their friends and families. Alex was with her parents, laughing about something.

'Interestingly, your ex-chief clerk told the cops that the last person he saw before the money went walkabout was Miss Sarah Wood. Tried to implicate her. Luckily, the detective saw sense. The basis for his accusation was that he'd caught her "stealing" one of his Dragon Fuels. Clearly, no one in their right mind would run off with that revolting drink. You don't suppose she was the one who tampered with it – you know, put the laxative in?'

'I don't know and, frankly, I don't care,' said Jonas. 'From what I gather, Wayne Turnbull has upset a lot of people over the past thirty-three years. Whoever decided that the least he deserved was a spot of tummy trouble was probably working on the side of the angels.'

Alex watched from the VIP area as Jonas bounded onto the stage, wrestling with the cheque. She had an arm wrapped around each of her parents' waists. They kept taking turns at hugging her and staring at her as if she might, at any moment, be spirited away by a passing comet.

It was her dad who'd found her hesitating on the outskirts of town, uncertain whether to proceed or flee into the wilderness she'd left behind. She'd realised as she began to pass groups of banner-waving fans and heard the approaching music and cheers that the wide open spaces and profound silences of the past month had forever changed the way she saw crowded urban environments. The thought of returning to them filled her with a mild agoraphobia.

Scout was experiencing something similar. After a child had popped a balloon under his nose, causing him to shy and come close to ditching Alex in the Columbia River, she'd dismounted to calm him down and check his heart rate. It would be galling to have made it this far only to fail the final vet check.

It was there that she was finally reunited with her dad.

'I thought I might find you here,' he said matter-of-factly, as if it was meant to be. As if he'd known all along that if he flew halfway round the world and waited under this particular tree at this particular time, his daughter would come loping along on a palomino mustang.

'I'm so sorry, Dad,' were the first words out of her mouth. 'Not just for going missing, but for the hateful things I said. I promise I never meant them. Think you could ever forgive me?'

He stopped her there, squeezing her tight. 'Alex, sweet girl, there was never anything to forgive. Believe me, you have had, and do have, plenty of cause to be angry with me. But what I'd like more than anything is for us to put everything behind us and be friends again. Do you think that might be possible? I'm hoping you might find time to come to Australia to visit your old dad. No, don't answer right away. Think about it. Meanwhile, I have something for you.'

He handed her a green folder. Alex opened it and her breath caught in her throat. It was filled to the brim with emails he'd written her and never sent. She closed it again quickly. She'd savour them later.

'Now, apart from having a skittish horse, what's keeping you from rushing to the finish?' he asked.

Alex looked sideways at him. He looked browner, healthier and happier than the dad she'd known in Surrey. Maybe they both thrived in big landscapes. 'I'm petrified,' she admitted.

'What are you afraid of?'

'Everything. Being arrested for stealing Scout, my mustang. Seeing Mum. Meeting your new family. Love. What happens next.'

337

'Ah, love. That's the biggest monster of all because it's always changing and takes on different shapes. Most of the time that monster is not about the other person, as we tend to imagine: it lives inside us. It's about being too scared to trust.'

'So what do you do about that?'

'Same thing you do with every one of your fears. Think about lions, tigers and bears. See it for the cuddly, beautiful thing it has the potential to be.'

Alex's heart suddenly felt a hundred times lighter. 'Lions, tigers and bears. Oh, yeah!'

The second hurdle she had to overcome was seeing her mum again. Jeremy, it turned out, was back in Surrey, filing for divorce, something Natalie seemed curiously unperturbed about.

'I could tell you that you're grounded for the rest of your life for pulling this stunt and worrying us nearly to death, but you'd be perfectly entitled to retort that we're grounded too for sending you to Camp Renew and putting you into the position where you had to flee from that madman Warden Cartwright. He's still missing, you know.'

'You're not going to make me go back there, are you?' Alex asked nervously.

Her mum was horrified. 'I most certainly am not.'

A microphone popped. They turned their attention to the stage. Alex allowed herself a lightning glance at Will. He was standing slightly apart from the other riders, hands in his jacket pockets, gaze fixed on his dust-coated boots. His expression was unreadable. She wanted more than anything to go over and put her arms around him.

'When I came up with the notion of holding a 1,200-mile distance race that took a month, most people considered me a lunatic,' Jonas was saying, 'particularly since I was adamant about having a flexible approach to both the rules and the route. But to put it into context, once upon a time Pony Express riders travelled 1,800 miles every eight days. By those standards, these guys and girls have had a picnic . . .

'Just kidding!' he said as laughter from the crowd was mingled with protests from the riders' camp. 'The point is, ladies and gentlemen, I wanted to create a race that fire-tested both horse and rider. My hope was that the degree of nerve, stamina and sheer willpower required to complete the race would produce a champion with the best of the qualities that made this country great. I can't tell you how much pleasure it gives me to say that, in my belief, that's happened. Before I introduce you to your winner, I have a confession. A small misjudgement on my part has meant there will be a delay in paying the promised $250,000. In short, it's been stolen.'

There were gasps of shock and a chorus of boos from the crowd. Jonas raised his voice. 'So without further ado—'

'Jonas, wait!' cried Gloria, rushing onto the stage waving a phone. 'You have an urgent call.'

'Now?'

'Yes, now.'

With one arm wrapped around the giant cheque and the other hand holding the phone to his ear, Jonas took the call on stage, as TV cameras beamed the footage around the globe. 'I see. I see. Good grief! Yes, I see. About that other matter . . . Yes, I think that would be for the best. Thanks, Chase. I'll be in touch.'

He clicked off the phone and slid it into his pocket. 'Ladies and gentlemen, I'm not sure how to tell you this. The good news is that the cash has been recovered. Gloria, my estimable PA, convinced me to put a tracking device on the case in which it was being carried, and the FBI followed it to Camp Renew, a teenage boot camp in Colorado. The money is on its way to Oregon as I speak and will be with the winner by the end of the day.

'Sadly, the man who is alleged to have stolen it was not quite so lucky. It seems he was – I think I understood this correctly – struck by a falling elk and is no longer with us. I'm sure you will join me in sending our condolences to his loved ones.'

'If indeed there are any,' Natalie whispered to Alex.

Alex was reeling. How the heck had Warden Cartwright got his hands on the prize money? Did that mean he'd been closer to her than she'd realised?

She felt unexpectedly sad. However much she'd detested him and his academy, she'd never have wished him any harm. The elk had not been quite so charitable. Strange, how it had got its revenge from beyond the grave.

On stage, Jonas had managed to recover the atmosphere of jubilation. 'I'm proud to announce that the winners of The Glory are ... GILL REDMOND and the irrepressible, unforgettable LAUGHING DOVE ESMERALDA!'

As Alex joined in the appreciation of her lovely American friend, a woman who'd now achieved iconic status in the sport of endurance riding, her heart broke for Will. Little Dove had beaten Shiraz by a nose. Without Wyatt Carling's ill-timed attack, Will would almost certainly have won.

Despite that, he was clapping louder than anyone else for Gill. He'd never forgotten her kindness during the night of the storm, and he was genuinely thrilled for her. It was only his body language that gave away his total devastation.

'Isn't that Will, the boy you were riding with?' asked her mum, following her gaze. 'Gosh, I can understand the appeal. Not that I approve of you camping alone in the middle of nowhere with a gorgeous boy I've never met, mind you, but he does seem to have done an extraordinary job of keeping you safe. Jonas tells me he's quite a special young man. Are you going to keep in touch?'

Alex's heart gave a painful lurch. She was about to excuse herself and go over to Will when Gloria approached him. Whatever she said brought about a visible change in him. His shoulders seemed to sag with relief.

'From the outset, I wanted The Glory to be a winner-takes-all race,' Jonas was saying. 'To me, that was part of its spirit. But, as many of you know, equine welfare is my passion. Early on, I secretly resolved to award a special prize for the best-conditioned horse. When the veterinarians and I looked over the records for the month, however, we were presented with a dilemma. Two names consistently came out on top. As a result, I'm splitting the prize. I can't tell you how much joy it gives me that the winners of The Glory Award for the Best-Conditioned Horse are also the youngest competitors in the race. They are Will Greyton with Shiraz, and Sarah Wood – or, as I believe she's more popularly known, Alexandra Blakewood – with Scout.'

Alex's legs nearly gave way beneath her. She had to be half-walked, half-carried to the stage by her dad. 'I can't believe it. I've never won a prize. Never ever. Not for anything.'

'I think you came first in a spelling test once,' her father said unhelpfully.

They reached the steps at the same time as Will. Before Alex could stop him, her dad was putting out his hand. 'I'm Sam, Alex's dad. I hear we're indebted to you for saving her life. Would you mind looking after her once more? I think she's in shock.'

Will smiled for the first time that day. 'Sir, it'd be my pleasure.'

32

The view from the stage was more terrifying than anything Will had experienced in the race. Flashbulbs, TV cameras and a sea of upturned faces. The Columbia River, coppery with the setting sun, provided a shimmering backdrop.

And then there was Alex, electrifyingly near.

'Like everything else about this race, this award is a trifle unconventional in that there's no actual award,' said Jonas. 'Not even a certificate. Instead I'd like to grant each of you a wish. I don't mean a Ferrari or a mansion,' he said with a smile, as members of the crowd started shouting out wish lists including everything from Caribbean holidays to concert tickets and smartphones. 'But something within reason.'

He looked at Alex. 'Before you answer, I have a message for you from Chase Miller . . . '

Will saw the panic flash across Alex's face at the

mention of the Camp Renew wrangler; saw the two enormous cops standing directly in her line of vision with shiny handcuffs and enough firepower to annihilate a small country hanging from their belts.

'He said to tell you that in light of recent events at the academy and of what you've achieved in The Glory, he can't think of anyone more deserving of Scout. The transfer of ownership papers are on their way to Hood River with the same police courier who is bringing Gill's prize money. In principle, the mustang is yours from this moment and by the morning it'll be official. With that in mind, would you like to tell me your wish?'

Alex was so overcome with emotion that for a minute all she could do was thank him over and over. Finally, she managed: 'You know my wish. It's the same as it was when I entered The Glory. To set Scout free.'

Jonas grinned broadly. 'I thought as much, and I've already figured out a way to help you with that. What I'd like to do is create a mustang sanctuary – a place where horses live a life of freedom and plenty and where those that are ridden are trained using natural horsemanship techniques. I have just the place in mind. A little bird tells me that a fifty-thousand-acre ranch in Colorado that, until quite recently, was home to a charming place called Camp Renew, has just come on the market. Is that something that would meet with your approval?'

Alex gave him a radiant smile and nodded furiously through her tears.

'In that case, if your parents approve, I was wondering if

you might consider coming to work for me rehabilitating wild mustangs. Gill Redmond, who has an endurance yard near Fort Collins, Colorado, has offered to take you on as an apprentice until our sanctuary is up and running.'

Will was so happy for Alex he was almost in tears himself. He wanted to wrap her in his arms, but if he did that he knew he would never let go. And that – more than prizes, more than finishing the race, was what today was all about – letting go. What other choice did he have?

So he gave her the warmest, most genuine smile he could manage and was saved from having to touch her by her parents, who ran on to the stage to congratulate her and thank Jonas. Far from objecting to their daughter moving to the United States at just sixteen, they were overjoyed. It was the opportunity of a lifetime and she'd be working with the horses she adored. Plus, it transpired that Natalie had always fancied a spell in America. The television cameras lapped it up.

Will was dreading the moment when they turned their lenses on him. Gloria had lifted his spirits a fraction by passing on a message from his friend to say that all was well back in Tennessee and not to worry. She'd also taken a weight off his mind by informing him that, as one of the top-performing riders, he and Shiraz would be transported back to Chattanooga free of charge.

But he'd never felt emptier. He'd fought with every nerve and fibre to win for his dad and he'd failed. He could hardly ask Jonas to pay for a $20,000 cardiac operation.

A commotion in the riders' area interrupted Will's bleak thoughts. Wyatt Carling ran up the steps to the stage. He'd shaved and showered and, apart from the bandage on his arm, looked every inch the rodeo star in a black Stetson, black and red cowboy shirt, jeans and elaborate chaps.

He tipped his hat to the delighted crowd, drawing whoops and wolf whistles. 'Apologies for interrupting, folks, but before Jonas gets around to Will's wish I sort of wanted to announce a prize of my own. Earlier today, partly through tiredness and partly because I can be a bull-headed numbskull on occasion, I made a series of stupid decisions, resulting in a fall. Against the advice of the paramedics I finished the race, but I ended in twenty-second place. In other words, I came stone last. My horse, Zephyr, who ran his heart out, deserved better. I'll always have to live with that.

'When I fell, I cut my arm pretty bad. According to the paramedics, things would have got desperate quite fast if Will and Sarah – I mean, Alex – hadn't stopped to help. At the time Will was in with a real shot at the title – a title, I've been told, that he only wanted because his father needs a heart operation. Because of me, he lost that chance. Now I'd like to make it up to him.'

Will was embarrassed. 'Wyatt, please, just forget it.'

'See, that's one thing I'm not prepared to do. Will, it so happens that a close friend of my father's is one of

346

Colorado's leading cardiac surgeons. He's spoken to key members of his team and they're prepared to operate on your dad for free if he'll agree to travel to Denver. I'll take care of all your expenses – flights, medicine and aftercare. What do you think? Would he do it?'

Will was aware that thousands of people were waiting for his response, but he'd lost all power of speech. He was dimly aware of Alex thanking Wyatt on his behalf.

'I most certainly would,' said a gravelly voice from the wings. Hundreds of heads turned to see an attractive silver-haired man with a pronounced pallor walk hesitantly onto the stage, leaning on a stick. A dark-haired boy of about the same age as Will assisted him.

'Dad! Tom! What are you doing here? How did you get here?' Will rushed to embrace his dad, each of them complaining that the other was too thin.

'We flew,' said Tom. 'Would have been here hours ago, but typically the plane had some technical fault. I did take your dad's TV away, like you asked, but he started sneaking over to the neighbours' house to watch the race every night. Once he got the notion that you were competing in it, there was no stopping him. He sold your grandmother's favourite painting to get us here.'

'Dad! How could you?'

Len was unrepentant. 'Oh, please, don't pretend you liked that ugly thing. It gave us both indigestion and you know it.'

'Dad, I'm so sorry about not being honest about the race. I didn't want to stress you.'

347

'You're apologising for riding twelve hundred miles across four states to do this amazing thing for me? I only wish your mother was here to see you now. She'd have been even prouder than I am.'

Jonas cleared his throat. 'Loath as I am to interrupt, we do have television cameras rolling and journalists with deadlines. In case you've forgotten, Will, you still have one wish. What's it going to be?'

Will didn't hesitate. 'Sir, if it isn't too much to ask, I'd like to take the girl I love to dinner in Paris. Paris, France that is, not Paris, Texas.'

Alex went scarlet. The crowd roared with delight, cheering and whistling.

'No, Will, I don't think that's too much to ask,' Jonas said with a laugh. 'Provided your parents agree, I'd be delighted to arrange for you to take your girlfriend to Paris. Rest assured, it'll be the one in France.'

Will grinned at Alex. *'Now* will you come with me?'

She looked away. 'I'm sorry to do this to you, Will, but no. I can't and I won't.'

There was a collective gasp from the audience, followed by deafening shouts from volunteers more than willing to take her place.

'This is why I've always considered the opposite sex an enigma,' Wyatt confided to Will's father. 'What kind of girl turns down dinner in Paris?'

Len was amused. 'One who knows her own mind, I suspect.'

Will felt as if someone had taken a sledgehammer to

the wreckage of his heart. That he'd been rejected in front of a global audience of millions hardly mattered.

Alex turned to Jonas. 'The reason I can't accept is because Will is the bravest, most selfless and all-round wonderful person I've ever met. I'm sorry to say this in front of my mum and dad, but if it wasn't for him I'd be dead. He risked his life to save me from a blizzard when he hardly knew me and again during a river crossing when he'd been badly injured himself. And it wasn't just me he helped. He stopped a horse from being stolen and, as Wyatt has already told you, gave up a chance to go for the title because he couldn't walk away from an injured man. So, no, I'm not going to be so selfish as to allow him to waste a wish on me.

'You're giving Will this award because he's taken such good care of Shiraz that she's in better shape now than she was when she started the race. His dream is to study veterinary medicine. Since I know he'd never ask you this himself, I'm going to do it for him. Is there any chance at all that you might be able to give him a college scholarship?'

Jonas was regarding Alex with something akin to awe. 'Not only is it possible, but I can think of nothing I'd enjoy doing more.'

Will's only wish was that the stage would open up and swallow him. 'Don't I get a say?'

'No, you don't!' his dad and Tom cried in unison.

Jonas laughed. 'If it helps, there's an excellent school of veterinary medicine in Fort Collins, close to where

Alex will be doing her apprenticeship, and I'm sure Gill would consider finding a spare stable for your horse. Would those things make a difference?'

Will looked at the girl who had his whole entire heart – well, apart from the corner that belonged to Shiraz. 'They'd make all the difference in the world.'

Late that night, after Jonas had delivered a quarter of million dollars in cash to Gill Redmond and Scout's ownership papers to Alex, he and Gloria sat on the cracked leather sofa at race headquarters sharing a pizza and a bottle of wine.

'Don't know about you, but for an idea that most people considered crackers I think the race worked out rather well,' said Jonas.

Gloria took a sip of wine. 'It surely did. The Glory was quite glorious. But let's get one thing straight. If you ever take it into your fool head to do something like this again, I'm resigning. No, don't look at me with those puppy-dog eyes. This was a one-off thing. Besides, by the time we're done dealing with all the lawsuits we'll be too grey to stage an egg-and-spoon race. And I, for one, will be quite content with that . . . Hey, what's with the teddy bear on the desk?'

Jonas helped himself to another slice of pizza. 'It was found by one of the marshals after the closing ceremony. A child must have dropped it. It's a bit battered but I like

it. It has personality. If no one comes forward to claim it,
I'm going to take it to the Green Power office. It can be
our company mascot.'

EPILOGUE

11.47 p.m., Cherry Pass Farm, Columbia Gorge, Oregon

She found Will where she knew he'd be, in the barn, close to Shiraz. When she leaned over the stall door, he was propped against a hay bale, reading a book by torchlight.

They'd barely had a chance to speak since the closing ceremony. There'd been a press conference followed by a meal at a famous local restaurant for the contestants and their families, during which they'd been seated at separate tables. It had been an evening of dreams coming true, but alone in her room at Cherry Pass Farm, a luxury guest ranch, Alex had been too restless to settle.

Will smiled when he saw her. 'Can't sleep?'

She sat next to him on the wood shavings. 'You know what's funny? Over the past month, there've been so many times when I've been freezing and soaked to the skin that I'd have sold my soul if someone offered me a steaming bubble bath, a soft bed, or food that didn't come out of a pouch or tin and wasn't burned on a campfire. And now that I have those things it feels weird. Wrong, somehow. I miss being on the road. I mean, Hood River is lovely and seeing my mum and dad again and knowing that they forgive me and love me is incredible, but I'm already pining for those starlit nights when it seemed as if there was nothing but you, me and the horses in the whole galaxy.'

'I miss the silence,' Will said. 'I used to lie awake listening to it. Even the mountains have their own music. I can't imagine ever adjusting to normal life again. I've loved the adventure, the adrenaline rushes and not knowing what was round the next corner.'

'I don't miss the rattlesnakes,' Alex put in with a shudder. 'Not one bit.'

'Nor me. I don't miss descending icy switchbacks in screaming gales, or being assaulted by masked lunatics, or the camp coffee. Let's face it, those things were grim.'

He took her hand. 'Come, walk with me down to the water's edge.'

On the banks of the Columbia River, they watched the midnight-blue ripples sliding lazily under the bridge. Somewhere in the distance fireworks fizzed into the sky, erupting in a haze of crimson and purple.

'We could always pretend that we're standing beside the River Seine in Paris,' said Alex.

'We could, but I'm not giving up on taking you to dinner in Paris one day for real. Veterinarians earn quite a good living, you know. As soon as I get my first pay cheque – or sooner, if it's humanly possible – I'm going to get down on my knees and beg you to come with me.'

She laughed. 'Don't be daft. Of course I'll have dinner with you in Paris, but we really don't have to go all the way to France. I don't care if it's the Bigger Burger in Chattanooga so long as I'm with you.'

'That's only because you haven't been to the Bigger Burger. I'm very relieved you didn't get to see me in the uniform. You'd never have dreamed of going out with me.'

'Oh, I don't know. I'm sure you look cute in blue and orange spots.'

'Don't,' Will said with feeling. 'I still have nightmares.'

'About dinner – aren't you forgetting something?'

He pulled her close to him. 'What's that?'

'I'm the one who owes you dinner. That's where I fell in love with you, you know – Betty's Diner. I fell in love with your right hand first.'

He gave a shout of surprised laughter. 'My right hand?'

'That was all I could see. Then I fell in love with your arms and your chest. You were wearing a flannel shirt and that hot white vest. When you turned to look at me, I fell in love with your face. And then when you did that conjuring act and saved me from being arrested for not paying the bill, I fell in love with your kindness.'

'When, dare I ask, did you fall in love with my mind?'

'Eons ago,' Alex said. 'Before I met you. I've been waiting for you my whole life.'

He kissed her then and it was a while before either of them could get it together to talk.

'So will you have dinner with me or not?' asked Alex. She pulled a $100 note from her pocket. 'I'm loaded. My father says it's money he was going to send me for my birthday a couple of months back, but somehow it never got as far as the post. I used to save every penny of pocket money and stuff it in my teddy bear, Pluto, in the hope that one day I could buy a horse. Now I have Scout, so I can spend it all on taking you to the best restaurant in town.'

'Sorry, Alex, but I can't.'

'Seriously?'

'Sadly, yes. The cardiac surgeon wants to operate on my dad before the end of the week. We're flying to Denver tomorrow afternoon.'

'Oh,' said Alex, trying not to sound too disappointed. She was over the moon for Will that his dad was going to get the life-saving treatment he needed, even more so now she'd met Len. They'd hit it off immediately. She just hadn't expected to be torn away from Will quite so soon.

He brushed her fringe from her eyes. 'Does your offer extend to breakfast?'

'Oh, it definitely does.'

'The thing is,' Will said, 'it's nearly one a.m. It seems a

shame to go to bed when it's already practically morning. We could stay up and watch the sun rise.'

Alex was so close to him she could feel the heat radiating from his body. 'Sounds good to me. How are we going to occupy ourselves till then?'

'I have one or two ideas,' Will teased. 'We could save them for tomorrow, but what if tomorrow never comes?'

'It has to come; I'm looking forward to it,' Alex said with a laugh. 'Then again, why take the chance . . .'

AUTHOR'S NOTE

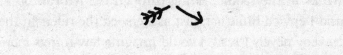

The sport of endurance riding is one of the fastest growing in the world and that, combined with a lifelong fascination with all things Western, made it the perfect subject for my next novel.

Like Jonas Ellington, I'm intrigued by the legend that is Frank T. Hopkins. Whether or not his claim to have ridden his mustang eighteen hundred miles across the United States is true, I've always loved the idea of it. Under the rules of the American Endurance Ride Conference (AERC), the maximum distance of any race is one hundred and fifty miles in three days, but I wanted to create a race in which horse and rider were tested to their limits and found out what they were made of.

Throughout history, cowboys, Pony Express riders, gunfighters, Indians, tribesmen, stockmen, explorers and numerous others have ridden thousands of miles across the American West, the Australian Outback and the deserts of Arabia, not because there was a big prize at the end of it, but out of necessity or because it was their job or in pursuit of a dream. There were no rules and no age restrictions. As many teenagers crossed continents or rode the range as adults.

When I was a teenager, I lived on a thousand-acre farm and my dad and I regularly went on two- or three-hour rides. At one time in his life my father had spent weeks in the saddle, riding through the African bush, and I envied him that, just as I envied the riders in the cowboy novels I read. I could imagine few things more wonderful than travelling through a vast wilderness on a beautiful horse.

Endurance riding is a sport with many and complex rules and regulations, the majority of which are put in place to ensure horse welfare. I'm afraid I've mixed and matched the rules and terminology of the US, British and Australian endurance riding associations in order to create a race that would work in fiction. I doubt that any one of them would sanction a month-long race. Apologies for any inaccuracies in terminology or any other aspect of endurance racing. I hope that the spirit of the sport remains intact at least.

As for me, I've finally achieved my own dream and got to travel through a vast wilderness on a beautiful horse – if only on paper. I've ridden every mile with Alex and Scout and Will and Shiraz and it's been a joy. I hope very much that you enjoy it too.

ACKNOWLEDGEMENTS

Almost my earliest memory is being in love with horses. Never did I imagine that I might one day be given the chance to write novels about them, let alone ride a palomino mustang through the mountains of Wyoming in the interests of research. If it's a dream, I hope no one wakes me up!

Thanks first and foremost to Fiona Kennedy and Catherine Clarke for making this book possible and for always being so supportive, wise and wonderful. None of this would have ever happened without you. A big thank you too to the amazing team at Orion Children's, including Lisa Milton, Jane Hughes, Jo Carpenter, Nina Douglas, Hermione Lawton, Fliss Johnston, Jo Rose, Alex Nicholas, Sarah Vanden-Abeele and to designer Abi Hartshorne for the stunning cover. A big thanks also to Julie Martin from Endurance GB for the rules advice.

As I've said in my author's note, I was fortunate

enough to grow up on a farm in Zimbabwe, where I spent hours riding through the bush with my dad and my sister, Lisa. Both understand the pull of horses and the wild and it means so much to be able to share that with them. Thanks to them and to my mom for being so tirelessly supportive and enthusiastic. To Jule Owen, thanks for the beautiful petroglyph illustrations and for sticking with me through death-defying storms and blizzards in Wyoming, twelve-hour drives across Idaho and Oregon, and on rides through icy creeks and up and down snowy mountain trails. I'd have been lost – quite literally – without you!

I owe a huge debt of gratitude to the staff and wranglers of The Hideout Ranch in Wyoming, especially Tom Bercher, the Head Wrangler, who understands horses better than anyone I've encountered in my life and was endlessly patient with my questions. I'll never forget Tom's Natural Horsemanship clinic. Thanks also to managers Marjin and Peter De Cabooter, and to Rebecca Bercher and the wranglers – Mel in particular – who help make The Hideout such a happy, special place. I'll treasure the time I spent riding Kicker through the Big Horn Mountains for the rest of my days. It was, for me, pure heaven.

Lauren St John
London
November 2014

GLOSSARY OF NATIVE AMERICAN INDIAN PETROGLYPHS AND PICTOGRAPHS

 Journey – The meaning of symbols and signs varied from tribe to tribe, but to most the horse symbol signified a journey, usually in the direction of home. The domestic horse was first introduced to North America in 1513 by the Spanish Conquistador, Cortes. Some escaped or were stolen by the Indians and quickly became integral to their lives, providing freedom through travel and prosperity through hunting and trading. The early Indians called them 'God Dogs' or 'Big Dogs.'

Hope – An eight-pointed star enclosed in circle and containing a circle. The number eight signified balance and the hope symbol was known as Star Knowledge, meaning hope for the future if celestial alignments were favourable

 Horse and Rider – Purity, Nobleness, Courage, Power, Independent Spirit, Freedom

 Mountain – Abundance, majesty

 Opposing Arrows – War

 Storm

Broken Arrow – Peace

 River – Constant Life

 Bear Tracks – Authority, Leadership,
Good Omen

Good

Bad

Help

 **Sad**

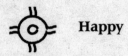 **Happy**

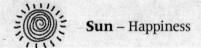 **Snake** – Defiance, Wisdom

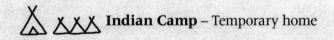 **Sun** – Happiness

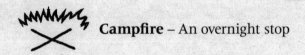 **Indian Camp** – Temporary home

Campfire – An overnight stop

364

Bear – A Power Animal. Some Indians believed that dreaming of a bear, touching or killing one made a warrior invincible

 Thunderbird – Symbol of lightning, thunder and storms, Sacred bearer of Unlimited

 Bison – A Power animal signifying abundance

 Great Spirit – The American Indians were a deeply spiritual people and the Great Spirit symbol represents all-seeing eye of God and the divine power they believed created the world. The Sioux called this power 'Wakan Tanka' – the Great Mystery

Days and Nights – Geometric symbols of celestial bodies signify time

 4 Directions – Paths Crossed

 Rattlesnake Jaw – Strength

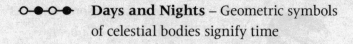 **Thunderbird Tracks** – Bright prospect

 Tree of Life – Sustenance

 Deer – A Power animal representing Healing, Kindness, Innocence or Compassion

Moose – A Power animal symbolising Long Life or a Headstrong character

Monster – Every tribe had numerous myths and legends about monsters. Those with horns were believed to have a spiritual power

Warrior

Hunter – Monster Killer

Bird – Carefree, light-hearted

Saddlebags – Journey

 Rain Clouds – Good prospects

 Crossed Arrows – Friendship

 Lightning Arrow – Swiftness

 Arrow – Protection

 Raven Tracks – A message from beyond space and time

RESEARCHING THE GLORY

For much of the first decade of my career, I was *The Sunday Times'* golf correspondent, following the men's PGA Tour around the world. Later, I wrote a couple of books on Americana or what was then known as New Country music, which gave me an excuse to ride around the US on the tour buses of musicians like Steve Earle and the Dixie Chicks, and spend a lot of time in recording studios and at the Pancake Pantry in Nashville, Tennessee.

For me, the abiding principle of reporting is to make the reader feel as if they're right there with you – standing on the 15th fairway at Amen Corner at Augusta National in Georgia, swimming with Hammerhead sharks in the Galapagos Islands, or hanging about backstage with Emmylou Harris and Linda Ronstadt at the Troubadour Club in West Hollywood.

For that reason, it's always been important to me to research my novels the same way, by seeing the places and some of the people or horses I write about in real life. Of course, the fact that I adore travelling and meeting interesting people and animals doesn't hurt either! Over the years, I've travelled to Antigua, St Petersburg, Cornwall, the Bazaruto Islands of Mozambique, the Namibian desert, Zimbabwe and New York, all in the name of research.

Researching this book was not quite so simple. The Glory is a long race and covers a lot of ground, much of it in terrible weather. Undaunted, my partner and I drove 1,800 miles across the American West, from Denver, Colorado to Portland, Oregon, in winter. On the first day of our trip, we drove for nine straight hours through snow blizzards on lonely mountain passes. The most surreal moment was negotiating Wyoming's Wind River Canyon in an almost total whiteout (we were the only people insane enough to be on the road) while a cheerful country song played on the radio.

I fell in love with the West. If you love wilderness and wide-open spaces, it's impossible not to. Added to which, you have natural wonders like the Yellowstone and Grand Teton National Parks, and charming towns like Jackson Hole, Boise and Hood River. The highlight of the trip, however, was spending nearly five days at The Hideout Ranch in Shell, Wyoming – a place so sublime that I felt I had to name-check it in my book.

At the time we visited, The Hideout had eighty-five of the calmest, happiest horses I've ever encountered. They lead a semi-feral life in which they're released into the foothills of the 650,000-acre ranch every evening and rounded up by a wrangler or two in the mornings. Those that are being ridden are separated and given breakfast in the barn. The rest spend the day in lovely pastures.

I was fortunate enough to ride a palomino mustang called Kicker, who'd been wild until about a year previously. As I mention in *The Glory*, the wild mustang, one of the defining symbols of freedom and the American West, is in crisis. Around 34,000 mustangs and burros are in Bureau of Land Management holding pens after being chased to the point of exhaustion by helicopter and vehicle in traumatic captures. Those over ten years old are mostly slaughtered for pet food. Less than 2,000 are adopted each year. In a heartbreaking echo of my own book, *The One Dollar Horse,* many sell for as little as $1.

Another 38,000 mustangs still live in feral herds in Montana, Wyoming, Oregon and Nevada. Like all wild animals, they're fighting a losing battle for survival as the human and cattle population grows and competes for water and grazing, but for the time being, at least, they are free.

Kicker, my wonderful Hideout mustang, was the inspiration for Scout in *The Glory*. He was a graduate of The Extreme Mustang Makeover programme and one of the best horses I've ever ridden. If I could adopt him now, I would. He carried me safely across icy rushing creeks and up and down sheer trails as snow fell in the Bighorn Mountains. It's thanks to him and the fantastic wranglers at the ranch that I was able, later, to sit at my desk in London and imagine how it would feel to be Alex and Will and to risk everything to win *The Glory*. I hope very much that you've enjoyed the journey!

Don't miss Lauren St John's bestselling
One Dollar Horse trilogy.

THE ONE DOLLAR HORSE

Fifteen year old Casey Blue lives in East London's grimmest tower block and volunteers at a local riding school, but her dream is to win the world's greatest Three Day Event: the Badminton Horse Trials.

When she rescues a starving, half-wild horse, she's convinced that the impossible can be made possible. But she has reckoned without the consequences of her father's criminal record, or the distraction of a boy with melty, dark eyes, with whom she refuses to fall in love.

Casey learns the hard way that no matter how high you jump, or how fast you gallop, you can never outrun the past.

RACE THE WIND

Casey Blue is overjoyed when her Badminton victory earns her and Storm an invitation to the Kentucky Three Day Event.

But when her father is arrested, she finds herself at the mercy of a vicious blackmailer. To make matters worse, Storm is behaving like the wild horse he once was. Faced with losing everything, Casey needs the help of her boyfriend, Peter, to win in Kentucky. But is he for her or against her?

FIRE STORM

Teenage eventing star Casey Blue has it all – fame, her champion horse Storm and a boyfriend who loves her. Then Kyle West walks into her life. The country's hottest equestrian coach is drop dead gorgeous and Casey knows right away that she's in trouble.

Winning means everything but as the Burghley Horse Trials approach it's clear that what is at stake is not just the Grand Slam but Casey's life.